What others are saying about
PHENOMENA the Lost and Forgotten Children

*(Formerly published as **SEACLIFF a Regular Boy Within**)*

PHENOMENA's characters are so endearing. The story winds through historical facts with ease and a gripping tale is introduced to the reader. It reminds me of *One Flew Over the Cuckoo's Nest*. It is very well written. What an amazing story! - **Margitte Reviews**

I enjoyed this book very much. It's introspective, but far from depressing. All the feelings, thoughts, and facts are put into words skilfully, finding the perfect balance between simple and complex, fiction and reality. I would recommend this book to all, because there's much more to learn from it than from a psychological anthology! - **Cristian-Zenoviu Drozd (writer)**

This book is amazing; it is honestly different. Tarr's result is a highly readable description of a slice of life few people were privy to. Interwoven into this historical work (a few actually funny stories, more unbearably sad) is the story of Malcolm. What happens to a child who has had no parenting, who is exposed to institutionalisation and whose stimulation is all wrong? A child who is not allowed to grow up? Read PHENOMENA the Lost and Forgotten Children and many of these questions are answered. - **T Laidlaw (psychologist)**

I've never read anything like it. It's not an average prototype of fiction. This story has a depth that could only come from life experience, from knowledge of the human psychology and behaviour. The author skilfully manages to sprinkle some humour in the darkest of situations. The ending is unexpected, with a twist that makes the reader want to start reading it all over again. A great book from a great author! - **Anca-Melinda Coliolu (author)**

Tarr introduces Malcolm to the reader as no one special, but it soon becomes apparent that he has many secrets. They begin to unfold as she hooks you in with imagery of many of the mainstay characters and the psychiatric institution called Seacliff. I loved, loved, loved Malcolm. At times it was very hard to read because of how descriptive Tarr was about his plight, but I just had to know what happened. I would recommend this book in a heartbeat and will definitely read it a third and fourth time. Best read so far this year. - **Allie Mataafa**

Tarr's voice is direct and her treatment is sympathetic and thought provoking. Definitely a true story you'll never forget. Seacliff is a part of New Zealand history that unfortunately is universal. - **Fancy Nancy Reviews**

The story sears the soul, the conscience and the mind, both celebrating humanity and revealing our darknesses. I had no inkling of the sending of "helpless souls" from England. I hadn't realised the extent of ECT use in NZ. I'm left feeling elated as well as ashamed after reading Malcolm's story. Thank you for your superhuman perseverance in making sure it was told. - **Kay Down (author)**

ISBN-13: 978-1534872424

PHENOMENA

the Lost and Forgotten Children

by

SUSAN TARR

ACKNOWLEDGEMENTS

PHENOMENA the Lost and Forgotten Children (originally **SEACLIFF: a Regular Boy Within**) was selected by The New Zealand Society of Authors' Mentoring Programme, funded by Creative New Zealand, and was guided into being by mentor and editor, Lesley Marshall.

Dr Tannis Laidlaw's incisive critiques helped me navigate the medical aspects of this story.

Inspiration for **PHENOMENA the Lost and Forgotten Children** comes from a multiple of sources, not the least being Malcolm. But also from a collection of personal diaries and old letters, photographs, personal and shared experiences of family, workmates and friends; from living and working at Seacliff, Cherry Farm and Porirua Psychiatric Hospitals.

Note: Some details have been changed to protect living relatives and descendants, though wherever possible and in most instances the correct dates, names and places have been used.

SPECIAL ACKNOWLEDGEMENTS

To Malcolm, with the greatest respect. To Jack and Nola Green, Campbell and Kathleen Pope, Doug and Marie Forrester, and all the other Seacliff village people I knew, as well as my work colleagues from the day who added to and filled my memories so colourfully.

To those who contributed their stories and wrote me letters once they knew I was doing this work – too many to list – love and thank you to each one of you.

But especially to my sister Kathleen Pope who worked tirelessly to provide me with accurate accounts of the times, along with photographs and video recordings.

Where **PHENOMENA the Lost and Forgotten Children** differs, is in the humour. Because it is such dark subject matter I felt strongly that there had to be some levity in it. You had to have a lot of stuff to break that up because nobody wants to read something that's just desperately miserable.

Susan Tarr
New Zealand

To my family

Michael and Anna, for their patience and faith in me
and my writing, with love always.

I may not have attempted Malcolm's story as it is if
it weren't for the friendship my sister Kathleen and I
shared. In many ways this story is a melding of both
our memories.

In Memory of

My sister Kathleen Pope
Kath McLeod

FOREWORD

I was raised within the community of Seacliff village, in New Zealand, during the 50s, with each of our family members working in the hospital at some time or another. We sometimes shared our primary school with young patients from the hospital. On turning fifteen we often worked up the hill, helping in the canteen, laundry, wards or occupational therapy. From a young age we absorbed the stories, and it was difficult to know where fiction ended and the greater truth took over.

To separate the truth from the almost-truth at this stage would be an impossible task as many of those concerned have died. Therefore I have blended together various stories in this narrative as representative of our family and friends' combined belief of what most probably did happen during the period covered by this narrative. Wherever possible, I have used correct dates, names and places. When there is a modicum of doubt in my mind I have changed names and details for the protection of those still living.

As a child I knew Malcolm, who was then a young man, since Dad often invited him home for meals. He was one of the lost children, those forgotten or abandoned by their family. We followed Malcolm's story from childhood to adulthood as best we could. Even after he was eventually discharged back into the community. When considering the tragedy and abuse of Malcolm's wasted earlier years, it is a story of immeasurable sadness. Yet he ultimately rose above it all, and with admirable strength, courage and innate resilience, was finally able to free 'the regular boy within' as he had always wanted.

This is Malcolm's story as I believe it unfolded.

Chapter 1

PHENOMENA the Lost and Forgotten Children

Non omnis moriar

I shall not completely die

(Horace)

Return to the Beginning – 1954

On nearing the house up Dunedin's Maclaggan Street, tucked beneath cherry blossoms, larch and pussy willow, Malcolm's old panic resurfaced. He'd mostly suppressed it during the journey back but now it threatened to break through his fragile control.

When he walked up the steps to the porch, through the front door with the coloured glass panels, how would that feel? He acknowledged his yearning to be back revolved around his memories of Julie's company, assured patience and optimism. How would it be without her, with just the other exhospital inmates who had also been transferred: Bob, Grey Lizzie, and a few new ones? Would there still be fights over the meals and the milk bottle tops? And what about his old bedroom? Would it be taken over by someone else? And who slept now in Julie's room?

And...and... Oh, there were too many questions!

Closer now, he could see the donkey-brown windowsills. Nearly home. Yet to be back here and without Julie by his side, guiding him into his future, would he ever be truly free from his old life in the hospital? His insides churned with doubts and fears. He had not expected that. And tears burned his eyes at the distant memory of Julie, the accident, her cold body whisked away beneath a grey blanket. But now he was older. He was an adult and, they told him, he should 'get out into the real world' now. So the old question returned: what did the real world hold for him, and what was real anyway?

Immobilised by nerves, he couldn't even make it out of the hospital van. He peered wide-eyed through the window at them all clustered together on the porch waiting to welcome him home. Grey Lizzie waved as if he were going on a day's outing, not returning from half a decade back at The Building. (That's what they all called the hospital.) She looked almost the same. Just more grey. Bob's ginger hair had faded too. But who were the strangers standing there, and where had the others gone?

After another prompting he clambered awkwardly down from the van. And Nurse West propelled him along when he would have stayed out in the street.

"Let's go inside and get you unpacked. And don't tell me you're shy, mister, a grown man like you?"

Malcolm clutched two brown paper bags: his farewell presents and his clothes. All he possessed.

Grey Lizzie craned her neck to peer over Bob's shoulder. Bob pushed his way to the front of the close-pressed and silent group to shake Malcolm's hand vigorously.

"So ya got glasses, huh?" he said gruffly. "Welcome home, then." And he turned away abruptly, muttering, "My scones are ready."

Malcolm was aware of the old familiar smells, hot and delicious, wafting along the passage toward him.

"Fresh scones," announced Grey Lizzie, beaming happily. "Don't let them burn, Bob, like last time. And make sure you wash your hands."

She rolled her eyes, but not before Bob had turned back and seen her.

"Mouthy bitch," he muttered, slowly shaking his head as he again headed toward the kitchen.

Grey Lizzie ignored him, turning sideways and pursing her lips so Malcolm could kiss her.

Nurse West bustled forward. "So which is Malcolm's room?"

Malcolm hoped she could bring order to this milling, indecisive group she was responsible for. And he'd thought it bad back at The Building.

"Who wants to show Malcolm his room?"

'Same one, third left," Grey Lizzie said. "The other chappie moved on last month. Gone home to his kin."

Malcolm allowed himself a smile – his same old room. Now he began to feel at ease. He'd lie on his same bed and look up through the casement windows to greet the smiling face of his moon. He followed Nurse West down the passage, past Grey Lizzie's newspaper-jammed room and stood patiently in the doorway while she gave it a quick once-over.

"It seems mighty fine to me, Malcolm," she said. "You settle in now and I'll be back in a week to see how you're going, all right?" Before she turned to leave, she added quietly, "But you'll be okay. Make conversation. The others will join in. Especially Lizzie and Bob. They've really come out of their shells since they've been living here." And she tapped the side of her nose with her forefinger. "I think he's taken a fancy to her."

Still he felt a stab of abandonment when Nurse West whisked into the van and off down the street. He would try hard, yet he was doubtful he could do it. Would he end up back at The Building, like before?

"Kettle's on. Go through to the sitting room. I'll bring tea."

That was Bob. He'd come to stand gawking with the others in Malcolm's bedroom doorway, to watch him unpack his paper bag, or to shyly touch his sleeve.

His return was a novelty because nothing much changed here at this house.

"Don't forget the meringues with the fresh cream, Bob."

Grey Lizzie was as bossy as ever though Bob was clearly still in charge of his kitchen, because he barked, "Stop with the bloody orders, woman!"

Even so Malcolm noticed Bob's voice was not as strident as it used to be when he spoke to her. And Bob nodded almost sheepishly as he followed his bark with a soft look in her direction. As she responded with a coy smile, Malcolm lowered his head to hide his own. Once upon a time he'd found Grey Lizzie aggravating with her constant carping and criticising, her obsession with germs. Now she was just Grey Lizzie who would talk to him.

Surely he could live here without fear. Some of these people, all transferred from The Building to live life on the outside, had been his family. Maybe they could be again.

Mooching closer to Malcolm, Grey Lizzie whispered, "I like your glasses."

Then he was alone.

He wandered from his bedroom along the passage toward the sitting room, first touching the light switch, and then running his hand over the familiar linen cupboard door. Next to it was the bathroom door. That was one room he never wanted to go into again. The hairs on his arms rose, and he made an effort to stifle the old horror before rejoining the others for tea and scones.

Chapter 2

Maclaggan Street 1947

Julie had been blind from childhood. Some traumatic event, was all they'd say, but then they didn't say much about Julie or to her. She was slight and bird-like in appearance. Someone had once commented, "Not at all pretty, that one."

Malcolm disagreed. Julie was not plain. Possibly she was beautiful. He couldn't be sure.

He knew he was not beautiful. He wore a built-up boot and his right hand was weakened. A mild man, with milky blue eyes, coarse sandy hair and a farm labourer's sturdy build, he was taller than most.

At twenty-six years old his sheer size was often regarded as intimidating, especially since he spoke little. Some knew him as trusting, gentle and kindly. He wore an old tweed cap that spent as much time fumbled nervously in his big hands as it did atop his craggy head.

Both Malcolm and Julie were different, as different from the rest of the world as they were from each other.

Folk used to call them lunatics, loonies or inmates. Or worse still, idiots. He didn't mind being called names by the taunting children leaning over the fence at Seacliff Primary School down the hill from the hospital. The girls were clean, their hair braided and tied with floppy ribbons, their cheeks rosy. Brown, black or red shoes highly polished.

"Loony, loony, out of the loony bin," the children chanted, their voices shrill. Swinging back and forth on the bottom strand of the wire, their hands tightly clasping the top strand, they sang in unison, "Looo-ny, looo-ny, looo-ny." Then a school monitor would ring the bell and off they'd traipse, giggling, to form a tidy crocodile in the school quadrangle.

Malcolm had long been conscious of himself and of something exceptional in his worldly position. The school children all seemed to belong to somebody;

they had a mother and a father. There was for each of them a group of other children, some younger, some older, whom he assumed were brothers and sisters, and who sided with each other in playground scuffles and brawls. They clearly made up part of a unit.

And now, after a long time, he considered how he too made up part of a unit. He lived in a regular white roughcast house with regular people, a supervised home in Dunedin up the top of Maclaggan Street not far from Speight's Brewery. The house was well organised for responsible adult patients – and he was considered a responsible adult patient – and run according to the scheduled orderliness of the Seacliff Mental Hospital rosters. The hospital kept changing its name: first Seacliff Lunatic Asylum, later Seacliff Asylum, and now Seacliff Mental Hospital. Whatever would they call it next?

Malcolm laughed aloud to himself. "The Loony Bin? The Booby Hatch?"

But it was already called by those names.

Here at the Maclaggan Street house he had his own room, quite unlike the hospital where he grew up. At night it was quiet: no snoring, farting or coughing. He was alone by himself and he could make whatever noises he wanted. Set in the end

wall was a tall casement window with the neighbour's high fence blanking out his view.

Often he'd sit on the end of his narrow bed, staring at that fence, counting the knotholes or timber
palings. If he stood on the bed he could feel the
warmth of the morning sun on his face, and he could
also see over the fence.

The neighbours behind the fence were dark-
spirited people. They didn't smile when Malcolm
smiled at them as they waited outside at the gate to
collect their pint of milk. They ignored Bob when he
said a gruff good morning by the fish vendor's van.
And if they saw Malcolm observing them as they
went about their business behind the fence, they'd
shake their fists at him and make their faces ugly
with dark gaping holes where their mouths should
be. They were like ghosts who never spoke, staring
from blank eyes and communicating through blank
open mouths. There'd been a few people like them
back at The Building.

The tall window had its own oiled blind that he
could pull down each night if he wanted to. If he let
it go too fast it would snap right to the top and stay
there. Then he'd stand precariously balanced on a
stool, coaxing the blind down, only to have it snap
back to the top again. Bob had come away from his

kitchen and shown Malcolm the trick of making it stay down. He liked Bob. Bob knew things. Bob was almost a regular guy even though he'd come out from The Building the same as the rest of them. He cooked some colourful strange vegetables. He also made an odd fishy paste that he spread generously in their sandwiches. Malcolm had become overly fond of this.

"Listen to this news, Mal. There's a huge fire in Ballantyne's Store up in Christchurch. They say it's much bigger and much worse than that fire in Ward 5. Lots o' people killed. Some of them youngsters too."

Malcolm smelled again the smoke, heard the roar and swoop of the devouring flames, the screams and howls – some from within the fire and some from the watchers. Sweat broke out on his forehead and his eyes pricked with unshed tears. Bob shoved a chair out for him and for some time both men sat in silence. They knew about fires and the insatiable appetites of fires. They knew that not everyone would be spared.

When the moon was high, Malcolm often left the blind up and lay beneath his blankets staring up at the sky. Round and white, the moon smiled down on him and listened to his thoughts. He had gained trust in the moon after a time and he began to wordlessly confide in it. The moon would keep his secrets; the moon would never lie...

Chapter 3

Contentment at Maclaggan Street

In 1946, Malcolm first rode into Dunedin in the Seacliff Mental Hospital van to live in the white house, to be a regular normal man. He was scared and remained scared for a long time. Mostly he stayed in his room, getting up sometimes to limp around the path to his side of the house and touch the knotholes in the high fence outside his window. He'd scratch M on it with a nail, then put the nail back into his pocket. It was a handy nail.

When the grip of winter took hold of the landscape, making the days short and dim and the pitch-black nights as long as a year, he began to sit with the others in the sitting room. He listened to the radio, taking from the voices and music a kind of anonymous friendship from afar. This bounty of happiness and the new ideas and revelations that came from the radio dispelled some of the lonely darkness.

Julie came in the van from The Building too. In the endless tide of moving – some in, some out – they never remembered how they had first met. They knew it was somewhere in their accumulated pasts, hidden among memories they could not share. Yet here they were. Julie, serene with corn-flower-blue eyes and a scar on her chin from an old gash, and Malcolm with his noisy cumbersome walk and braced boot. Yet he found himself wishing they had met properly, earlier.

Julie had the end room beyond the bathroom, past the linen cupboard and along the dark passage. Her room had two casement windows, one on each outside wall. She also faced the wooden fence. Her other window overlooked the back garden though she couldn't see that either. Malcolm wondered if she closed her blinds at night, if the white face of the moon disturbed her. And since she had no sight, did she know it would listen to her thoughts?

During the day she wore a shapeless floral print dress made by the women inmates in the hospital sewing room. The buttons on her cardigan were mismatched. Only the top two were the same.

He sensed Julie was sometimes frightened. She reminded him of the field mouse he kept in his pocket, turning her head as if to ask him a question, yet not speaking. Sometimes the mouse would quiver as he stroked it or fed it crumbs from Bob's kitchen. Like the mouse, Julie sometimes needed a strong friend, someone to tell her about the step at the bathroom door or about the sharp piece jutting out at one corner of the worn stone bench.

Initially he had looked away when she stumbled or fell down, closing his ears though she made no sound at all. With all his being he wanted to help her, but he felt powerless to act. Fragmented memories of beatings and The Treatment dealt out when he dared intrude in the problems of others back at The Building kept him still and silent. He was working to overcome this.

She didn't talk much, but then neither did he. They lived in a world full of silent people. It was by chance they sat next to each other in the cosy kitchen at the back of the house that overlooked the washhouse and vegetable garden.

By chance they ate together at the kitchen table covered over with an oilcloth. In the sitting room their armchairs were cramped close together in whatever space was left. His hands lay limp in his lap as he watched hers move and touch, respond, curve and prod. She had a bag of cut lengths of multi-coloured rags and a rectangle of sacking.

One day he spoke to her in his rasping disused voice. "What are you actually making, Julie?"

"A rag rug." She flicked her blank eyes in his direction, and smiled warmly.

He watched, mesmerised, as her nimble fingers plucked and hooked the coloured strips through the open weave of the sacking, creating an endless mass of fiery colours.

"It looks like the Queens Gardens."

"Does it really?" She smiled toward him again.

"Yes. It's real pretty."

But he was looking at Julie, not the rug.

In the kitchen, Bob lit the coal range, endlessly feeding its insatiable appetite. The range burned hotly, sometimes, it seemed to Malcolm, for months on end. Especially through the winter when it never stopped heating and feeding, feeding and heating. There was a tap on the tank at the side where they could get hot water for washing dishes in the enamel sink, and a wetback for the bathroom. A kettle constantly simmered on top for teas and cocoas. The water heated, and roasts and rice puddings were cooked in it. It was Bob's coal range. No one else touched any part of it or what was on or in it.

Except Malcolm.

At 5am he pulled his clothes on and headed straight for the kitchen. His job was to take the cooled ashes from the range out to the garden, leaving a few remaining embers in the grate. Then he'd polish the warm range with black Zebra Nugget and a brush from a wooden box he kept beneath the sink.

At 5.30am, Bob re-stoked his range with newspaper, kindling wood and coal. He blew gustily onto the embers until the newspaper flared. Every morning he told Malcolm the same thing. "There's an art to getting it just right, m' boy. Gotta make sure there're always embers under them ashes, under the burnt coal. Right?"

"Right, Bob."

Malcolm helped the coalman with his deliveries. Oddly enough, he liked coal and the bucket of Southland coal he carried in sat ready on the polished hearth for Bob to feed his fire.

Every morning Bob told Malcolm, "This coal is full o' dust and chemicals. It'll ruin the roof. I've told

Sister Evans a dozen times to get the shiny black Kaitangata coal."

"Right, Bob."

Malcolm admired Bob. He liked his rough and rugged manner. And ever since he'd arrived at the house, Bob had kept his eye out for him.

One of the others polished the front porch step with red Nugget until it shone as rosy as an apple.

Julie couldn't see Malcolm's limp. She never saw how his jacket hung over his broad shoulders with sleeves too short for him, or his much fumbled tweed cap. To her, he was just Malcolm, always nearby in case she needed someone to talk to or help her.

As their friendship grew into a second year, Malcolm gained confidence in it. Julie lived in the same house, shared with him and laughed with him. Sometimes he could believe they danced together and loved together, just like his mother and father had in their front sitting room.

She had never been out walking so he asked Sister Evans' permission to walk her into the city sometimes. He promised to take care of her and make sure she was safe in the traffic. And keep her dry if it should rain.

One fine spring day, the pair set out for a little walk into town. Even though Julie walked deliberately and carefully with her white cane tap-tapping ahead, he saw how excited she was. Whenever they came to a corner he would touch her arm and tell her what the intersecting street was called. She'd repeat the name and tap her cane around the curbing until she found the road below. With another light touch he would guide her across to the other side. The first time they went walking they made their way slowly to the Queens Gardens.

One day he said, "If it's the Queens Gardens how come I never seen no queen here?"

They'd been walking out regularly now. On fine days, they walked all the way north to Wilson's Distillery where he liked to count bricks. On colder days they stayed snug inside the house up Maclaggan Street.

Julie thought about his question before she replied.

"Maybe the queen comes at another time."

The gardens were at the bottom of the steep street beyond Moray Place, opposite the NZR Bus Terminal. Sometimes they walked across the busy road while drivers tooted horns, brandished fists. He held her hand tighter. They stood in front of the wrought iron fence enclosing the steam train.

Still holding her hand, he said, "It's Josephine."

"Josephine," she repeated, like she always did. "It's a good name for a steam train. Is it a girl?"

He laughed from deep down in his belly. He knew she was kidding. They liked to laugh.

"Girl steam trains," he chuckled again as they crossed back to the park, her white cane tapping in front of her. "Whatever will you say next?"

Mostly they sat on a wrought-iron bench with lion feet on each corner. He watched the pigeons dance and squabble on the Robbie Burns statue.

"They're doing it again, Julie. Shitting."

She responded with a sweet sound, turning her face toward his. "Well, that's pigeons, eh."

The sun was setting beyond the stone buildings and factory chimneys. Pink streaking an orange sky. The air was burdened with the sickly stench of MacLeod soap and Cadbury Fry Hudson chocolate.

Malcolm explained to Julie how the three names, Cadbury, Fry and Hudson, were first joined together in 1930. Fry was Swiss chocolate, Hudson made biscuits and Cadbury came from England. He gained great pleasure from sharing his learning from the radio.

Before long, darkness shadowed below the sunset, smouldering and intense, reminding him of the smithy's furnace back at The Building, at the hospital. He turned from the brightness and watched as she faced it with her sightless eyes.

"Tell me about today's sunset," she said quietly.

Watching the evening progress, he saw how it changed Julie into the prettiest person he had ever seen, touching her eyes and her nose with its rich colours. For a time he simply gazed at her face, her smile.

"It's red and orange in places with darker blue patches. Oh, and there's purple too."

A bird angrily demanded crumbs. Julie tilted her head, listening.

"That's a sparrow. It should be in bed by now."

"Yes, light brown feathers, black eyes like raindrops on the road. It's a girl."

He didn't take his eyes from her face, and his chuckle made her smile.

They sat close together in silence as cars roared and buses ambled by with the occasional toot. In the distance a siren wailed. With Julie, he wasn't shy any more. He'd learned to laugh at jokes, and he'd learned to make his sentences longer because she listened to him, and she didn't make fun of his stilted speech. Like last night when they'd listened to *Life With Dexter* on the oak valve radio. He'd explained how HMV meant His Master's Voice.

"It's on the front of the radio. You can feel the little dog with your finger. The radio is my learning. It can be yours too, Julie."

As the seasons blended one into the other, the two were rarely apart. He picked flowers from their front garden. She would hold and smell them while he collected a vase.

That autumn it was cold with a white frost, clean and crunchy underfoot.

"We've got new neighbours," he said. "No one has met them. We've seen them, watched them. Bob tried to speak to them. They keep to themselves." Then he grinned a bit. "I heard them saying it could be dangerous, the lot of us living next door. They talk about what we get up to in here, a house full of the likes of us right next door to decent-living Christian folk. They said we should be locked up. Permanent, like. Hah!"

"Why do you think they say that?"

When he didn't answer, she said, "What do you think about them saying that?"

"I think if they feel that way then they best build a wall, a fortress to keep their family safe from us." Silent for a moment, he then added, "But I think they're the crazy ones."

Chapter 4

Grey Lizzie

"Milkman's coming!"

Grey Lizzie shoved her head through the heavy brocade and velvet curtains.

Malcolm ambled down the narrow passage, his bulk almost brushing against each opposing wall. He stepped outside as the early morning autumn sun streamed through the panes of red glass. On the radio, Aunt Daisy talked about the sun shining right up her back passage. Same as here, he thought. Sun shining…

The milkman passed the white picket fences, the clapboard houses and the roughcast terraced cottages, rattling crates, bottles of milk and cream.

"Open the door, Malcolm," snapped Grey Lizzie. "He's gone. Get the milk. Go on. Don't forget my newspaper."

She spent her life hunched over newspapers, more often than not refusing to tidy the bathroom or mop the floor dry. Germs, she insisted. Germs everywhere. Especially on the floor. And when she said 'germs' a shudder of disgust ran through her, making her look stiff and terrified as if she'd come into contact with some filthy dangerous animal.

"I won't forget."

"You will."

"I won't." He set his jaw firmly, and made his way to the gate. Two pints each day and don't forget Grey Lizzie's newspaper.

"You did yesterday," she added once he returned.

"She's a fool, that one. The woman takes no mind 'o me," Bob said. "I'll skim the cream off for tomorrow's porridge so put them in the safe on the back porch for now. And God help anyone who opens the fresh milk first." Bob said this last sentence loudly right into the sitting room. "And ya lot save the tops. Especially the red cream ones."

He bellowed on a bit about keeping house rules, scowling around the group. Someone was getting into the milk, drinking the thick cream right off the top.

Each of them had to promise to pitch in and do their best when they moved into the house. No staff, no nurses, no attendants. Just Sister Evans once a week to check up on them, bring stores and collect soiled linen. Today was Monday so at 10am sharp Sister Evans arrived. She wore a white uniform, stiff white veil and a blue woollen cape lined with red. She came in the hospital van that delivered bags of fresh linen, before collecting their dirty laundry, which Malcolm had stuffed into empty bags. He carried the bags to and fro because he was the strongest person there. Sometimes he'd carry two bags tossed one over each shoulder.

So everyone sat around the kitchen table. After pouring herself a cup of strong Bell tea, Sister Evans took grocery orders and heard out problems and grievances, all the while blatantly counting heads: no one escaped, no one sick, no one dead.

"If anyone has a problem they should bring it up now," she said abruptly. She always said this to make sure the meeting wouldn't drag on with needless piffle. "Or hang on to it until next week."

No one made any comment though there were a few shuffles. Then Sister Evans honed in on Grey Lizzie, her face sullen, mouth curled down as thin as a chicken's beak, waving her hand in the air.

"Lizzie?" Sister Evans invited.

"Crikey Dick," Bob groaned. "Another beef?"

Sister Evans frowned. "Wait your turn, Robert."

Bob crimsoned, tightened his mouth, his ill-fitting false teeth clamped firmly against each other.

Grey Lizzie stood up, as if addressing a real and important meeting, and away she went. She complained, moaned and grizzled, endlessly skirting around her issue.

Malcolm watched and listened, wearing a face of exaggerated understanding.

Finally Sister Evans said, "That's more than enough, Lizzie. Smartly now, what's wrong this specific week? And get to the point."

"Well, it's not that I'm trying to be critical – or hurt Bob intentionally – on purpose. I'm just showing him – helping him – when he does things wrong," Grey Lizzie mumbled. Then added loudly, "He's filthy."

A grin stretched Malcolm's face. How carefully Grey Lizzie chose her words to forestall the moral dilemma of her attack. This was going to be very interesting.

Bob hauled himself to his feet, planted his hands on the table, his long fingers stretched wide apart. His face bulged and dark red, and spittle shot out of his mouth as his teeth clacked away.

"Ya shut the hell up, ya rotten grey bitch!"

And that's when the real fighting began. Lanky Bob with the grizzled ginger hair and dour Scottish temperament lammed into Grey Lizzie.

"Ya dare call me filthy in my kitchen! Ya bloody newspapers put ink all over the show. That's filthy, that's what it is," he raged. "I'm sick to death of ya snivelling and whining about every bloody thing I do. First it's too hot then it's too cold. Ya don't like my Neenish tarts and ya don't like my rice puddings. My sago's got lumps in it. My gravy's got lumps in it. If it's got no lumps it's burnt or it's too runny. Or it's full o' germs! Go back then. Go back to the bloody building so we can all get some peace. Or shut the hell up, ya devil-bitch woman!"

Grey Lizzie constantly moaned about Bob's lack of hygiene in his kitchen.

"We-ell," she said, slowly and deliberately, "your lemon Madeira cake was dry and your rice pudding was burned. I couldn't eat a mouthful."

She lifted her teacup to her mouth, her hand ingrained with printer's ink, a smudge on her forehead.

Malcolm watched Julie. Her head darted this way and that as each person spoke. Kinda like she was watching a game of ping-pong.

"I like it burned," he said suddenly. He liked Bob. "That's exactly how I like it."

"But it was completely burned, wasn't it?" Grey Lizzie smirked maliciously at Malcolm, wanting to draw him to her side of the argument. "I couldn't bear to eat it. Not a mouthful of it."

He again sought to rescue Bob. "Just the bottom."

"It was not burned," Bob said ominously, smouldering, his internal combustion slogging away.

Someone else rallied to further support him. "I like it burned too."

But Grey Lizzie was unable to contain herself any longer. "Burned!"

The whole problem, Sister Evans said, was that they had two cooks in one house. "Perhaps you can share the cooking."

But that was the last thing Bob needed to hear.

"With her? All she's good for is peeling spuds!" Righteously indignant, he sprayed spittle over the lot of them, and his false teeth landed on the table to grin mockingly up at Grey Lizzie.

He bawled gummily, "See what ya done now, ya pernickety scheming bitch!"

"Robert Millar, you are not to use that kind of language in this house," commanded Sister Evans, not unreasonably, and she slapped the table so hard the milk sloshed out of the top of the bottle.

Julie nearly fell off her chair. She hadn't expected that volume of discussion. Grey Lizzie sucked back her next words and her bottom lip, and Malcolm held his breath, watching Bob turn his most brilliant puce yet as he pulled himself to his full height.

Bob gripped the edge of the table in white-knuckled fists. "She can do the whole bloody lot then and go to buggery as well!"

Grey Lizzie made gagging sounds, ready to cry for real, holding her hands to her ears, shaking her head sideways. "Can't hear. Can't hear. Can't hear."

Sister Evans calmly ordered Bob to apologise.

Bob looked first at Grey Lizzie then back at Sister Evans. He took a precautionary step back from the table. "It's my kitchen! She can be damned!"

Grey Lizzie scarpered off to her bedroom.

Malcolm knew exactly how she'd ease herself through the narrow gap between her door and the jamb, her room being crammed wall to wall, floor to ceiling with newspapers dating back a decade. Whenever she got up to her shenanigans, she always scuttled away to hide in her paper lair.

Sister Evans closed the meeting as if nothing had happened. All sorted. No changes necessary. See you next week. Goodbye, then.

The next Monday, when Sister Evans arrived all starched and clean, she sat at the kitchen table to work out new rosters so as to spread the housework more evenly, though ultimately each person did what they wanted to, what they could. For the most part it worked all right. And Bob continued cooking and baking. They all knew, and occasionally said, he was a damned fine cook and generous with his servings. The kitchen was his domain.

Someone else was in charge of dusting, sweeping and polishing the front porch. Grey Lizzie was in charge of keeping the bathroom clean and dry. This she did only when somebody complained about the mess, and then she laboured on about all those germs mixing up together and not wanting to touch other people's doings.

Each evening Malcolm and Julie did the dishes. And he collected and bagged dirty laundry for Mondays as well. He also brought in the daily milk, along with Grey Lizzie's newspaper, which he thrust into her impatient hands.

Chapter 5

Talking

Wednesday was coal day. As soon as Malcolm heard the truck, he ambled off to open the gate ready for the burly coalman. Once he'd got the first sack hoisted, Malcolm led him past his bedroom window and Julie's corner room, along the cold concrete path to the coal bin by the washhouse.

The coalman dumped his load into the bin.

Malcolm was in charge of the wide-mouthed coal shovel so he shovelled up any scattered coal. Each evening he filled Bob's coalscuttle and set it by the range ready for Bob to bank the fire for the long night. And he filled it again first thing in the morning.

It was in the lee of the house, by the coal bin, that the early morning sun first took hold on the coldest of winter days. In these pockets of faint heat, he let the warmth stroke his ankles.

In the sitting room there was a gramophone and some black records. Malcolm and Julie often listened to the music, existing in the security of their private world. But when there were hot scones to pull apart, they joined the others at the kitchen table.

Julie asked Malcolm about his parents.

"Did you have any?"

She snipped the coupon off the yellow tea packet. As if each of her fingers had an eye sewn into the end, she was methodical in her snipping.

When he didn't answer, she said, "Some people don't, you know," and she spread all the saved coupons onto the table and counted them. "There's three dozen now. Did they tell you how you got to be at Seacliff? Why you got there?"

He thought hard and then told her what little he could remember. How his mother was 'slowly fading' in their house where he lived when he was little, up the steep street where nearby pine trees grew tall and swishy in the wind. He recalled the grownups saying the words 'slowly fading'. He told her how

he'd go to his mother's bedroom before catching the
school bus at the corner, how it was his job to dust
her neck with rose geranium talcum powder.

"And you did that every morning? Dusted her
neck with the rose geranium talcum powder?"

"Yes."

He stirred his tea, first to the right and then to
the left with a definite pause in between when, abso-
lutely still, he held the spoon straight up. Stirring
helped him remember.

"I had a stick sword. I made shields from rhubarb
leaves. Bella came to live with us," he ended abruptly, a scowl on his face and in his voice.

"Bella?" The hot scones distracted her, her nose
twitching at the enticing aroma.

"She was my cousin." He spoke flatly. "She came
to help with the dishes and things."

"Oh, dishes." Julie slid her hand in search of plum
jam and butter.

He helped himself to a scone. He didn't help her.
He didn't need to. She mostly did everything for herself. He chewed sullenly.

"I saw them."

Part of the scone broke and fell to the floor. He
stared at it, and then ground it into the linoleum beneath his boot. Bob wouldn't be happy since he'd

already mopped the floor. But, right then Malcolm didn't care. The darkness swooping...

"Uh?"

"I saw them," he growled. He wished she would stop inviting the darkness in. Daddy and Bella...

"Where did you see them? What were they doing?"

"Things. Nothing," he mumbled, thoughts clouding...

After a long pause it was light again. Calm and safe. The thoughts trapped inside.

"So that's how you came there, then?"

He grabbed another scone, heaped butter and plum jam on top with a knife, and squashed it down.

"Yep. That's how."

"Brothers and sisters?"

He focused his full attention on a third scone and chewed noisily, crumbs spilling onto his trousers as he ignored her question.

She pressed on, rewording and fine-tuning.

"Was it just you, then?"

"Yep," he said shortly, through a shower of crumbs, before draining his cup down to the tealeaves, his hand shaking. "Just – me."

He sat on the concrete wall while Bob dug over the garden in the backyard. Birds sang and the days were clearer now after a harsh winter.

Bob said, "Ya gotta get rid o' the couch grass and dock before ya can grow spuds, carrots, parsnips and silver beet. Maybe a cabbage or two. But the white butterfly..." He straightened his back, shaking his head. "Reckon Sister Evans will get me derris dust?"

"No." Malcolm was emphatic. They'd been through this a million times. "It's poisonous."

He followed Bob inside. He liked listening to Bob.

"...and then they took the tower down off the main building. They said it was too dangerous. Ah, but what a sight that must o' been. I wish I were there to see it come down. So how long ya been here, lad?"

"Two years this Christmas. I like Christmas. All those decorations and things. And the special grub you make us. Little crossed tarts and steamed pudding."

Each year, Sister Evans brought in the almond icing and the tree for them to decorate. Christmas was always a good time.

"Ya watch Grey Lizzie with the mistletoe. Don't ya go getting caught out again."

With that Bob slapped his thigh real hard and guffawed loudly. Malcolm remembered how he'd spent the whole week avoiding Grey Lizzie and her puckered lips. Yeah, they were good times all right.

"Mal, if ya grab those bottle tops from the shed ya can string them across my garden to keep the birds off. Reckon ya can give threading a crack if I get ya started? Fourteen silver to one red."

That was how much milk and cream they went through in a week. Bob showed Malcolm his hidden stash, though Grey Lizzie had burned some more of them.

"Silly bitch thinks I don't know," Bob grumbled. "A handful here, a handful there, but I'm on to her. I got too many reds, not enough silvers. I've a mind to burn her bloody newspapers." Bob was fair stewing now. "Light the whole bloody lot right there in her room. Her in it. That'll teach the meddling bitch."

Bob grabbed Malcolm's sleeve, such was his agitation, and Malcolm listened as Bob worked through the various tortures he'd like to exact on Grey Lizzie. He finally settled on one, and they both agreed it was the best.

At dinner, Bob stood at the head of the table prior to serving. Sometimes someone might say grace. But he thumped his fist on the tabletop, startling everyone, cutlery clattering. His face wasn't even red. He just grinned shrewdly, staring down at Grey Lizzie until she averted her eyes.

"Some folk collect things we want and need so ya better keep an eye on ya newspapers. I got matches."

Whilst Malcolm and the others sat in morbid anticipation, Bob dished up slices of succulent roast mutton, crisp roast potatoes, onions, pumpkin and parsnip, gravy, to everyone – except Grey Lizzie.

In tears of rage and frustration, she raced down to her room bellowing like a hungry calf.

Bob grinned from ear to ear.

"My bottle top stash will start to grow pretty quickly now." He spooned out bright green peas.

Malcolm did the dishes, while Bob hummed *Ghost Riders in the Sky*. They'd heard that on the radio all week. The radio alone was democratic, making no distinction between those diminished or undiminished. The notes of the music or the words of the singer or speaker did not alter for anyone. But it could be turned off. Bob was oddly unaffected by Grey Lizzie striding down to turn the radio off in a way that would normally annoy him. He just mentioned he was going to build a chook run from a stack of old timber and netting out back.

"From now on we'll have fresh eggs for sponges with whipped cream on Sundays. No roosters though. They be noisy critters. I can't abide the noise."

Malcolm agreed with a vigorous nod of his head, forking leftovers into his mouth. He imagined fat brown hens squatting in the dust, sleepy and squawking as they fluffed themselves up. Bits of straw, feathers and invisible grains of pollen floating in the air. It would be like that at nesting season. Or at least when it was warmer. Or whenever it was those chooks might lay their brown eggs.

Sundays Bob fried bread in dripping for breakfast.

"I'll wring their bloody necks if any o' them chooks turn out to be roosters."

Malcolm guided Julie into the sun, past the washhouse and the dunny draped in succulent, ripe yellow passionfruit.

Once they were settled, she said, "Did you remember more about your daddy and Bella?"

He scuffed his wired boot in the freshly dug dirt. A worm. He watched it for a moment as it wiggled and squirmed. He didn't want to talk about – things.

Do you remember...

"Do you?"

"No."

"So you don't remember?"

He squashed the worm beneath his boot, slime grinding into slime, as the blackness came over him. He got up and went to his room where he stared through his window at the knotholes in the fence.

Weekly, now that the weather had settled, they extended their walks to farther parts of the town. He talked softly all the time.

"...either fast or slow, the Leith River is sometimes brown and churning or clear and shallow, as it flows out to the harbour, out to the sea and beyond..."

This time they walked all the way north to Wilson's Distillery so he could count some more bricks.

Facing up into the valley beyond the brick factory, he said, "The river starts up there." And he guided her hand in that direction. "It flooded, you know. The Leith. Years ago, in 1923. I think they said that, but anyway they told me about it. I was little."

Julie smiled.

"Wilson's," he said. "Built in 1862 by George Duncan. It burned down in 1872 and they rebuilt it from stone. But the three-storey malt house and kiln weren't built until later in 1876."

As they crossed the busy road to the Botanical Gardens, Julie sniffed the air.

"Polyanthus," she said. "Sometimes our summers are like that. Days after days of flower smells."

He watched as her nose twitched and her blue eyes glistened. Though he was silent from then, still he watched her. He always watched her. He didn't speak again until they were inside the Begonia House.

"The roof is high." He said this suddenly without looking up. "It's made of curved glass. Built in 1863. That's well before we were born." He paused for a moment, stilling her by touching her arm. "And now we have to be very quiet, Julie."

He was not about to tell her how he'd careered into the goldfish pond the year before, breaking exotic begonias and water lilies, splashing noisily, terrified of drowning. The glasshouse keeper was fearsome as he hauled him out, and he didn't mince his words either. Even when he'd explained about his boot, how he'd slipped on the wet concrete.

"Blathering idiot! Get out of here!" the glasshouse keeper bellowed. "And don't you come back, you hear!"

But he did go back when he'd seen there was a new glasshouse keeper. Now he vividly remembered that wet trudge home, the people pointing, laughing, him like a wet scarecrow, the water in his socks blistering his feet. Yes, he clearly remembered the wet walk.

To Julie, he described only the fish, glinting and slippery. Its cold eye fixed on him through the water, watching him. A memory poised in his brain. Was it slippery? Could he catch one and rescue it from the water? Elusive memory...

Julie spoke in her soft musical way as she wandered along in the wet humid air. "I love hearing the water, and the silence beyond the water."

Outside the main gates of the Botanical Gardens they walked on, winding around the streets in no particular order. Past Speight's Brewery, Malcolm touched her arm again, to stop her. He had something special to tell her.

"This is how I count bricks on the street wall."

He scratched with an old nail on the first brick.

"Hear that noise? That's me. I'm counting and writing my name." Most of the bricks already had M on them. "I count off twelve bricks then I scratch my name on that brick. The most I've counted to is twelve. Not sure what comes next. Just lots, because that's what's left over after twelve."

When they had left the house that morning, Bob had been in a surly grump. Even so, he packed them a picnic lunch.

"She's prodding my plants with her stick, Mal. We strung those bottle tops to keep the birds from doing just that. Ah, but she's ya sweetheart, so keep her off my garden, eh."

Now they fed their crusts to the squabbling ducks before they crossed Princes Street, Malcolm dragging Julie by the hand, her other hand clutching her white cane.

"Idiots!" A motorist yelled at them, tooting his horn, shaking his fist. "You loonies should be locked up!"

Malcolm tugged at his cap.

"Was that us? Idiots? Loonies?"

He didn't answer her.

"Malcolm? Us?"

"Nah, just some idiots farther down the street."

He'd often thought about the world's particular attitude toward himself, and the others, and the reason for it. Something within him responded to an apprehension within his own heart, that he did not belong in his life, but somewhere else. At night he sometimes dreamed chaotic, multi-coloured dreams and in the daytime his thoughts still lingered in them.

He didn't talk for a while, but then he suddenly started up again. "Mummy and Daddy took me in the cable car. Right to the top. For my fifth birthday."

"What's a cable car? Can we go in the cable car?"

He thought about that particular birthday when he was a regular boy with a regular family. He remembered that ride, sitting on the outside bench seat or swinging from the leather straps, held up in his father's arms. He talked for a while longer about riding the cable car, sometimes as far as Roslyn or Mornington. But those memories were distant. Yet he could see in his mind the timetable board and the clicked tickets he tucked into his shorts' pocket.

"Can we? Where's the cable car?"

He reverted to the safety of dates, saying, "It started in 1881. But it's all gone now. We went a long time ago but you would have enjoyed the ride."

Chapter 6

Going Back

Malcolm was content.

As he saw it, all was mighty fine in his life. He'd lived at Seacliff Mental Hospital and at Maclaggan Street for most of his life, and this house with Julie was surely as good as it could be.

Until she fell.

Someone – to be specific, that grey-faced, grey-hands Grey Lizzie – hadn't bothered to mop up the spilt water on the linoleum in the bathroom because of the *germs*. So Julie slipped and fell against the hard surface of the bath. It was some time before anyone found her, her tiny broken body in a growing puddle of red. She never screamed for help; that was not her way. She lay shocked, growing chilled until someone complained that Julie was hogging the bathroom. That same someone pounded on the door.

"You've had enough time! You know the rules!"

The querulous voice of Grey Lizzie insinuated itself through a crack in the door. For good measure she wrapped the doorknob in her hanky and shook it. With a clatter, Julie's cane slid from its resting-place against the jamb.

Julie's dead! Julie's dead! Julie's dead in the bathroom! The words chanted and buzzed through the house like the singing of summer crickets on the telephone lines. *Get Malcolm! Julie's dead! Dead!*

"Julie? It's me. It's your Malcolm."

His voice soft against the crack in the door, willing her to speak, to be alive, his whole being shrouded with fear, still hoping, dreading.

He played with the doorknob, rattling and squeezing it long before he turned it. Opening the door a fraction, he tilted his head sideways so he could peer through the slit into the bathroom with his one good eye. He spoke sideways, through the gap.

"It's me, Julie. It's your Malcolm."

Her naked thigh turned translucently white with cold, the red tide beyond on the black and white linoleum. He saw this. Opened the door wider. Her face, a strange colour, lips as purple as pansies. Fair hair, dark like wet string, stuck out from her head like a crooked halo.

His throat closed down, strangling his words. His eye squinted against what he saw.

"Julie? Are you all right?"

The others crowded, clamouring, frustrated by his bulk. Whining. Petulant. Grey Lizzie the loudest.

"It's our bathroom too," she said. "It's our home too. We want to see what's happened, so shove over."

To Malcolm they'd turned animal; wild dogs excited by the smell of blood. He stood firm, barring the door with his body.

Grey Lizzie was relentless, bawling, "C'mon! Let's see Julie!" Punching his shoulder repeatedly.

Barely registering the blows, he considered carefully what he should do. He held the doorknob tightly so there was no chance anyone might wrest it from him. Then he turned his body slowly and placed his hand firmly in Grey Lizzie's clamorous face. When he released the doorknob, he used his other hand to shove at some anonymous blue woollen jersey. Fists and elbows, shoulders, everywhere. With his boot, he manoeuvred them all back until he was able to slip inside the bathroom.

He was with Julie, his bulk filling the small space from side to side completely. The door shut tight behind him.

Squatting, he brushed the back of his fingers against her cheek. He reached up the cold damp wall to the rail above for her towel, and covered her nakedness. She was so small lying there, so still and broken. The upper half of her body slumped down against the bath, whose feet had cruel claws like a lion. Like the park bench at the Queens Gardens.

Like that they remained, stuck in time. Malcolm and Julie, together, on the cramped floor space of the bathroom in the white roughcast house up Maclaggan Street.

An ambulance arrived. It's siren blaring noisily.

People galloped up the front path.

Bang went the front door.

"He pushed me!" Grey Lizzie bawled. "He hurt me!"

Someone clouted her a good one and shoved her into the sitting room, slammed the door on her squeals.

Heavy feet pounded down the passage, past the linen cupboard. Stopped outside the bathroom. Huffing and puffing. They thumped, and they shouted through the closed door. They ordered Malcolm to stand up, open the door from the inside. Come out.

"Just get up, man, so we can open it from here!"

"Damn you, boy! Damn you to hell!"

He was unmoved.

"Come on then, lad. Do as you're told. There's a good feller."

He shut his ears to both the yelling and cajoling.

With a fire axe, they smashed the door from its hinges, and so the ambulance crew, the hospital staff and all the others crowded into the doorway.

"Has the dirty bastard killed her?"

"Get him out of there!"

"Easy, lad, come away then. Easy does it."

"If you don't get out of the way, boy, I'll make you, all right."

Someone's heavy boot kicked his left buttock while a hand grabbed a fistful of hair. Then someone climbed onto his back, hooked him beneath his jaw, forcing his head painfully backward.

Malcolm unfurled his great body. Silently he rose to tower over the ambulance officers, who immediately stumbled backward. He walked from the bathroom into the crowded passage. And stood there. Motionless.

"There's a good lad, then. There's a good lad. Easy, easy."

"You can't trust that lot, I say. They shouldn't be allowed out. They're too bloody dangerous."

Julie was whisked away efficiently by the ambulance men and a squad of white uniforms, crisply flowing veils and swinging, navy blue woollen capes, out to the ambulance on a stretcher, covered over with a grey blanket.

Malcolm, gawping from behind the others, saw everything yet saw nothing.

So – Julie was gone.

Julie's dead. Julie's dead. Died in the bathroom. Died in the bathroom. Julie's dead. Julie's dead. Dead!

The strains of that ridiculous chant started up, crickets filling the house, filling his mind, clouding his thoughts and blinding him. Grey woollen cardigan, blue woollen jersey, shuffling footsteps, chanting, singing, all idiots, all crazy bloody animals, should be locked up...*locked up...locked up...*

"One of you needs to clean up this mess."

Julie – a mess. Softly merging pink and red shades of her life, of her inner beauty drifting toward the drain hole with its black hollow eyes waiting to drink her up.

In silence, he registered that everyone's eyes turned accusingly toward Grey Lizzie.

"It's all her fault," Bob growled. "She should have done her job."

Grey Lizzie slunk off, grey knuckles stuffed into her quivering grey mouth. Back to her paper lair.

With everyone gone and the others seated at the table, Bob dished up dinner. But Malcolm turned and walked silently toward the bathroom to stand in the empty space where the door had been. Crouched down, he put his finger in the congealing blood on the linoleum and he stirred it. He did the same with the blood in the bath and it seemed to respond, first performing a swirling dance away from his finger then back again.

Cupping his hands together and lifting the rosy pink film to his face, he cradled it against his cheek. His silent tears merged with Julie's life and he moaned her name over and over.

When Bob came to find him, Malcolm was covered in cold water and blood; he was cupping up the mess, trying to save her from the drain holes. Trying to save her life.

Bob just patted Malcolm's shoulder a few times. Then he led Malcolm to his bedroom, and stripped him of his wet clothes, dressed him in his pyjamas and saw him into his bed.

When darkness fell, a deep and impenetrable silence shrouded the house.

Malcolm believed he had not looked after his Julie.

It was Monday when Sister Evans next came. Grey Lizzie wiped and mopped busily, a look of guilty disdain on her face. Bob scrubbed the wooden tabletop and cleaned his coal range. He muttered to Sister Evans about the rust patches from the coal dust already showing on the roof. Malcolm sat on the hearth stool and stared blankly at nothing.

With Julie gone his days were a continuous fog. Outside, the dark clouds seemed never to depart. Dank misty mornings, dank misty afternoons, and dank misty nights. The trees in the park had no green leaves; only drifts of dead leaves surrounded him. There were no more bright little flowers. No more birds. Alone in the park, maybe he would see the queen.

He ate nothing, his chest aching with pain so intense he wondered if he might die. He hoped he would. Haunted by memories of Julie, of smells familiar, he stayed in bed, but even sleep wasn't safe. Into the slow hall of time marched the night's dark and dreadful hours. He didn't sleep again. He went outside to the dunny or he wandered the house, checking and rechecking the bathroom from outside the door – but going no farther.

Winter's grip tightened about the house up Maclaggan Street. Snow banked against the windows. He stood outside, his frozen hands deep in his pockets, facing Julie's window, the one facing the back garden, not the one facing the neighbour's cold wall; the wall built to keep them out: keep *them* safe.

Using his nail, he scraped the build-up of snow on the windowsill. But he couldn't see through the net curtains. He stood there letting wind and sleet snatch at him, as winter swathed him.

One day he ventured along the far end of the passage, past the new bathroom door, to Julie's bedroom. After a long time, when he did turn the knob and push the door open a crack to see inside with his good eye, there was no one there. The room was musty from disuse. The casement windows were iced up. Green mould formed on the sill.

Julie was indeed gone.

He heard the deep groan pass through his open mouth as he sat on her bed, shaking his head in disbelief. He grabbed her pillow to his face, masking the appalling noise of moans from deep within, too painful to express through his throat.

And he clutched at Julie's dressing gown, with the tufts of candlewick missing from the front. She'd picked the tufts free, rolled them into balls, put them in her pocket.

His fingers closed possessively around them. And he dragged the garment about himself, the fabric seeming to hold her smell and warmth. His head buried in the folds, he moaned his grief.

The others were drawn to the dread howling that came from down in Dead Julie's room. That's what they called her now, and like shadowy ghosts they watched from the darkened doorway. He was oblivious as each slipped away, most back to the cosy sitting room, Bob to stoke the coal range, make another batch of scones. Whip the cream.

While the moon crept silently across the square windowpane, he remained in the darkness, emptying his mind of everything except the night noises. The moreporks hooted mournfully – owls crying too. In the deeper reaches of his mind, in his secret valley, a dense mist had gathered, tender and insidious as the memories of things best forgotten.

It was safer in the valley, on the inside.

It was peaceful.

Chapter 7

Obliterated

Sister Evans shook him vigorously. The others crowded, necks craning, around the bedroom door.

"Malcolm! Talk to me!"

He was passive when Sister Evans returned with an army of male attendants to escort him back to Seacliff Mental Hospital. Parked out front in Maclaggan Street was the hospital van – its open door a dark and hungry mouth waiting to swallow him up.

Curtains were whisked aside as he walked down the footpath, unresisting, between two uniforms and was settled on the hard leather seat in the back. He heard the van door slam and the click of the lock. He stared blankly through the window, distantly noting the others on the front porch waving as if he were going on an outing. Perhaps to the beach for a picnic.

He was unable to fully comprehend anything.

His thinking shut down.

Through rain and sleet, town and countryside, the van chugged and ground on toward The Building, wheels skidding, shimmying on loose rock and gravel, mud and slush spraying out the back.

The familiar morgue stood solemnly to one side. The van manoeuvred the main entrance gates of The Building. Double-storey wooden barracks alongside featureless main blocks sculptured from grey stone bricks with neither ornamentation nor personality.

Yet who told him it used to be a beautiful castle? Who had he listened to? He looked up at the narrow barred windows. He knew those cell doors had slits in them. It was inconceivable The Building had ever been a castle.

Mrs Green was sweeping the path outside the canteen, and opposite, behind the high wire fence, the big children wandered aimlessly about. The van bypassed the admission block, driving straight to the men's ward.

He was walked to an iron-framed bed next to a locker where he would keep his toothbrush and comb. This minor detail of his toothbrush and comb in the locker encroached into his brain – it must be attended to carefully because the major details of his life were now in chaos.

Voices. "…and in this ward you'll have no other possessions. They'll be placed in store for you…"

For later

For when

For if

A staff nurse, white cap, white uniform, green epaulettes, was talking to the attendant. Something to do with his general size, weight and measure of medication. Passively, he swallowed the pills from the plastic eggcup. And he lay down on the stiff bed and waited for the dark sleep, to die and be with Julie.

But they hauled him off, sat him upright on a chair, and left him there. He folded his hands and waited. He didn't want the drowsiness to creep up on him, sneaking him away into a deep silence. He wanted to greet it, note each step it took. He thought about the van, The Building. Now the waiting.

The Staff Nurse returned. Someone said he would need to evacuate his bowels. Why didn't they say shit? Someone said he should be ready. Ready for what? Ready for Julie? Yes, he was ready.

He was escorted to the communal bathroom, and he offered no protest as attendants stripped him naked. Obediently he lay on the concrete floor, closing his eyes, drawing his knees up to his chest, his mind shut to all things unpleasant. He stood as they dressed him in pyjamas, was compliant when they dragged him onto a trolley with a rubber sheet stretched across it.

Out of the ward and down the endless corridors, the trolley wheels drummed soothingly, rubber against rubber. Through the doors, push and bang, more rubber. Sterile white and green painted walls, the ceiling a swimming whirlpool of electric light bulbs racing above him, all voices merging into one.

Rubber against rubber, faster now, and thrumming...

Leather straps were fastened securely around his wrists and ankles as attendants pressed down on his knees and shoulders.

Julie smiling down at him. Nearly there.

A nurse dabbed cold paste on each of his temples before fitting strange things to his head. Efficiency. The white team working in unison. Working fast. The Box; he knew what it was – they'd talked about electroconvulsive therapy in the wards, and at the house. A doctor spoke of voltage as he held two black things like the long earpiece of a telephone.

Ready now, drifting peacefully closer to Julie.

When the shock registered, his brain screamed. His body instantly convulsed. Eyes wide open; the agony of it. Eyes clamped shut; the agony of it. His whole body arched with the great force. He fiercely ground something in his mouth, bounced backward onto the trolley, fighting with all his might against the leather straps trapping him there. But still he bounced. His feet strained downwards, ankle tendons stretched to ripping. Hands curled into tight fists, nails drawing blood from his palms.

More voltage. More high-pitched screaming in his brain, accompanied by lightning flashes, blue and red. Then white. Growling and howling deep inside. Animal noises. Deafening. Competing with the red agony...

The flashing lights inside his brain subsided, replaced by a haze of senseless pain coursing through his entire being. Around him, the team moved on; he was non-existent. The swish of starched uniforms, hard little caps, navy woollen pants, squelching of rubber soles on painted floors. So vividly clear, yet somehow slowly distorting, dark shadows moving away...

The silence. Soundless – drifting on and on.

Constrained by leather straps.

A voice that soothed and consoled, then other voices of satisfaction and approval over a procedure gone well. And the levels of medication? Who was really sure? He was a big, big man.

Everything gone...

Obliterated...

When Malcolm finally woke to the drug-induced echoes of moans and whimpers, he wondered who could be so desperately miserable they would carry on like that. He was aware he was soaked in cold piss. His jaw ached interminably. His head pounded relentlessly while his entire body throbbed and jangled. A gurgle of sound. Who was that? He wished the whimperer would shut up so he could sleep.

Someone slapped his hand.

Forever he drifted, sometimes hearing the whimpering and gurgling, sometimes being bathed and changed, only to be soaked in piss again. Water forced between his cracked lips into his bruised mouth. Tablets. Medicine poured down his throat. Ulcers formed, stinging. Glycerine on gauze sticks swabbed around his tongue and gums.

Pink nurse? Why was he at the foot of his bed? Why was the wall at his feet?

Pink nurse?

When is it?

Where is it?

He sat in an armchair in the dayroom, the smell of piss stronger, stinging his groin. Everything he saw through his aching eyes was blurred. Sometimes a stray thought. Occasionally the thought honed in acutely on one memory or another; the lucidity and clarity strangely frightening.

Other times nothing to prompt them. Just dull. Not totally dark. Just dead. He wondered if he had died.

Someone said, "There's been another execution."

A passing attendant wiped the drool that dripped into a sodden mess on the front of Malcolm's pyjamas, tied a towelling feeder around his neck.

His mouth hung slack.

Execution?

Was it him?

Was he dead?

Chapter 8

The Green Budgie

Clarity: for today, and memories of Maeve Murphy and her green budgerigar. Malcolm attempted to recall every word she had ever spoken to him. His intention was to fill the dark void in his mind, fearful that his memories would become lost or spill out if he didn't hold onto them. Today was Maeve's day.

Sometimes she lived in isolation higher up the hill at the women's ward. This ward overlooked the drab stone buildings and the little village nestled safely farther down in the valley, toward the open sea. Maeve was the one who'd called The Building a castle. Maybe from up there it was. From where he was it was more like a prison. She came from Quarantine

Island off Port Chalmers up the Dunedin Harbour. They rowed her to the Seacliff rocks in a dinghy, across the Pacific Ocean.

Maeve said she'd seen the lighthouse. "Not many people have seen it, you know. Like when it's daylight. I saw that lighthouse up real close."

She'd been escorted over the slippery strands of black kelp and sharp mussel-clad rocks, past blue penguins and paua, up the steep climb to the road high above. He knew this part was true because he'd been down to the rocks, before he lived in Maclaggan Street. He knew the tang of salt spray on his face, the smell of seaweed and crabs, the joy at being totally free on the rocks. Alone except for seagulls.

She had walked up through the buttercup fields that joined into the rocks, she'd said, and up the uneven rocky pathway that was the high road, past the hall, past the primary school. Up, up the hill. Even beyond the main gates, higher than anyone else, to the women's ward.

She was right proud to be up the hill.

"I survived tuberculosis. Not many did. It's a regular hospital there. It's better than being down in the loony bin. From up there in the hospital you can see right across the Pacific Ocean." Or so she said.

One day she showed Malcolm her storybooks. Strangely enough, he knew the stories by heart, though he didn't know how. Besides the books and her trip in the rowing boat, he thought she was daft. She'd kept her budgie on the end of a string. If that wasn't mad, what was?

Maeve said, "Old Mrs Abbott cut the wings off her budgie so it couldn't fly. That Damned Cat ate it. We had a terrible job settling. We cried all night."

He pictured a ward full of crying women.

"It was horrible," she said louder. "We were very upset."

So she tied her green bird on a string. She'd thought by warning That Damned Cat about how she'd skin him alive if he moved a whisker in her budgie's direction, she'd keep it safe. He knew the story by heart, how she and her budgie paraded up and down the long hall. In contempt of the cat.

"It was Christina who got hold of my budgie." Maeve said this with a sob in her voice. "She dragged him around on his string, him half-flying or bouncing on his back. I tried to get him, but Christina ran into the domestic woman driving the electric polishing machine. Killed my green budgie."

Maeve bawled loudly as she described how she beat up Christina, pulling out most of her hair. She

wailed long and hard about how the domestic woman had finished off her budgie yet blamed the patients.

"She said if we were still using mops I'd still have
my budgie and Christina would still have her hair.
And there wouldn't be all those bloody feathers to
clean up. She was so nasty, Malcolm. Malcolm!"

He'd surprised himself by laughing loudly when
she got to this part. She'd rounded on him smartly.

"You've got a mean streak. I wish I never told
you. I hate you! I'll hate you forever."

He stopped laughing. He didn't want to be hated
by anyone. And he didn't know why he'd laughed
anyway.

His thoughts wandered away from her. He once
wondered what it would be like to have a cat. Sometimes he'd deliberately left the rubbish bin lids open
so kittens could climb inside for a feed. But Maeve –
ah, yes, there she was again – blabbed to an attendant who dragged up all manner of health issues:
mange, ringworm, fleas and worse. What could be
worse than mange, ringworm and fleas?

He sat, unmoving, in the armchair in the dayroom.

It was time to eat: sausages, peas, mashed potato and gravy.

It was time to sleep. He rolled his clothes in a bundle and put it outside the door. In the early morning someone tossed it back inside.

It was time to get up. 6am.

Lining the hall outside the bathroom were wooden benches, back to back, where the patients sat, some still in pyjamas, some already naked, waiting to be bathed, others dripping wet, waiting to be dried. Donkey stood naked and still, his penis, much bigger than the other men's, hanging down, flaccid, his balls like red oranges. There were three bathtubs and three wooden chairs in the bathroom. Everyone had to be bathed, dried and dressed by breakfast time. Two inches of hot water in each bath, emptied when it was cold and scummy from repeated use.

As he let his pyjamas drop, Malcolm felt the chill rise up from the soles of his feet. Waiting in front of the baths, the basins and the lavatories with no seats and no doors, he glanced at his awakening body. His shoulders were broad. The thick matted hair on his chest extended across them, down to his belly button. His eyes followed the rough curls below his hollow paunch. Flesh hung in a fold over his hips. It used to fit him – now it was too big.

Donkey was saying he didn't need to piss. A nurse threatened Donkey with The Treatment for not standing in the open urinal and pissing when she said so, though he had nothing to piss. Malcolm tried sending him a message through his eyes. Just piss some. It's easier that way. He understood why Donkey, like some of the others, preferred to piss in the bathwater where no one would see him do it. But, no, Donkey had to stand in the open and piss because he was told to. And that was how it was. He stood there, his hand holding his penis, pissing a little in the open.

Malcolm knew Donkey would finish it in his bath.

"Get over here, sissy. I haven't got all day," snapped a stout nurse as she leaned across to turn on a tap. Air bubbles gurgled and blurted through the tap, clanging in the pipes behind the walls.

The bath water was shallow.

Donkey pissed.

Nightly, the patients left their false teeth in labelled pottles on a bench in the bathroom. A junior nurse on night duty would collect them and gingerly place them on a tray. Sometimes she had to get them out from a patient's mouth first. Once he saw her drop the tray onto the floor, her left standing in the midst of them. He imagined them snapping at her feet.

She scooped them back onto the tray, mixed and mismatched, audibly dry-retching.

He grinned, glad he didn't have false teeth.

Outside. "The sun will do you good after this long winter," the bald attendant said. "You go for a wee walk. Off you go then. Don't forget lunch, boy."

Malcolm felt apathetic and vague as he wandered through the main entrance, down the uneven road to the tennis courts. Someone had pulled weeds from the edges, and the nets had been tightened and the lines re-painted white. Someone apparently had his old job. The tennis courts were for the use of patients like The Twins – Leonard and Margaret – and the staff. The Twins waved to him. Inseparable, they moved in complete harmony with each other. If one stood they both stood, if one sat down they both sat down. If one was scolded or got the belt they would stand together awkwardly, arms at their sides until the punishment was complete. Afterward, they comforted each other in a special language the staff didn't understand, chirrups, mumbles, and vague hand movements.

Malcolm waved back, then lowered his head and limped on. This was his first time outside on his own since he'd come back to The Building nearly a year ago. The Building, as it was called by Malcolm and the others, had been born from The Castle ruins.

Glancing up at the red brick walls of Clifton House, he noticed the ivy had grown considerably since he'd last seen it, stretching out tentacles, steadily claiming the bricks in its path. He remembered some time in his recent past when he'd walked to Speight's Brewery in Dunedin, but he couldn't remember why he'd walked there. Wilson's Distillery had bricks. Did it have ivy too?

He shook his head, removed his cap and scratched his forehead. His thoughts blurred. Why could he remember some things clearly and others not at all? A welling up of frustration swamped him, making him more determined to do his memory exercises even on those days when he didn't want to.

As abruptly as he'd stopped, he moved on. His head was down; he didn't know where he was going. Following some instinct not connected to thought, he doggedly traced the narrow path between the tennis courts and Clifton House, his boots splashing in shallow puddles. A startled rabbit sprinted away for a few yards, then stopped.

What would it be like to have a rabbit?

Sister Evans had taken his mouse when he came back to The Building last year, before they gave him the pills: one white and three pink. She smoothed its fur down before wrapping it in her handkerchief. She promised she'd find it a new home. She also took his nail, the one he used for writing his name, M.

He wandered on, barely noticing the cold. He considered the dreamtime after he'd had his shocks, how he was borne along on the wisps of memory.

On the winding driveway that lead down beyond the Medical Superintendent's house, he stopped to view the huge trees that surrounded the house: magnolias, walnuts, kowhai, elms, the tall and stately yew, the rhododendron bushes tucked in at the bases to form an almost impenetrable force of foliage. The spindly cabbage trees. There were many more he didn't know the names of. Some thorny, some so tightly packed with hard little branches and leaves a boy would have no joy in climbing them. Though such a tree would make an excellent hiding place.

He studied the differences between each tree; some were in full bloom, others not; the shape of the leaves, the flowers, the tree as a whole. With the rhododendrons he tried to memorise the different colours and the variation of each bush's leaves.

Then there was the grand white wooden house secreted in the midst of this fine garden. Was Cynthia still there, making beds, shaking mats for the Medical Superintendent and his family? Cynthia spent all her days inside. It had upstairs verandas with rows of painted carved wood to support the railing on the top, like a capped picket fence. Did Cynthia still clean and cook, only returning to the ward at night?

He was surprised. So soon after thinking about Cynthia, he saw her approaching from the side of the house, wringing her hands in a most unhappy manner, tears dripping off the end of her thin nose and chin.

His throat tightened.

"Oh, Malcolm," she said, as if he'd never been away, "I know it's my problem and they keep telling me that but..." She clutched at his jacket, as nervy and worried as he'd ever remembered her to be. "...it's just that I might do something wrong. I might chip the teapot or I might leave an eye in the potatoes..."

She gulped for air, her face contorted and strange.

He moved a step farther away but she tightened her grip with both hands.

"...or a crease in a pillowslip..." She rushed her speech, no hesitation, no pauses. "...and they say it's part of my problem that I have to make it all perfect because I see myself as an imperfect person..."

She let his sleeve go. He stayed dead still.

Eventually she stopped talking, chewing her nails, the ends of her fingers bleeding and frayed.

"I'm so tired...it's all this thing..."

He knew of her compulsion, her incessant tidying and neatening of the ward furniture, straightening the curtains, ensuring the cutlery was set perfectly for meals.

The women who shared her ward regularly reported her to Sister. "She whimpers and keeps us awake with her fidgeting and straightening her sheets. And she's in and out of bed a dozen times or more. She's worse than the bloody cockroaches, she is."

As Cynthia's hands continued to twist and wring, he saw how that might annoy.

"...and they moved me to a corner and said I could make my bed as often as I wanted and that the others were heartily sick of me, and Sister too..."

And so she continued to explain and apologise for the next fifteen minutes. Now he felt too sad. He didn't know what to say or what to do. Eventually, he wandered off leaving Cynthia behind, wringing her hands, and sobbing still, with her face tear-wet.

Chapter 9

The Siren

Beyond the white house, Malcolm ventured farther, seeking the giant walnut trees, lofty and eternal. He walked on their kindly carpet of dead leaves while rays of sun fell through their crowns, and he held his breath. Safe and at peace, he stretched out a hand to re-introduce himself, overcome with a feeling of rediscovery, of renewed gratitude, and possession. This place was entirely his: the moss, the walnut trees and damp leaves, the sun motes, secrecy. He watched blackbirds take flight and waited for the wood pigeon, the woosh-woosh of its wings, but he neither saw nor heard it this day.

He remembered how, as a youth, he'd climbed the trees dragging a stick with him to whack off walnuts, and then he'd clambered down and gathered them into a pile before peeling off the rotted outer layer. Crunching two shells together in his strong hand, he'd expose the treasure within – either a juicy kernel or an equally tempting black dried-up kernel. Either were good grub. He kicked aimlessly at the leaves, inhaling the familiar smell of decay.

Soggy leaves stuck to the toe of his boots and the cuffs of his trousers. He knew these leaves. He stood before one particular tree, the branches beckoning him to hide within their leafy safety.

"No," he said abruptly, making the branches stir and the leaves rustle in defiance. "I'm too big to hide. I'm a grownup now."

He looked beyond the grove of trees, out to sea, across the dusty Coast Road, which wound above Seacliff village. With his eyes fixed on the horizon, he wondered how long it would take to row from the rocks below back to Port Chalmers, across the Pacific Ocean. How long would it take to visit Maeve's lighthouse? He longed to go down to the cliffs where he could inhale the salty tang of the sea, perhaps see a little blue penguin scrabbling on the rocks. In the far distance, the lighthouse sat patiently, guarding the treachery of the open harbour entrance.

A dog howled.

A car tooted.

Cold now, he lay beneath the tree, comforted by the familiar smell of squashed onion flowers.

The hospital siren began to wail, rising and fading, setting his teeth on edge, and causing his muscles to tense. He covered his ears and pressed his shoulders deeper into the leaves. But it was not calling him.

He set to recalling all of the times he had heard the siren wail, what it meant. He numbered them off on his fingers as they came to mind. He vowed he would keep those memories close and often go over them so as not to lose any. Sometimes in the dark of night the sirens would sound. The hospital vans and cars would start off to be joined by cars from the village. Like some dark and secret order they would first unite and then disperse in well-planned teams. Always, they searched the cliffs first. Sometimes the searchers didn't make it in time; there would be an empty bed in a ward and no one talked about anything.

Another visit to the morgue.

Another secret.

Teddy Hopkins was found without the sound of a siren. He had ridden away in the dim early morning on a bicycle in his pyjamas. Doug, a young farm employee from the village on his way to bring in the cows had cycled past Teddy whom he later described as 'peddling at a leisurely pace in his pyjamas' down the main road, near the railway station, past Reid's farm. A hospital van and two attendants were dispatched to return Teddy to his ward. He was not escaping. He wanted to ride the bicycle he found leaning against the ward fence. He happened to be in his pyjamas. It was early in the morning.

Malcolm recalled the time the siren wailed for a youth missing from the village. The youth's parents worked at the hospital. Malcolm knew this for he had learned to listen well. They found the youth's motorbike on the top of the cliffs and for days they searched the cliffs and the caves, and the paddocks rolling down to the sea. And the surrounding dense native bush. The village women made stews and soup and delivered plates of buttered scones with homemade jam and cream to feed the searchers who apparently never found the youth. It might have been a rumour, but he'd heard how the same youth lived from then on at Sunnyside Mental Hospital in Christchurch.

Another secret.

Another shame.

Clouds gathered overhead, the temperature dropped, the weather breaking with gusty squalls ripping through the carpet of walnut leaves. He clambered to his feet and made his way back up the road that circled the hospital, his prison, her castle. The siren finally stopped, leaving the air bruised, the birds unsettled.

Sometimes the siren went off and it meant nothing to the patients.

To Mr Waldron, one of the staff from down in the village, it meant something. Malcolm knew his story by heart. He decided to retrieve every separate part he had ever heard, as part of his memory homework, and make it into one whole story. Starting at the beginning, he recalled when Mr Waldron brought his bride out from England to settle in the new country. He heard how later everyone was sorry for him; the young couple had only been married a few years. And everyone had their own ideas on how the unfortunate event took place.

That day the sirens had wailed and faded and the hospital wards buzzed with questions. Who's escaped? Who's scarpered? Who's done a runner?

Who's gone over the fence? Who's out of the booby hatch?

But the problem wasn't up at The Building. It was down at the village.

According to Mrs Roger, the Station Master's wife, Mrs Waldron said she had left the baby sleeping in his bassinette. She'd said the poor wee tyke was exhausted from his colic and it seemed a pity to wake him. But it was Mr Waldron's birthday and she needed the icing sugar.

They said the sun was out, the washing on the village lines drying on that otherwise perfect day. An old goods' train rumbled slowly from the station toward the level crossing. Malcolm recalled talk of newer, faster trains, those that sped along reducing the trip from Dunedin to Christchurch by hours.

So Mrs Waldron had paid the grocer a shilling for her icing sugar, then set off down the path toward the crossing, past the other shop set among trees and wild sweet peas, her long hair billowing behind her. Mrs Roger was by then at Seacliff Railway Station, where she stopped for a cup of bright brown tea. As she glanced back, Mrs Waldron had neared the level crossing. How exasperating it must be to find the goods' train fully stopped, she told Mr Roger.

Malcolm recalled how it often shuddered into movement across the street when he occasionally went down to the village. Then it would blow out a cloud of steam, whistle loudly, shunt a few yards forward, then back again, and come to a complete stop. Often, he had to wait a long time for it to clear the track.

Everyone imagined the young woman becoming upset, her thoughts turned to her baby, and to the cake she'd left cooking in the range. Mr Waldron had said the little chap was plagued with colic and awake for most of the night. Mrs Waldron was fair exhausted. But her baby? Awake and crying? No doubt those thoughts hounded her as she made her final decision.

It was suggested she had held the bag of icing sugar between her teeth before touching the greasy coupling with both hands. It was gritty and grimy, often with not the slightest hint of a shudder for several minutes. Perhaps she'd taken her chance, swung herself up into the couplings, astride the huge shackles.

No one knew exactly how it went though various opinions supported the idea that the train had started with a lurch and Mrs Waldron slipped between the two units. Someone ventured that had she slipped right through she might have been able to lay flat on the ground, avoiding direct contact with the underside of the train, the heavy steel wheels and steam. She might well have survived.

It was further opined that her long hair became caught in the grease giving sufficient purchase for it to loop around the coupling. But, whatever, back and forth shunted the noisy train drowning out all sound barring its own.

The bag of icing sugar was found intact.

Though he hated that story, recalling all the details was a means of keeping his memory alive.

Without his memory he was no one.

Chapter 10

Mrs Green

Mrs Green ran the hospital canteen. To Malcolm, she smelled like fresh flowers, and being gentle she often provoked something in his distant memory, a hint of someone else. She understood more than some that he didn't always feel the need to talk, not that he couldn't. Mondays, Wednesdays and Fridays she opened the canteen at 9am selling writing pads and envelopes, chocolate fish and Buzz Bars. She even sold the new Pinky Bars. He signed M in her journal for mixed lollies like Eskimo men and milk shakes, jubes and jellybeans, and a few aniseed balls for good luck. Mostly the men signed for Government Issue tobacco. He didn't smoke. Mrs Green wore dirndls gathered at the waist with shirring elastic, buttoned from the collar right down the front to the hem. Mondays she sold mutton pies sent down from the Palmerston bakery. He liked those mutton pies, hot and peppery.

His best mate, Sandy, rode in the cab of the delivery lorry. He always called out, "How's ya been, Mal?" when they were still some distance away.

Malcolm turned his head away, but he couldn't contain a grin as he raised his hand.

Sometimes they were in the same ward together.

One day Malcolm asked him why he was there.

Sandy said cheerfully, "An infection got in my head, ya see. Did I tell ya I see ghosts? I see their shadows. I smell them."

"I don't smell them," Malcolm said. Then, "Sandy, what's your real name?"

"I dunno, cobber. Maybe Sandringham."

They doubled up laughing, talked about some other weird names like Buck, Satan and Mouse. They weren't real names. Just nicknames. Like Donkey and Snake.

Malcolm thought of Mouse whom he'd met at the men's lockup – Mouse, a timorous, hesitant grey soul, cowering and all hunched over. Too afraid to die, more afraid to live. And he understood why

Buck was called Buck – his sharp yellowed teeth, like a big old rat. But Satan he never understood.

The canteen was near the boys' ward, Tamariki. While Mrs Green scooped tuppenny ice creams he asked her why some of the boys were so big.

"Some are as old as you, Malcolm," she said. "They just never grew up. Some might grow big while others stay small. But their minds are still very young."

Girls were kept in The Annex along with newly admitted patients. He'd heard there were nine nurses looking after them, and each nurse had a private room in The Annex. Staff and patients alike shared the big bathroom with its three baths. Once they commenced night duty, junior nurses moved into the Nurses' Home. Though he never understood why they moved, he knew lots because he listened.

He wanted to know more about the big boys at Tamariki. Their playground had swings and a sandpit, and he watched them plod aimlessly around, vacant faces staring at the ground, at the fence, at the sky. Some had enormous heads, like the boy an attendant was carting around in a wheelbarrow.

Malcolm went back to the canteen to ask Mrs Green why some had big heads.

She explained about hydrocephalus, how they'd got sick when they were little kiddies. He went outside to stare at them.

The boys never spoke. Had they so little? Small glimpses into happiness, or nothing? One grinning boy beckoned, so he walked closer to the fence. This boy had tufts of hair pulled out, no eyelashes or eyebrows. The boy dribbled and grinned inanely.

Malcolm began to move away.

The boy beckoned again.

Malcolm left.

The farmer in the dell the farmer in the dell hey ho the derry oh the farmer in the dell the farmer takes a wife the farmer takes a wife hey ho the derry oh the farmer takes a wife

This fine spring day, a year on from when he last visited the walnut trees, and Mrs Waldron was killed by the train, Malcolm walked down to the bottom of the steep road and back up again toward the hospital's main entrance. He viewed it all from a different angle: the library settled peacefully among gardens of neatly tended rhododendrons and yellow and purple bushes, azaleas, and the morgue with its little high-up window. What was it they were afraid of? That a corpse might try to escape – a dead body on the loose? He chuckled to himself and decided to tell Mr Antonio, the cook.

Mr Antonio laughed loudly, clapping his floury hands together, punching Malcolm's arm.

"Once you're in that morgue, you're in to stay. So you'd better behave yourself then, eh."

Mr Antonio cooked in the main kitchen, baking bread twice weekly. He fed Malcolm bread crusts with roast hogget dripping. The kitchen radio was always on.

It was good to know Mr Green too. Now he was retired from his job at the hospital, Mr Green often visited the kitchen and Mrs Green at the canteen. He called her his missus.

He said, "It's time you called me Jack, son."

Malcolm looked away, still called him Mr Green. He told good stories, calling them yarns, but Malcolm wondered if Mr Green was fibbing. Sometimes he found it hard to tell who was on staff and who weren't at this place called The Building, nestled in the hills above the cliffs where the blue penguins bumbled around on the rocks and the black seaweed glistened.

At the hospital everything moved slowly, like fog. He tried to remember where he'd been heading when he first moved out, down to Dunedin, to Maclaggan Street. That was in 1946 when he was about twenty-five years old. But something had gone wrong because now he was back at The Building. He'd been back a couple of years, he'd been told, so he thought he must be at least twenty-eight. Maybe even older.

He cursed his foggy brain, half-recognising the nature of his own condition, dimly recalling a previous existence. Sometimes he felt he didn't live anywhere any more. He just existed among the rotting remains of dead people. Sometimes he thought he might sift through those remains, might even read the remains. Sometimes he searched for signs of his passing, for the scent of his prey, his memory, so he could hunt it down. That was all there was left – the scent of his memory. The rest was the mess he left behind when he passed through.

Some things he knew for sure though. Mondays were Pinky Bars and mutton pie days. Thursdays were the days he visited the main kitchen.

"Routine is best for you," he'd been told by Yorky, who pronounced his words funny, who always talked about the weather compared to back home. Wherever that might be. "Don't vegetate. Get out and live, lad. You're more fortunate than most. Look at that lovely sky. It's not raining, is it? There's no smog." Yorky said all this. "And you could talk more. You used to talk the hind legs off a chair, before you came back. But, ah, laddie, I don't know about these new-fangled schemes. We don't have 'em back home so I just don't know. Remember what you were like then?"

Remember...

Do you remember...

Do you remember?

"Do you?"

"Yes," he said, though he didn't.

He waited to feel the need to talk. He felt nothing. There was little he could remember and nothing to encourage him to take an interest in his life. If he used to be different, like they said – and sometimes he knew they were right – they must have taken his thoughts captive and left him with only fringes and tatters, not enough to live with. He wondered where they stored his stolen thoughts. Maybe they stored them in the morgue with the little high-up window. Hah! As if memories would try to escape.

Maybe that was the secret.

The delivery lorry pulled away from the parking bay alongside the boiler room. Malcolm scuffed his boots in the coal grits considering whether he could stand there until it ran over him, like Jock did. Jock had lost his reasoning since all his shock treatments. Malcolm wondered if it might hurt as much as The Treatment. The driver tooted. He stood still with his eyes clamped shut. The driver tooted again and yelled. Someone pulled him roughly to one side.

Sandy climbed down from the lorry and gently took his arm.

"Come on, Mal," he said almost confidentially, which was a surprise as usually he yelled. "I've something to tell you."

Once they were on the footpath, he said, "Ned The Accountant escaped."

Malcolm knew Ned The Accountant. But escaped? He hadn't seemed the type, and yet what was the type? There was always covert excitement when someone escaped. The word went around like a whispered breeze and the siren set up wailing. But a patient could be 'at large' for weeks before being found, or persuaded to return. Sometimes the alert would go out to the locals to lock their doors, but mostly with some food or a beer in their belly the patient would happily return to his ward alone or under escort.

He shook his head to clear his thoughts. "I heard the siren," he said. "I didn't hear the name."

Sandy said, "He went over the lockup ward wall this morning before lunch."

Chapter 11

Jack Green's Yarn

Mr Antonio was in the main kitchen, his hands warming on the outside of the immense enamel stove doors, flour right up his hairy arms, laughing and joshing. Some got right on with the monotony of their task, peeling onions, scrubbing pots. But there was always someone who would join him in laughter. Today it was Malcolm.

"*O solo mio*," Mr Antonio sang in his deep baritone from way down in his big fat belly. Though the radio words were in English, he often sang in Italian.

Malcolm stood quietly at the bench and considered the sacks of spuds. He would peel them, remove the eyes, wash them and put them in buckets of fresh water. Someone else would tip them into the steamer while he scrubbed the concrete floors. Mainly women worked in the kitchen, but he liked to spend time there. The kitchen was safe.

When Mr Antonio sang, Dorothea, who was once an opera singer, cast scowling glances at him through wet eyes, (she cried easily) muttering indistinctly. She disliked singing and would often stride over on her stiff or trembling legs to turn the radio off.

Mr Antonio said, once he'd finished making custard and come to sit at the large table, "You wanna tell me about that home plan down in the big smoke? You've been back a few years now, haven't you?"

Malcolm tilted his chin. "Yep."

Custard! Suddenly, he remembered last Christmas, the steamed puddings and ladles of yellow custard. Throughout The Building there were decorations and fancy trees with coloured lights. Christmas trees too – some over eight-feet tall. In his ward, theirs stood in a brightly decorated tin bucket. The soft fragrance of the pine permeated each corner of the dayroom, now decorated with tiny lights encased in square plastic lanterns, each with a dusting of European snow. Amongst all that winking brightness, miniature baubles frosted with crystals twinkled delicately.

From his chair at the table in the kitchen, if he squinted his eyes, he could clearly see that tree, brightly sparkling and winking. There was an angel on the topmost branch. Sister Hodge bought it to replace the fat Santa, which normally adorned the spot. That Christmas, the ward windows were draped in newly created paper streamers. He'd helped make those.

Young nurses retaped the paper-chains from the previous year, those that had come unstuck during the annual storage. Then they fixed them in draped garlands above the doors and windows. One nurse pressed little buds of Sellotape to the walls to secure the tinsel, and above the ceiling lights another draped lengths of shimmering foil string. Cottonwool was stuck on every available surface to represent snow, and cardboard stars coated in glitter hung from the ceiling.

Christmas cards were arranged on the sideboard so anyone might reach for one to read, and then another and another.

From the outside, the hospital grounds had looked like fairyland. The folk from the village joined the staff to walk through the grounds singing

Christmas carols. He recalled how he joined in, wandering from ward to ward with the group growing larger by the minute. Some had great voices, booming out in the still clear night. Yes, those were good times: Christmas, sports day and the concerts. They were the best. He made a pledge to focus on those three occasions as part of his current memory exercises.

But today he'd come to listen to the radio, clean potatoes and scrub floors. Even though Dorothea had turned the radio off. She reminded him of Grey Lizzie back at Maclaggan Street.

"You were gone some time, weren't you?" Mr Antonio continued. "What was it like out there for you?"

"It was too big."

"Too big, huh?"

"Yep. Too big."

Mr Antonio bustled about in his floury kingdom.

"Here, lad, try this mutton casserole."

As far as Malcolm could tell, there was no difference between his casseroles and the stews Bob made at Maclaggan Street. They were both meaty, floating with peas, carrots, turnips and dumplings. Malcolm figured a casserole used to be called a stew. Casserole was maybe its nickname.

A bell announced morning teatime. Dorothea stopped scrubbing porridge pots to bring out crockery cups and enamel teapots, which she thumped down onto the tabletop next to a jug of milk. Mr Antonio produced a batch of scones with crusty cheese on top. This batch was baked in a slab, though it was creased with a knife before cooking. Just not separated first.

Dorothea sailed into her seat and clasped the handle of the first teapot. She started right in to pour tea. It had always been her job to pour. A new patient had attempted the job only to end up scalded as Dorothea asserted her claim over the boiling water. She was the longest serving person in the kitchen. So, with her constantly wet apron patch from leaning against the big sinks, she finished pouring then backed away to stand behind the others. To Malcolm she was like a dull ghost in a wet pinny.

Mr Green arrived with a cheery, "Gidday, everyone," and seated himself beside Malcolm. Immediately, he started in on one of his yarns.

"Did you hear the one about the bikie gang that came to me house?"

"I d-don't like these s-scones." That was Dorothea. "They're not p-proper s-scones."

Those there when Mr Green first came in and spoke, gawped, scones halfway to open mouths, butter dripping down fingers or off their chin.

Mr Green said, "Just cut different is all."

She repeated about them not being proper scones, her lower lip quivering, legs all a-tremble.

Mr Green leaned closer to her, grinning.

"Crickey dick, woman, don't eat 'em then. There you go, if they're not proper, don't eat 'em. They'll probably kill you if they're not proper, eh."

Malcolm slurped his cup, his mouth moist and grinning, and his eyes darted from Mr Green to Dorothea and back again. She poured more cups of tea, slopping them deliberately as others continued to arrive. Mr Green's head cocked from one side to the next like a rooster, watching their varied reactions. Some didn't know whether to laugh or cry. Malcolm burst out laughing and then the rest followed. Dorothea stomped back to her bench in a sulk.

Then Mr Green said, "All right, so I can get on with me story?" He set his eyes on Mr Antonio who'd gone to thicken his stew, and he yelled, "Toni, you hear the one about me bikie gang?"

"Not that one. Dorothea, pour me another cuppa, lovie."

Mr Antonio ambled back to the table, wiping his mitts on the front of his apron, scraping up a chair to sit on. He slurped long and hard at his teacup. But, after he'd swallowed, he said to them all solemnly, "Just so you know, young Ned The Accountant made it as far as Christchurch. Did you all hear about it?" No one responded. Some looked away. "He must've been feeling right proud of his efforts because he went to the Police Station to get directions to his sister's place."

"Ned, poor bugger." Mr Green took up the tale. "He told me missus his sister had stopped writing to him and hadn't sent him any Pocket Edition or Sante bars since last Christmas. He wanted to know if she was all right, her and her kiddies. Nothing else. Just wanted to see with his own eyes they were all right, is all." He shrugged his shoulders, his big hands open and empty. His voice choked up. "Guess after he'd seen 'em he'd have come back here. Back home."

Mr Antonio coughed.

"The policeman gave him the address, and seems he thanked him. He was like that. Being an accountant it stands to reason he'd have good manners. You wouldn't have rude accountants, eh. He says thank you as he's leaving the station. But he pulls out his

Government Issue tobacco. That's what done it. Dumb bastard. He was cuffed and taken straight to Sunnyside Hospital while they arranged escorts to get him back here."

A few boot scuffs, but nothing more.

Malcolm drained his cup and swallowed the tealeaves before setting it down on the saucer. Mr Antonio reached over and refilled it from the teapot – Dorothea didn't do refills.

He said, "I hear they got a new treatment in Sunnyside, Jack. They operate right into the brain now. Call it a leucotomy. Ah, what with the insulin treatment and electrical-convulsive therapy it makes me wonder what they'll come up with next."

Some of the others quietly stood up and walked outside into the brisk fresh air.

Malcolm stayed. He wanted to learn more. He'd heard staff talk about Sunnyside Mental Hospital, about the new treatment trials. Or when someone died there. Of the other mental hospital nearby, Orokonui, he heard little, just that the same staff worked between both hospitals – Orokonui and Seacliff.

Mr Green started on again about the bikies, how they looked downright menacing in the tranquil village, how he was wary of gangs.

"I wasn't scared, like," he insisted. "But all me neighbours were out gawking. Then bugger me if the bikies didn't stop right in the middle of me bloody drive." He shook his head a few times for emphasis. "Seven of 'em noisy contraptions."

He grinned a kind of quirky grin that started with his rheumy eyes and then spread out from there. With age he was getting rangier and a bit more crooked, kind of like one of the farm scarecrows or the gnarly roosters who pecked around the pigsties. Those pigs were lucky pigs, Malcolm thought, fed big buckets of slops daily. But, like the roosters, Mr Green had strange rolls of red flesh around his neck. Maybe his skin was too big for him now. He recalled an earlier Mr Green in a bushman's shirt and corduroy pants bundled together with a brown leather strap. A memory formed in his mind. He'd been in Mr Green's backyard near the concrete copper.

He said loudly, "Copper."

"Right on, son. Me old copper used to be a good 'un for boiling up crayfish back in the day." He chortled some more. "So me and me missus are a bit narked to see our Barb race out to these thugs. Couldn't tell one from the other. All looked the same, black and shiny, silver studs all over their get-up, buckles on their boots and strides. Anyways, I says hello."

Mr Antonio said, "You can't be too careful, Jack. At your age."

"You're dead right, cobber. Anyways, I just grinned at the lot of 'em. Barb was clinging on the arm of one and me missus was taking cover behind her ironing table."

As Mr Green told it, he got out a box of spirit bottles full of his home-brewed apricot wine. He was that proud of his brew.

"I tell you what, though," he said, "I was fair crapping meself."

Dorothea collected the cups and saucers to wash in the sink. Her next job was to rub grease on the shells of several dozen trays of fresh eggs for preserving for winter baking. Mr Antonio gave his stew another stir, and Mr Green was off on a whole new bent. Malcolm waited for him to refocus but Mr Green's memory wandered around to when he played the piano accordion in his band. At last he got back to the bikies.

"So they were swigging away and calling me bad names too. But I'm not as daft as they think." He absent-mindedly scratched his bulbous nose. No chance that nose was ever handsome, Malcolm thought. "They forget I used to be a youngster."

The late morning cooled. Mid-day mist crept down over the hills and covered the buildings.

"Having swigged all me wine the gang were fair gurgling and rolling about on me back lawn. One of 'em cracked his head a beaut on the copper so I nipped inside, left 'em to it."

Malcolm saw how Mr Green hobbled around, tiring from his great age. And he somehow knew how this story ended.

"You know what, Toni? One of 'em had the cheek to call out Hey, old codger, ya got any more? Cheeky young sod. Well, I gave 'em some fig wine," cracking a smile a mile wide, "and sent 'em on their way."

Dorothea stalled greasing eggs to rejoin the group around the table. She who was normally as sullen and silent as the dough worked by Mr Antonio now piped up.

W-what happened?"

She stared, unblinking through her pale weak eyes, lost within the convolutions of Mr Green's story.

He smiled angelically, and his eyes became moist and vague.

"I used to be a fine cook in this kitchen. Before the Italian arrived. In my days a stew was just a stew. I used to bake Lamingtons and cream brandy snaps for the patients. And butterfly cakes. Ah, but I got too old, ya see."

He once told Malcolm he used to tramp above Blueskin Bay, just past Warrington but before Orokonui, high into the manuka lines, collecting supplejack to weave into crayfish pots. He had a special twist he used to keep any ornery cray from reversing out the entrance, but it was also so he would know if Tanner or Carson meddled with any of his pots. They were all mates yet they still didn't know about the special twist.

He trusted Malcolm with his secret and that made Malcolm feel smooth.

"Ya know why I hate casseroles? All because one night I cooked dinner for me missus. I got a tin from the cupboard. Casserole, it said. Damned company making casserole for cats. I added salt and pepper and it made a good meal. She ate it, said it was nice. When she did the dishes she saw the tin with the cat on it."

Everyone liked Mrs Green and it seemed wrong to laugh over her eating cat food. So no one did.

Meanwhile, Dorothea was getting upset.

"W-what about the g-gang?" she whined, wringing her hands together beneath her apron.

"The gang? They got on their bikes and rode off."

Dorothea huffed her disappointment.

"Well, me missus gave me a right telling off for what I did with her Syrup of Califigs and Senokot granules. I cleaned out the bathroom cabinet to make that little brew. I reckon they'd have been crapping in their leathers before too many miles."

Dorothea blanched – she knew first hand the rigours of that mixture. Mr Antonio shrieked as best a baritone could, tears streaming down his cheeks. Mr Green sat with a happy grin slapped across his face. Malcolm let rip with a bellowing laugh – one spoonful moved him quite smartly. And it was later, when he was thinking about that story, he thought maybe Mr Green's one purpose in being on this earth was to bring laughter to those who couldn't find their own.

Chapter 12

The Gardens

On a Saturday morning in December, 1950, a warm still summer's day, Malcolm saw Lionel Terry making his way outside The Building's grounds up to his private garden on the slopes of nearby Mount Charlotte. Trusted patients could walk the roads outside the main gates, walk pretty much anywhere they wanted, and since Lionel was trusted he would often bring back flowers or strawberries he'd grown in his garden. With his white flowing hair and neatly trimmed beard, he was indeed the most well known patient around.

Farther along the road, Malcolm, who was also trusted to walk outside the main gates, saw a group of junior nurses carry bedding giggling among themselves. They were also headed for the grassy slopes. This wasn't the first sunny day he'd encountered these young women. He'd often considered the reason for their expedition, and decided they'd be part of the night staff that needed to sleep during the daytime away from the unavoidable noises around and inside the Nurses Home. He had fully planned on climbing Mount Charlotte this morning, only not when Lionel Terry was around, or the nurses. He figured it would take him closer to heaven. He might see Julie, so he wanted to be alone.

His memory had started coming back properly – he remembered Julie – but he told no one and no one asked him *Malcolm, is your memory coming back yet?* He remembered from way back some of the things Mr Green talked about, like the special crayfish pot twist and the copper in his backyard. But he acted no different from any other day. He knew what happened if you acted different. You got The Treatment. He determined not to lose any more memory and he intended to recognise his friends. That part had been particularly hard for him, not wanting to ask *Who are you?* And for some sectors of his brain there was only a gradual return.

So he remained the same, whatever that might be, all day and every day.

He now recognised some of the attendants from a long time ago. The female nurses seemed to move on but not the attendants; they stayed for years. The younger generations followed in their footsteps. They looked like their fathers used to look.

Each school holiday, youngsters from down in the village or the nearby farms would traipse up the hill to their holiday jobs. Some helped in the laundry folding clean linen, some in the kitchen peeling vegetables or helping Mr Antonio with his baking. Even the Occupational Therapy Department benefited from these youngsters who revelled in making sheepskin teddy bears with huge glass eyes and joints that moved, and learning basketry, or dancing a waltz with the older patients. Others would toil in the gardens or the boiler room while some even worked alongside trained staff as junior nursing aides. These ones often stayed on at the hospital when their schooling was complete.

During the school holidays there was a lot of laughter from both the young people and the older staff members. The days were somehow brighter and everyone somehow more light-hearted. Malcolm and most of the others looked forward to these times. They were some of the happiest times he could remember at The Building.

As scheduled, and on time, he obediently took his medication from the eggcup. There was no choice or the pills would be forced through his closed lips and into his mouth. Some of the patients still put up a battle three times each day. He couldn't see the point – your mouth bruised and bleeding, the staff exasperated. He opened his hand to receive the pills, different colours with no explanation, and closed his fingers over them.

The water went down but more often than not the pills stayed between his fingers. If the others did the same they wouldn't have to suffer the bruising. Later he would tuck them into the lining of his jacket pocket along with Julie's candlewick balls. No one noticed.

Sometimes days passed during which he became increasingly agitated, with his memory flitting in and out. He asked the faceless moon to help him, to save him from...something. But the moon over Sea-cliff ignored him, no longer listening to his thoughts. In Maclaggan Street it had turned its face to him. Now he only saw the dark back of the moon's head, its face gone.

Do you remember?

Do you?

He surely remembered the preparations for his last shock treatment and lived in perpetual fear of repeating whatever it was he had done to get it. He knew some of the others got many treatments. Some said fifty, one said one hundred. Was that more? How many was fifty? These were numbers he could not fathom. And once a day or several a week?

He did know that each session was progressively stronger than the last, some taking place in their own ward and some in the long wooden building like a prison barracks beyond the engineer's rooms. He couldn't remember where he'd had his treatments. Or why. He'd lie wherever he was, terrified, waiting for the agonies, then the nothings, then confusions when he woke.

And he listened, silent, when the attendants talked of the death rate within the hospital.

He could smell death, a sour tang like earth and mildew. He often considered the others' damaged brains – those patients the attendants spoke of as surely enjoying a better life once they'd had The Treatment. Were their brains already damaged, or had they become damaged after they were shocked? The attendants said The Treatment was to stimulate the brain, but who could be stimulated or feel like himself any more after so many sessions?

He remembered vividly the agony of the skin tearing on his ankles from his last session. Some of the others lost control of their bladder or bowel, or from then on had seizures, like Davey McPherson, or became feeble-minded. And there were those who emerged with fractures and broken teeth.

No one talked about them.

Some who had The Treatment were still children. Some had transgressed in that they would not eat all of their dinner and that made the attendants angry. Sometimes they hadn't obeyed the rules about making their bed. Or, worse, they wet their pyjamas. In Malcolm's thoughts he whispered those horrible truths. In the dark of night he cried silent salty tears. Those were the ones he sorrowed for the most, the kiddies.

What could they have done so wrong as to warrant The Treatment? Surely they were the innocents. And then he'd seen others sink deeper into their melancholy until darkness claimed them. He remembered how Jock stood rigid in front of the coal lorry. Jock died. Willis stopped eating and drinking and no one made him. He died too.

Malcolm knew what he knew. And his growing collection of memories would one day set him free. But sometimes he sat alone with his face in his hands, silently grieving the enormity of what he knew. Other times he existed in daytime dreaming, full of vivid colour, confusion and clamorous noise. During those times he didn't remember anything new; he didn't even contemplate remembering. And on other days his memories were as fleeting as the shooting stars in the fair night sky.

For some inmates, he knew, there was no comfort and nothing left for them to remember with after they'd been dragged screaming, or docile as cattle, for personalised electroconvulsive therapy. Their minds had died though their bodies lived on. Those he empathised with and grieved hard for. Some never came back to the wards. Those he grieved less for.

That was another secret.

And they needed bodies to satisfy the morgue's great appetite, and for student nurses to learn how best to take care of the mentally ill, for the post-mortems, the tutorials. But what did they do with the bodies that went through those doors? Chopped them up, buried them there where they once lived?

All of this he wanted to know if he only knew how to find the answers?

Seated tidily in the visitors' chairs in the dayroom, one woman leaned toward another so alike as to be her sister, and said huskily, "They may never have wanted their lunatics in the city, but I must say, my dear, they have housed them rather poshly. All through our taxes, I might add." Nodding her head, her veiled hat stabbed through with a bulbous pin.

To escape the chill wind, Malcolm had taken refuge in this sunny dayroom. He carefully noted her smart shoes fastened with four button straps. Oddly enough, he suddenly recalled an elderly woman from many years ago who wore a dark woollen coat complete with fox fur. This woman he remembered had stood beside his father in their front room with its vases of white lilies placed on the various furniture. He wondered what else that day might have meant to him.

As he pondered the similarity of the elderly woman from so long ago to these sisters seated opposite, he became increasingly intrigued.

Like many visitors, these women appeared to assume the patients were deaf or incapable of comprehension. They directed their conversation to each other with only the occasional gesture of inclusion toward the other patients sitting nearby and keenly listening.

Malcolm decided the specific patient they had come so far to visit hadn't yet arrived. So he listened, pretending they had come to visit him. To see what that was like.

The sister, if sister she was, replied, "I heard it was a considered move to the country for the benefit of the inmates' health rather than a sop to concerns about social stigma. Despite the flash exterior I hear the interior in the main building is quite plain."

Both sisters clutched handbags in gloved hands. Both wore stockings. Just like that long-ago elderly woman in his past.

On another visiting day, weeks later, as he sat soaking up the warmth of the dayroom, the same sisters arrived. The patient they had travelled so far to visit was not well; he was confined to his bed with a cough. Malcolm noted that this was the second time he'd been present when the women had made this same journey in vain. The previous time the man was confined to his bed with dysentery. Perhaps he didn't want to meet with them. Some didn't like visitors – their forced concern, their protracted goodbyes that came hot on the heels of hello.

The women seemed unconcerned. Indeed, they barely mentioned the absent patient. And had he been present, would they have made an effort to communicate with him? And about what? Now, since the burden of their journey was lifted and since they had time to spend before their train was due to leave, they nattered about the gardens: how manicured the lawn was, the borders planted with primroses and pansies, the areas around the larger trees. The azaleas. They considered the lawns to be immaculate.

He learned their names – Sylvia and Maretta.

Sylvia commented to Maretta, "It used to be virgin bush, my dear. Imagine the weeks it must have taken to prepare the land for those immense gardens. It must be most beneficial for them to walk in such beautiful grounds. And the views. No matter where you stand, you're always assured of the views."

He was interested in the sisters' dialogue as long as he drew no attention to himself. The warmth was pleasant, the perfume from the vases of flowers peaceable.

From these sisters, he'd gleaned a different fact – that the need for a new asylum in the Dunedin area was also because of the Otago gold rush. He'd not heard that reasoning before. He added this new fact to his store of other facts.

Then he was nearly jolted off his chair when one sister said the original building contained four and a half million bricks made from local clay on the same site. He became lost in wonder at the magnitude of so many bricks. As the sisters discussed the length and breadth of The Building he mentally lined up the bricks and counted them off in lots of twelve.

And so the sisters kept up their chatter until they felt inclined to stand up. Perhaps they walked outside to get away from the pervading stench of piss and sweat.

He dawdled along behind them, not because he was interested in them as women, or even as sisters – which they might not have been – but because he was so taken with the voluble facts with which they regaled each other. Sylvia insisted the bright yellow glossy ranunculi were simply buttercups growing as opportunistic garden weeds. Maretta said she knew her plants, citing how these particular ones were more often white but still with the bright yellow centre, and how some were annuals and some biennials. And how a few had orange or red flowers. She said it was not uncommon to find them with six or more petals, or with none at all.

Right then he decided he'd count the petals on each of them and make a mental note of which was a common opportunistic flower and which was not.

Chapter 13

The Fire

The siren pierced the stillness, rehashing in Malcolm's memory that dreadful time when he was about twenty-one. Those sirens started at 9.45pm on 8th December, 1942 and wailed all night. The women and children screamed briefly, those in their rooms or in the twenty-bed dormitory with locked shutters that could only be opened from the inside with a key. Though some of them didn't make a sound, climbing under their iron beds or beneath their mattresses, hiding from the noise, the smoke, and the smell of burning people.

The fire spread through East Wing, Second Block, Ward 5, rapidly devouring the wooden structure and those inside it. An attendant gave the alert and the firemen tried to fight it with water from a nearby hydrant. There were no sprinkler systems. That two-storey wooden structure, an afterthought added on-to the original construction, was completely burned out, reduced to ashes, which smouldered for days. Thirty-seven of the thirty-nine Ward 5 inmates burned to death.

One hour later it was all over, all gone.

Except for the smell, the sickly cloying stench.

And at the end of it all – the searing heat and flames and ashes, the screams and cries of staff and patients, the great silence that followed – only two women survived. One was saved from a room that did not have a locked shutter. An attendant pulled the window's grating off. The other patient was res-cued from the first floor.

Malcolm heard that of the two survivors, Lil con-tinued with her job of delivering the mail, but from then on Esther didn't speak. When her family visited with new clothes for her, she sat and picked at them until they were in shreds. She picked at the healing flesh on the side of her face and head as well. She was allowed to go home for the weekend, to her family in Dunedin.

She never returned to the hospital. Malcolm heard her family tell the staff that her hair remained curly on one side, but went straight on the other, and it all became forever snowy white, like her face. She mostly sat in her chair and plucked out her eyebrows, afraid of the fireplace.

Everyone operated in a state of intense grieving after the fire. Nobody could answer the questions in the inquiry except to say there was a nursing shortage, and there might have been an electrical short circuit due to the shifting foundations. There was no fireplace in Ward 5. It was steam-heated.

Dark-suited men asked more questions: *Why were the patients locked into bedrooms and dormitories with no staff on duty? Why were the high-up barred windows fastened and shuttered with no access from outside?* They suggested it was hard to believe those trying to get in to drag the patients out could not do so.

Conclusion: Insufficient staff – a ratio of ten to one – and the source of the fire was never established.

Who cared, really? The patients were the detritus of society, nothing more. That's what Mr Antonio said, that the general consensus out there was that they were the detritus of society.

Chapter 14

Ned's Secret

Malcolm walked past the morgue, eyeing it with distrust before averting his gaze so as not to be held in the glassy stare of the high-up window. He passed through the main entrance and out onto the gravel road. Opposite was a cluster of trees: willow, larch, flowering cherry, and others unnamed, small and tangled.

Studying trees and plants at the hospital was one of his greatest pleasures, along with remembering dates and facts, and counting bricks. He knew many plants by name, some by smell. But here, standing before the cluster of trees, he decided on the best way to Mount Charlotte. It would be in a straight line directly over the fence on the far side of the road by the boiler man's house with the black barking dog.

Once over the fence, he waded through the bog holding onto the lower branches of the willows, making sure the roots couldn't hold him stuck there in the thick dark water. His boots filled with fetid water and muck. He remembered talk in general about the poor drainage and the unstable land on which The Building was established, causing cracks to appear in the ceilings and walls. For a moment he panicked, struggling to get his boots out from the bog, grasping hold of a spindly branch to pull himself toward the trunk.

One foot in its woollen sock came free. Now he had one boot on and one wet sock. The other boot was stuck in the bog. He spent ages working out a plan to retrieve his boot. How long would it take? But what did time matter? On a tiny weed-woven island, he emptied the muck out of both boots, becoming in the process wet and filthy to his waist. With his boots back on, he pulled himself along a few yards by clinging to the lower branches. Closer to the trunks the water was shallower.

Glancing down, he saw ahead of him another set of boot prints, each swirling with oily film and insect larvae.

He began to take long slow breaths to calm his laboured breathing. When he was scared, dark things happened.

From the tree that blocked his progress, a man's trouser-clad leg hung down, nudging his head. Each nudge released myriad blowflies.

He kept both eyes fastened on the bog water so he could stay upright. If he fell into the bog, he feared he might not get up again. His soaked clothes were heavy enough already. He would surely get into trouble back at the ward, probably get sent for The Treatment.

Standing still now, his eyes fastened on the extra prints. He was kind of waiting for the man in the tree to move aside. The man who had been alive but who was now dead. Whose remains, incorrigibly lanky, derelict and terminal, were dangling, slowly turning.

Shocked rigid, Malcolm waited, not knowing what to do. The man moved slowly away from him, then slowly back to press against Malcolm's down-turned head. Two men dancing in the willow trees in the miry bog.

You poor, poor bugger, he thought as he stood where he was, his head bowed in respect for this man he once knew, who was no different from him.

Ned The Polite Accountant swayed a little this way and a little that.

After some time Malcolm returned to his ward. He decided not to tell anyone what he'd seen. He would let the man have his peace in the clustering trees. Soon enough someone else would find him.

"Look at the state of your boots, boy. You'd better clean them up before dinner. And your trousers! Where the hell have you been?"

He winced at the sharp blow to his head. Dinner? He didn't want dinner. He wanted to go to bed and think about Ned The Polite Accountant, recall every-thing he knew about the quiet man. But he had to wait until 7.30pm.

"Come on, off with them, you dirty bastard!" The attendant flicked Malcolm's forehead with his belt. "You think I've nothing better to do than clean up after you mongrels?"

The attendant watched him strip out of his dirty clothes outside, then turned the icy water hose on his nakedness.

"You're getting The Treatment for this!" he roared.

When Malcolm was in bed, he thought more about Ned The Polite Accountant and his years at The Building, how he helped the staff in the administration office, and how he was often seen walking between the various wards with a clipboard of papers tucked beneath his arm. His clothes were always immaculate. He was just a regular guy. But Malcolm figured you maybe didn't have to be smart to be a regular guy. Couldn't anyone be regular?

He felt his face, surprised to find it wet with tears.

Chapter 15

Smooth

Early in the day Malcolm crossed the yard to the main kitchen. He scuffed the coal grits that had fallen from the lorries constantly going back and forth from the boiler room to the wards, or up and down from the railway station. He limped slowly and unevenly because his head ached, and his good eye was still closed from the belt buckle cut. Abruptly he stopped walking and raised his hand to his jaw. He flinched from the swollen bruise there. His tongue probed the place a tooth had been. But though several days had passed since his beating, he still had not been called for The Treatment.

Inside the kitchen, the steamy warmth and the radioman reporting the world news were comforting. He had discovered there was another life beyond this, a life in which there was even more for him to learn. Though he lived under a rule of 'fear and obey' he was learning how best to get on with it.

He sniffed at the beginnings of savoury smells, tried to guess what they might be. Mince with potatoes and onions? Shepherd's pie was his favourite. Sometimes Mr Antonio piled the top with grated cheese. Shepherd's pie and golden syrup pudding with ladles full of bright yellow custard – these two foods calmed and soothed him.

For him this particular day could have passed like all the others – a retreat to the end of a narrow garden to sit on a mossy bench in the shade of a giant elm, keeping out of trouble. Clearly, he saw his mother's face, like the touch of her hand on his back or on his shoulder. She was at a window, staring at him. He had more often seen her like this, but she never came out to speak to him. And he told no one.

The new young doctor, Dr Burt, leaned in closer to ask Malcolm his questions. "How do you feel, Malcolm? Tell me how you feel, what you're thinking. Take your time then." And though he didn't ask him about his visible bruises or black eye, he did ask, "Is there anything you would like to talk to me about? Is anything worrying you?"

Malcolm sat opposite the doctor at his desk spread with papers and words written in black and red ink. This man used Brylcreem on his hair, making it seem set like plastic. He'd buy some of that Brylcreem with his next Comforts Allowance from the canteen.

"Very well, then." Dr Burt scribbled on a paper, and after a lengthy period of silence, said, "Why don't you want to answer my questions, Malcolm? Why don't you want to talk about things?"

It wasn't that Malcolm didn't want to answer or didn't want to talk. He simply had nothing to say.

"What do you feel?" the doctor continued gently. "How do you feel?"

"I feel-," Malcolm felt obliged to provide the good doctor with some sort of answer, "-smooth."

And it seemed to excite the doctor greatly because he scribbled furiously on the fast filling up sheets of paper. Then he leaned forward again, smiling.

Malcolm gave him a smile back and then looked down at his boots, which were dry now.

Well, their little chat together certainly had the doctor nodding away as he scratched down some more notes. When he eventually stood up, he said, "Malcolm, I want you to remember you can talk to me any time. And you're coming along just fine."

Malcolm considered the doctor's words about how he was coming along fine. But how far had he come, exactly, and where had he come from? Those words indicated he'd come from somewhere, so if he had come along fine, from somewhere, where was he going to? Often these strange questions formed in his mind, so he set himself to figure out what the answers might be.

He felt in the lining of his jacket pocket. The balls from Julie's candlewick dressing gown along with a collection of tablets was growing steadily.

It was Sunday. Some day. Some new day. It was always some new day. Today it was Sunday.

It was the day before mutton pies, Pinky Bars and Pixie caramels.

While sitting on a bench in the gardens, Malcolm thought suddenly of his parents. Surprised, he sat upright. His mother was right there again in his memory, only this time she was fading slowly in her bed, smelling of rose geranium talcum powder. She smiled at him with tears in her eyes, seemingly tired. He remembered how after school he'd crept down their passage to her room and found her sleeping. He sniffed her neck and slid his hand down under the sheet to find hers so he could pat it gently, maybe even squeeze it a little and tell her it would be all right soon.

So did he have a father? And if he did, what was his father doing? He wondered these things more often now as his memories came back in starts. If he really concentrated and squeezed his eyes tight shut, he could just about see his father. His father was smoking a pipe. Suddenly he remembered the smell of the rum-flavoured Borkum Riff tobacco, but sometimes his father rolled his own cigarettes with Pocket Edition and Zig-Zag rolling papers. Mainly it was the pipe. He was with Bella. Smoking his pipe. There it faded.

He wanted to know what his father was doing with Bella. Mr Green could tell him because he knew about things. And Mr Green had trusted him with his secret crayfish pot twist.

But when Mr Antonio greeted him, "Hello, young man! What are you doing in here so early?" Malcolm awkwardly lowered his gaze and turned his head away.

Mr Antonio was breaking eggs into a bowl. "Sponges," he said. "The Medical Superintendent has a special luncheon on so if you stick around you can beat the cream."

Malcolm waited by the window for hours for Mr Green. As he beat bowls full of cream, Mr Green gave him a wave and walked on by. Not every day was the same. But later Mr Green did come into the kitchen. He came over with slices of freshly creamed and jammed sponge.

"Pull up a chair if you want, son."

Malcolm shuffled his feet and shoved his hands deep in his pockets before taking them out to fiddle with his cap before he put it back on his head again.

"Have some sponge. Tell me what's bothering you."

Malcolm sat on the chair. "Mr Green?"

"Call me Jack."

Maybe this one time, because it was important.

"Got all day if truth be known so don't rush."

Eventually Malcolm got down to the question. "Jack, what was Daddy doing with Bella?"

Jack uttered some oath and scratched vigorously at his balding head. He rubbed his nose around on the front of his face as if it were made from India rubber. Then he nodded toward the teapot.

"Grab us a cup, then." He leaned on his elbows for a long while. "Ah, crikey dick, I dunno, son."

Malcolm stared incredulous. His mouth dropped open. He'd believed Jack would tell it and it would be so.

Jack cursed under his breath some more, scratched his whisker stubble. "Best let me start again because truth be known, I don't know. But – well, you never know, do you?" Jack's eyes softened. "You tell me everything from the beginning, son."

Malcolm told Jack how he remembered the rose geranium talcum powder, how, when he was six, he'd saved his pennies for his mother's birthday. One day he'd come home from school to find her crying over a bloodied sheet. Normally, he liked to watch her do washing, soap suds sliding down the wooden scrubbing board, her singing jingles. But he'd never seen her cry before so he didn't know what to do.

Then he remembered how, just the previous week when he tore past the dunny, down the concrete steps, and slammed into the coal shed door and howled loudly, his mother had run down the side of their house, calling, "Where does it hurt, little man? Show Mummy so I can kiss it better. There's my brave boy."

He'd shown her his head with its bump forming and she kissed him three times, and it was all better. Then they went inside to find the biscuit tin.

He knew what to do.

"Tell me where it hurts, Mummy. I can kiss it better."

Well, she laughed and cried some more and hugged him tight. When she'd eaten some crispy biscuits and drunk the cup of milky tea he poured for her, with three spoons of sugar, her tears had gone.

But from then on she cried often.

At night his father wrapped her in a blanket and held her in his arms, rocked her back and forth. When Malcolm tried to cuddle his mother, his father pushed him away. "Off you go, boy. Mummy's not well."

Malcolm was sad. He knew she wasn't well, but he was her boy. He made more milky tea. He spilled the tea.

His father cuffed the boy heavily. "Get out of here! Go to your room. Get off with you!"

He later peeked through the door and saw his father standing by the window, crying and cursing at the wind.

Mr Brown The Rawleigh's Man called to their front door with its four panes of coloured glass. The sun shone all afternoon making patterns from the fret-work on the veranda. Only important people came to the front. Regular people came to the back.

His mother bustled along the passage, wiping her hands on her pinny. She welcomed the man as if he were the minister or the doctor.

Mr Brown The Rawleigh's Man's visits were excit-ing. Like a fat brown duck, he waddled into the kitchen with two leather suitcases. One he placed neatly on the tabletop, the other on the floor. Mal-colm knew what was in each: tall brown bottles: cough medicines and disinfectants held in place by frilly elastic ribbons, smaller jars of ointment and bottles of Mercurochrome. He was allowed to look inside the suitcases as long as he didn't open any lids. He peered at the contents as Mr Brown The Rawleigh's Man and his mother went into the sitting room.

Down the passage the swish of the heavy curtains being opened caught his attention. He raced along just as the door closed, shutting him out. Scuffing his boots on the carpet runner he returned sulkily to the kitchen. He studied the contents of the open suitcase and picked up a brown bottle. There was no special smell about this bottle, only the combined smells of all the bottles and jars, mysterious and inviting. He twisted the cork.

Up the passage...

Murmuring...

He resented being shut out.

This was his house and she was his mother and he was her little man. Back up the passage he stomped. The door stayed closed. Down to the kitchen he thumped. One suitcase open on the table, the other on the floor. He kicked it until it fell over. He picked the crusty scab on his knee. Big Billy had pushed him off the tree hut ladder five sleeps ago. He slid a grubby nail under the scab, grasped it firmly and yanked, gasping at the sharp sting. The blood oozed.

But he knew what to do. His teacher told his mother he was an intelligent boy and he would go far in this world. He was a big boy and would take care of himself. Mr Brown The Rawleigh's Man and his mother behind the closed door. The little brown bottle. Peeling blue paper from the cottonwool. He ripped off a wad, tugged the tight cork from the bottle. Red everywhere. Red like blood. He was covered with blood. The table and the rug were covered with blood...

"Jack?"

Malcolm's voice reed-thin, recalling a previous existence. Terrifyingly, he glimpsed the scale of his loss.

"Mummy was bleeding. Dying. That's why..."

"Take it easy, son."

Jack patted Malcolm's shoulder.

Tears filled Malcolm's eyes and rolled slowly down his cheeks, spreading sideways along each crease. His mouth hung open. A great intake of air sucked to the depth of his grief. His broad shoulders caved. His head hung low. He bawled.

Jack continued patting him on the shoulder.

Dorothea poked her head around, squinting through her glasses, screwing up her mouth in dislike. She turned back to her sink, scrubbed freshly pulled turnips, muttered loudly, "Don't be s-s-slow. Don't."

Scrub, scrub. Scrub, scrub. Scrub...

His bawling gaining momentum. Dorothea stuck her wet fingers into her ears, waggled them, chanted, "C-c-can't h-hear. C-can't h-hear. Can't hear!"

Malcolm drew breath, enough for his next bawling, before two attendants escorted him back to his ward, him stumbling and banging against them.

Grief-stricken, yet knowing, he submitted to the preparations for The Treatment in the long wooden ward. He howled his terror as they discussed his medication: two pinks, two whites and a yellow.

One said, "Can't have a disruptive patient. Once one gets started they all get started. That new feller, Doctor Burt, he said Malcolm was coming along nicely. He's likeable enough but he's young and inexperienced. Well, I guess they can't hope to get them all right. Did you hear about that kiddie in...?"

Whispers. Fuzzy. Mixed up. Quiet inside. White.

sometimes snow sometimes hail sometimes sunshine sometimes mist sometimes fog sometimes fog

sometimes summer sometimes winter sometimes summer sometimes winter sometimes sometimes

He hadn't always been in this ward, whichever ward it was. After The Treatment, he woke to find himself with new people. Most of them sleepy. He was sleepy.

One day he remembered his jacket pocket lining. He had two secrets, his pills and Julie's candlewick balls. He felt smooth and content. But when he thought about it now, he knew in his heart he didn't have the secrets – they had him.

He tried to understand the progression – or not – of his personal behaviour, emotional or physical, that had earned him another shock treatment, but nothing was explained to him. He had The Treatment in clusters with no recollection of what had built up before each of them. Then he'd wander among the others, sleepy and confused, with their pillows clutched to their chest, crooning or yelling, banging the walls, eyes full of fear or pleading.

When he realised he was outside the enclosed grassy area he somehow knew he'd wandered back to the wrong ward. His home kept shifting. But he recognised that this last treatment took place near the laundry and the main kitchen.

He dreamed he would find the perfect sleep, but when he found it what would he do with it?

Chapter 16

His Boots

There was an old lady who swallowed a fly I don't know why she swallowed a fly perhaps she'll die

"Get a move on, Malcolm, or they'll leave without you."

The hospital bus was packed with patients dressed in picnic clothes. Dorothea wore a straw sunhat that mice had eaten a hole through. His thoughts flicked over to his mouse...

The good ones were going to Warrington Beach for a picnic on this glorious day. He was a good one – he'd kept his nose clean for some time. Mr Antonio organised sandwiches and orange cordial. A nurse sat in the front seat opposite the driver. Two attendants sat down the back.

Eventually they arrived at the camping area beneath the tall skinny pine trees. Dorothea howled when someone shook out a grey blanket to sit on. She got sand in her eyes. The nurse waited while Dorothea took her glasses off, then she peered into her eyes. She pulled her own upper eyelid down over her bottom lid to show Dorothea what to do. He thought this nurse was kindly when she spoke, though mostly he couldn't understand what she said. She was newly out from England.

Dorothea's hands were cracked from years of scrubbing piles of pots, podding mountains of peas, peeling acres of potatoes. Those raw hands peeled her upper eyelid down.

"That's better now, isn't it?" The nurse moved on to unpack the picnic box.

Meanwhile, with her back to everyone, Cynthia sat wringing her hands and fretting. She stood up, flicked and twitched her skirt about herself before straightening the picnic blanket. She smiled, but her mouth quivered. She forced it back into another tremulous smile. Her eyes watered and she wiped them with her frayed fingers. No one sat next to Cynthia.

With the patients finally organised, the nurse left some of them sitting on the blanket. She pulled on a skullcap. She wore her swimsuit under her uniform. Some of the others followed her down the beach to where the waves splashed flatly onto the sand. They trailed into those waves to stay with lips blue and teeth chattering, huddled like a bunch of softly-hued tulips in a vase. Then some splashed unenthusiastically while others stood rigid, or paddled at the water's edge like tired old children, watching the waves and gulls without pleasure. One older woman, round as a turnip, swam as languid as seaweed the length of her mentally designated short beach.

"Malcolm, you join in. Off with your boots now."

Malcolm sat on the sharp beach grass and undid his laces. He took his boots off.

"Socks off too. Come on, come on! The tide's going out. Get your wits about you."

"I'm not overly fond of water," he said quietly to no one. "I really am not fond of water."

His eyes were drawn to the seams of his boots where traces of long-dried bog dirt remained imbedded. In trepidation, he peeled his socks off, rolled them up, and dropped them in tight little balls next to his boots. There he sat, unnoticed.

A group of barefoot footballers stood waiting for direction. Phaedrus got to kick off first. Cackling raucously, he kicked the ball, which landed among the sharp beach grasses in the hot sand dunes. Phaedrus straightened up, crowing like a maniac, making it clear he wasn't about to get his feet cut up.

One attendant muttered, "He's away with the bloody fairies again."

The other said loudly, "Stupid bastard!" and went to retrieve the football, cursing the razor-sharp grass. "It's a bloody waste of time, this gadabout!"

He kicked the football expertly to land at Phaedrus' feet. Phaedrus watched, unmoved, as it rolled a few times before it came to a halt a couple of yards away.

"Come on, then. Try it again!"

The attendant shook his head in frustration.

Phaedrus caterwauled as he picked at his trouser front, sliding his hand down to his swollen crotch.

"Get your hands out of your pants or you'll get The Treatment. I'm warning you."

Malcolm turned away. He'd heard that several patients had been committed to the hospital due to 'excessive and indiscriminate masturbation'. Some reportedly made indecent proposals to women. And men. Phaedrus was a fine example of excessive and indiscriminate masturbation. On this happy hospital outing to Warrington Beach he had tuned out the cursing and threats.

An attendant delivered a firm kick to his backside. His head jolting forward, Phaedrus lurched face first into the sand. Some of the others watched idly as he pulled himself upright, spitting out sand, still cackling.

"Just kick the friggin' ball!"

Phaedrus kicked as half-heartedly as before. This time the ball went in the opposite direction, surprisingly high. There it stayed, wedged between the topmost branches of a nearby pine tree.

"Bugger me days!"

Malcolm limped over to where lunch was being served. He reached for a sandwich before sitting on the edge of the blanket, away from Dorothea and her constant blinking, closer to Cynthia, who smiled her teary gratitude. Phaedrus sat down heavily next to him and started in on the sandwiches, giggling inanely, one hand groping again in his crotch.

Dorothea glanced beneath her sunhat at everyone ignoring her. When her eyes lit on Phaedrus, she gagged repeatedly. After one almighty shudder, she moved to the furthest edge of the blanket to show her disdain. There she sulked with her back to everyone, refusing to eat or drink anything more.

Someone said, "Give it a rest, Phaedrus. You're making Poor Dorothea puke."

"You're making her eyes water. You're making her cry, so give over."

"It'll fall off. You'll go blind like Poor Dorothea."

"Like Poor Dorothea," Cynthia murmured.

The focus had shifted from Phaedrus and his tugging hand to Dorothea. Then no one spoke again until one bloke announced, concerning his sandwich, "It's that bloody tinned corned beef. It's not fresh. I bet it's not all beef either."

Phaedrus cackled loudly. "Ya reckon there's cocks ground up in it, do ya?"

The nurse, towelling her damp hair, said sternly, "You shouldn't say that word, Phaedrus. It's not polite. There are ladies present."

But the bloke with the sandwich opened it and poked his finger around inside it.

"Well, my oh my. I do believe that's one of them things right there!"

The nurse slapped his hand. He dropped his sandwich into the sand. Phaedrus cackled some more.

Malcolm hid his grin in his sandwich. He thought the blokes were pretty funny.

Lunch was over.

The youngest attendant retrieved the football from up in the pine tree in time to board the bus. The other attendant collected an assortment of bathing costumes, boots, socks and sandshoes, tossing them into a box strapped to the rack at the back of the bus. There were a few sandwiches left on the sand, curling in the sun.

"Come along. Hurry up there."

"It's been fun, hasn't it?"

"It's time to go."

"Put your cardie on."

The staff adroitly dispensed these small kindnesses.

"Keep warm."

"Pick up that towel. Don't drag it in the sand."

"Be quick now."

"Have you had a good outing?"

"Everyone had a good picnic? That's nice," said the nurse. "Oh, I know what. Before we go, why don't you sing us a little song, dear?"

This she directed at Dorothea whose face and neck blotched violently. She wrapped her arms tightly about her chest, swinging left and right. Then she began humming, making a faint noise Malcolm had not heard before.

"Yes, sing us a wee song, lovie," said the bus driver. "Me mam used to go to the town hall in the Octagon. She'd go all that way in the bus just to hear you sing opera. She said you were a right little corker. When you were young, like. So go on, sing us a wee song. Do it for me mam."

Dorothea clenched her jaw lest her mouth betray her and burst into some glorious aria she'd never forgotten. She was a shy woman, decidedly plain, unattractive. She got flustered whenever she had to speak. On each occasion Malcolm had heard her, she stuttered. Her hands would sweat and her legs tremble. In short she was pretty much like the rest of them.

For now her face relaxed a little and a smile began at the corner of her lips and her reddened eyes were wet.

She tilted her head upwards and she saw something no one else did.

The older attendant said, "Nope. It happens every time. She sings but only to herself where no one can hear. Inside her head, like. No one knows what happened except mid-performance she just stopped singing. Beyond recall, that one."

The conversation moved on to the hospital hall. Malcolm listened avidly as they talked about how it was finally finished after extensive redecoration and restoration, and then discussed the equipment on its stage, and the lighting for the upcoming drama and musical performances. Clearly the staff were proud to provide accommodation and facilities of the highest standard for the earliest performances of the New Zealand Ballet Company, and to advance the musical entertainment provided by its own orchestra consisting of both staff and patients.

Even though Dorothea turned up religiously to watch she couldn't be persuaded to sing on stage, or off it. One time when she was absent from the kitchen, Malcolm found her standing alone on the stage in the dim light, head held high, tears streaming down her face. Soundless. He never learned what her secret was, why her singing was trapped inside her. Even Mr Green didn't know.

The young attendant tossed the football into the bus box on top of the boots and sandshoes.

"Hey, Brian, you hear any more about that young feller who hung himself?"

Malcolm's body prickled instantly, while Brian, the other attendant, choked over someone's smoke.

"Young Ned, the accountant chappie? Nothin' more. He sure was polite, eh. You know where they found him? In the willows above the primary school. Below the boiler man's house in that mucky bog."

The conversation went back and forth between the two men. Malcolm listened to everything they said. He clearly remembered the man hanging in the tree. For one part he was glad Ned had been found; it wasn't right that he should hang there, alone, forever. But he was shocked now they were actually discussing it.

One scratched his head, organised some more patients onto the bus. "Yeah, the bloke that found him said he was just hanging there like an ugly kite."

The rest milled around. Malcolm stared blankly at the fine white sand, he couldn't move. Sandflies settled on his neck. Dorothea screwed her fingers in her ears, turned in aimless circles.

He forced himself to walk to the back of the bus to get his boots. He set to digging the bog dirt from the seams with a stick. When it broke he reached into his pocket for his nail. It was long gone.

"Come on, Phaedrus! Climb aboard, Dorothea. Malcolm, where are you going now? You can clean your boots later. Who've we got so far? Allen, Bert, Eliza, Alfred, Leonard and Margaret, and you, Cynthia. The rest of you'll miss tea."

Once the attendant clamped the door shut, he stood braced in the aisle totting up patients. Seated in the fifth row next to the window, Malcolm was number seven. It wouldn't do to leave a loony loose on Warrington Beach. The driver started the engine, letting it idle unsteadily before beefing up the revs, selecting first gear and then swinging the heavy steering around. Malcolm saw how he released the clutch with a jump. He watched as the bus lumbered slowly away from the glistening sands and creamy foam skirts of the beach. But he couldn't take his mind off his boots.

The driver yelled down the bus to the attendants at the rear, "It's odd. When you come to think of it, that is. Hung himself. So how'd he manage that?"

"They think someone might have helped him. One of his cobbers."

"Why's that, then?"

"Too many boot prints in the bog."

"You're pulling my chain!" the driver yelled. "Fair dinkum? Suppose there'll be a bloody enquiry now."

Malcolm swallowed the bile that surged up from his gut. He tucked his head lower and tried to clean the remaining bog dirt off his boots with his fingernails and spit. He wanted to shake the sand out of his socks, but they were back in the bus box. He wanted to do something, anything at all, except listen to what the men were discussing. How Ned The Accountant had help to hang himself, because of the extra boot prints in the bog.

Chapter 17

Father Teague

The Twins, Leonard and Margaret, had been at the hospital most of their lives, like Malcolm. The only real difference he could tell was they had a surname – Sutherland.

Dick told him their story.

"They were not always mad," Dick said. "Just their mum was. Their dad went back to England to make a better living. Something to do with the unions, as it happens."

Malcolm sat quietly on the bench alongside the tennis courts and listened.

"He planned to save his money and get them all back to the homeland, but no one heard a word from him. His wife went mad with worry, literally, so they wanted to commit her but her kiddies wouldn't let go of her, screaming and hanging onto her legs. Six-years old they were, like peas in a pod. And no one was willing to take on twins born of a mad mother. Like, who knew what might happen?"

Dick scratched his head, blew his nose with a sound like a foghorn. "So they let them come with their mum. And they did all right until she died of pneumonia. Now those two are inseparable."

Malcolm remembered something. When he was first admitted to the children's ward – not The Annex – the kiddies were already there. He had watched them walk around, hand in hand. They sat together and walked together and ate together, speaking only to each other. And they mirrored each other's movements.

Back then, he spoke to no one. Mostly he sat and listened, or walked and listened. But sometimes he didn't even listen. He remembered The Twins, Leonard and Margaret.

Beyond his aborted attempt to climb Mount Charlotte, he still harboured a deep yearning to be closer to heaven, closer to Julie. He studiously avoided the area by Ned's willow tree. Of that dreadful time a couple of months back he'd heard nothing more, not since the attendants and the bus driver had discussed it. It was as if a tide had come through and simply washed all trace of that life away. Daily, he became more relieved that perhaps he was not going to be blamed for helping with the hanging. He was also saddened that a man such as Ned The Accountant could so easily be forgotten.

But had the hanging been forgotten?

Were they even now searching for the wearer of the other pair of boots – him?

How long did these enquiries take?

He vowed he'd stay vigilant for as long as it took. And he would be as discreet as possible.

This particularly fine day Malcolm chose an area above the boiler man's house and struggled with the barbed wire fence until he was behind it. His boots were soaked by the time he reached the base of the hill, but having made it so far he was exhilarated.

Gasping and panting, he finally reached the top of the extinct volcano that was Mount Charlotte.

In his chest was that all-familiar yet strange sensation: a quickening, a thumping. He shuddered as sweat ran in rivulets down his back. What did this recurrent feeling mean, this powerful erratic pulsing inside? Vowing anew not be different from anyone or anything, he decided he would keep it a secret. Yet it happened a lot lately when he thought about Julie, or when he remembered things, or thought about the hanging and the subsequent enquiry.

Sheltering from the biting wind low beneath a copse of trees at the summit, he snuggled into the base of the gorse bushes. In the village where most of the staff lived, smoke from their fires whipped up into the pale sky. And in the deep gully to his right were naked dead trees. There was also golden gorse, and the sweet scent of them carried on an upward draft.

Mr Green had said in some places the moisture from the underground stream was closer to the surface, and that was where the willows grew. Toward the main road, he spied a cottage with a rusting roof cloaked in road dust. Opposite was the railway station.

Never before had he seen the sharp contrast of the houses and roads down the hill, the dark macrocarpa hedges. Black demarcation lines where one property began and another ended, farms began and farms ended. He could see as far south-east as the hills above Blueskin Bay, where Jack confided he climbed to get his supplejack for crayfish pots, and the mist shrouding the cars travelling south along the Kilmog. North was Christchurch, where Ned The Accountant went. Yet how did he know Christchurch was north when he'd never been there? He only knew Seacliff and where he had come from, south.

Confusion muddled his thoughts with roiling patterns. And the wild sea at the bottom of the cliffs had never looked so inviting.

His mind turned to Julie who existed only in darkness. She told him her parents had disappeared while she was spending a day with her grandmother. Tea was eaten, it was night time, and still they never came for her. Her grandmother continued to care for her. It was years later when blind Julie was found by the neighbours, along with her dead grandmother.

Malcolm knew what happened to people like Julie. They were deposited, confused and bewildered, into the care of the mental hospitals for the unloved and unlovable, the uneducated and the unwanted – soon forgotten, feeding the insatiable appetite of the institution, placating the guilt of the knowing masses. Deposited there to be described, measured, weighed and quantified, labelled, segregated and finally, cattle-ised – as had happened to him.

Seacliff Mental Hospital was a solid stone-block wall that encased the frail, the feeble, and the despairing, a milling herd of now compliant cattle.

That's how Julie had come.

His chest pounded again, and he gulped cold air into his lungs and allowed himself to grieve for her.

Whilst he had forgotten much, he was surprised at the intensity of the memories newly slotted into his mind. When eventually he wiped his eyes clear of tears he glanced toward the hospital growing into the hillside as if it had been birthed there. It surely did look like a sprawling prison, no different from the real prison past the Robbie Burns statue in the Queens Gardens, opposite the railway station in Dunedin, past Josephine…

Josephine?

He knew Josephine was somehow connected to Julie.

But now as he stood on top of Mount Charlotte, overlooking the rolling hills, the ocean, the village and The Building, he finally understood what Jack had said about the land inevitably slipping toward the sea. He'd spoken to Julie of these things. It had made little sense to him then. Jack had said that even the houses in the village would slide into the sea one day and some farms would go before them and other farms would go after them.

He clambered back down to the road, and then walked down to the village to see how he fitted in. Sundays were when the farmers and village people stood on the steps of the stone churches to catch up on news. Did he fit in? he asked himself. Not yet. But one day he too would stand on the steps of a stone church and talk of mundane happenings.

The hospital had its own chaplain. Malcolm often wondered about Father Teague – always in a hurry, always carrying his well-thumbed Bible as if it were part of his uniform. Sometimes Father Teague visited a ward Malcolm happened to be visiting as well.

Father Teague would stand there on the fringe of a group gathered together for whatever reason, and he'd smile nervously before saying, "Good morning, everyone. How are you today?"

Mostly he was ignored and his awkwardness would increase until a patient responded to his greeting. He might get spat on or told to sod off. Or perhaps he was mistaken for a family visitor and regaled with news as far back as the turn of the century. But Father Teague was blessed with infinite patience. And while he might not have been blessed with the courage of Robbie Burns, the bronze statue in the Queens Gardens, he was patient and caring. He would sit, if it were appropriate, and safe, and nod and listen, sprayed all the while with spittle or cake crumbs. He neither flinched nor moved away. Malcolm thought perhaps Father Teague *did* have the courage of Robbie Burns. Sometimes, when he stood up to leave, Father Teague looked like a moist Lamington.

A fly landed on Mr Desmond Markby's shirt. His hand darted out like pincers. He plucked the fly off his shirt mid-buzz and popped it into his mouth. Malcolm stifled his immediate laughter as he saw Father Teague visibly flinch.

Father Teague had come to visit Old Sammy this day. Malcolm watched them sitting opposite each other in the dayroom, the heat of the morning sun creeping through barred windows that broke the sunlight up into a grid of interlocking little squares. It warmed up the furniture polish so it scented the room, disguising, ineffectively, other odours like piss and shit and rotten teeth.

Old Sammy was struggling to come to terms with exactly who his visitor was. Each time he selected a name, he was wrong.

"Ah, Luke, young man," said Old Sammy to Father Teague. "How nice of you to pop in and see me. I was telling my dear lady wife, Beryl, how I look forward to our little chats."

Father Teague smiled angelically, clunking his heavy teacup against the saucer.

Old Sammy nodded his head keenly. "And how's that sweet little wife of yours, Adam? And are your children doing well? Little Mary is such a treat."

"Listen to him going on," Alfred growled into his teacup. "From Luke to Adam to Micah to Zephaniah and he'll keep going until he's covered the whole bloody Bible. The Messiah himself will be next on his friggin' list."

Mr Desmond Markby delicately removed a tiny black leg from between his teeth.

But when Old Sammy called Father Teague 'Joshua' all hell broke loose in the dayroom.

"He's not Joshua!" shrieked Alfred. "Joshua broke down the walls of bloody Jericho, you flaming old coot. He's not friggin' Joshua!"

Everyone stopped whatever mindlessness they were engaged in. Phaedrus' hand remained motionless in his crotch. The teacups stopped clattering on their saucers while Mr Desmond Markby held his pinkie finger out from his delicate hand and moved not a single muscle. Old Sammy was caught mid-slurp and Patrick froze with his gummy mouth wrapped around his saucer.

Malcolm was highly amused and he drew his gaze level with Father Teague, who said, "Right you are there, Alfred. It was Joshua who fought the battle of Jericho. Well, I never... Oops, is that the time now?"

He said this last bit as he craned his neck around to locate the wall clock even as the words left his mouth.

"I must be gone then."

Chapter 18

The Lobotomy

Malcolm watched silently from the dayroom as the sullen rain splattered its misery against the window-panes. The dayroom was over-crowded, today no exception. Sometimes the numbers dropped, only to rise again. The staff alternated between amiable patience and marshalling the patients like cattle into trucks on a train, shunting them from here to there. The impression Malcolm gleaned was that mad people shouldn't speak. It only caused trouble and more work. They should sit and be quiet. Quietly mad.

Eating in overcrowded dining rooms reminded him of happier times with fewer numbers elsewhere. Julie? Right now he could not remember all of her story or details of their lives together, just snatches here and there. Or why he was often brought to tears at the mere thought of her. He knew she had died but he could no longer remember how or why.

He wondered often if The Treatments were to blame for his loss of memory, and if this happened to him after each session. He strove daily to avoid drawing any attention to himself that might result in further treatment. But he worked tirelessly at garnering each and every new memory as it surfaced. He sought to know more about Julie, and his mother.

Today, there was a distinct undercurrent running through the ward. Staff talked of a new procedure.

"Does it truly require invasive brain surgery?" asked one male nurse.

"Yes," another replied. "It's called a leucotomy though some call it a lobotomy."

"What's it supposed to do exactly?"

"It makes mad disruptive patients normal. Cynthia's on the list. I can't wait to see how she turns out. No more crying all the time and tidying the furniture, realigning the cutlery in the dining room. She'll probably be discharged to go home, along with the other patients when they become normal."

Normal? For the men, a pair of sharply-pressed serge trousers, a white shirt with epaulettes, and shiny shoes? Was that the normal they spoke of? Like male attendants?

Hah, he scoffed to himself. I'd rather be quietly mad.

He thought rotters like his ward's bully should have been inside rather than on staff. The man was more physical with the patients than Malcolm ever thought necessary. But the hospital was understaffed and what staff they had was overworked, and some were probably unsuited for the role they undertook. As a rule, those on staff were kindly even though they were sometimes frazzled.

He'd taken note of what happened when other patients swam against the tide: the deprivation, punishment, and the dehumanising loss of memory – both present and past. Now there was this discussion on the new procedure, The Leucotomy. And whilst it gave hope to many, it also caused panic among the patients and a fear they might be in there forever. In the lockup. In the loony bin. In the booby hatch.

Someone asked him how long was a lifetime and what came after?

He had no answer for other patients' questions. He had enough unanswered questions of his own.

"Come on, man. Get up! You've been warned. Now move it or you'll get the hose again."

Shivering in the liquid darkness, he was drenched and cold. He wanted to ask what he'd done to warrant the hose but who could he ask? He was no one and worth nothing. And this attendant was a bad man. Malcolm heard the jeers, the coarse laughter, how he would be a good candidate for The Leucotomy, how with half his brain gone he'd talk more or talk less.

All he wanted to know was what was fact and what was truth and where the rest of his memories were. He existed under the constant threat of solitary confinement, the straitjacket, the padded cell and all that involved, the fire hose, The Treatment or The Leucotomy – or was it The Lobotomy? – if he was disruptive or disobedient or if he wasn't *quietly mad*.

Always, all ways, under the total direction of someone else and yet how was he disagreeable?

This saddening nothingness disturbed him immensely, growing bigger each day, darker and hungrier, consuming some of the others. He saw it reflected back from their vacant eyes, blank nothingness. Steadfastly, he hung onto the belief that he wasn't the same as them; he knew he was different, that he didn't belong here with them. So he stood apart from them as the winds of change blew them from place to place – stood apart and listened.

The idea that there could be another punishment even worse than The Treatment caused a stir of vast proportions. Names were read, and those who were noisy, those not content to sit quietly and be mad in silence were herded away for this latest form of correction. When they did return, with cloth turbans wrapped around their shaven heads, they were from then on – and forever – silently submissive.

Malcolm, when he saw them, feared he would be grouped irrevocably among them, irretrievably claimed as one of the walking, eating, sleeping dead...

"Evil is such a lazy thing," Satan ranted to no one, tearing at his hair, his eyes boggled and frenzied. "It piggybacks along the way. God has everything. God! Has! Everything!"

Malcolm stood silently outside the high-fenced lockup and watched Satan drop to his knees, sobbing. Satan was a nickname. Everyone called him that.

"He's lucky," Satan howled to the sky before jumping back onto his feet, arms outstretched, screaming at the top of his lungs. "But heaven is empty while hell is bursting at the seams!"

When he caught sight of Malcolm behind the high wire fence he loped over to him, imploring him to believe.

"The Bible, it's all there. Read it for yourself. This one begat that one, that one begat this one and begat and begat... I don't understand any of it."

Abruptly Satan's voice and face changed again, dark and thunderous. "It's a big wild world out there. Devils and hell! And the loneliest of them all is Father Teague."

Malcolm leaned closer to the fence, filled with a new interest and compassion for the terror of this man's hell, of his God, of him not knowing the difference between them.

"He'll despair, you know, and then he'll fail. The loneliest. The loneliest. He's just a man after all."

Satan's voice had dropped lower, heavy with pain.

Malcolm, compelled to look straight into Satan's eyes, saw the horror and the insanity. He realised he did not fear the man.

Satan asked him quite calmly, "Do you know why you're afraid when you're alone?"

Malcolm shook his head. He was not particularly against being alone. He enjoyed his solitude.

"No, I don't," he said, just as calmly, curious to hear Satan's answer.

"I do," said Satan. "Secretly I don't want to be scared anymore. You won't tell anyone my secret, man? You won't tell?"

"Of course not," Malcolm said, though he had little idea of what Satan referred to.

"You feel it inside like you're falling down fast," Satan growled. "Stand still, man!"

Malcolm stopped scuffing his boot in the grit, and stood rigid as directed.

"When the voices get mad it gets cold. I want them to leave but they won't go. The existence of God has destroyed us. And now the devils are gone. People are still mad, but that's just people. Will you forgive me, man?"

"Yes, I will forgive you." He could do that.

Satan slunk away.

His rants were soon replaced by a sharp hissing sound. The approaching madman was the new patient, nicknamed Snake. He hissed and bobbed his head, arching his neck like a cobra. The hissing came from inside his red mouth where his tongue had been neatly sliced to form two prongs that vibrated with the noise. He left Snake to his hissing. He had other things to do.

After a lengthy time of quiet non-disruptive reflection, he was drawn to Father Teague and his Bible. He wanted to find out what happened after this life was spent. He wanted to find out about Joshua who fought the battle at Jericho. So he sought out Father Teague on a regular basis. Weekly he joined a group within the holy house called The Chapel.

Mostly it was quiet still and cool. In winter, though, it was bitterly cold with icicles formed on the coloured windowpanes from which prisms of light glanced off the walls. In the centre was a large wooden cross. He eased himself inconspicuously into a back pew while others wandered around. Some cried, and some knelt on floor cushions mumbling prayers.

A man who regularly had fits during each service clung to his Bible, mouth wide open, teeth in a permanent rictus, eyes tightly closed. Others stared, mute and unmoved. He stared, mute and unmoved. It was safer to be a non-person.

Now he was troubled by a spate of nervous yawning, which he suppressed with a frown and a flaring of his nostrils – it would not be to his advantage if God thought he was bored. He even worried he might be capable of behaving stupidly or explosively in such a place. He further worried he might be potentially dangerous. Could he trust himself? He'd been referred to often as 'one of those quiet types'. Whatever that meant.

Kneeling on the wooden pad in front of him, he prayed silently to God that he wouldn't become lodged between the two pews, knocking over the one in front which would then knock into the one in front of it, all of them crashing to the floor like dominoes in the dayroom. Whilst he made this ardent prayer, he put his hand over his mouth to cover the grin that came unbidden at the image of what he was praying against.

Most earnestly, however, he prayed for his mother and Julie.

Over a period of Sunday services he learned to give thanks to God for all things. He learned there were situations in life worse than any of theirs, though he couldn't begin to imagine how that could possibly be. And he learned of the love of Jesus and his saving grace. Maybe he could talk to God about going to heaven straight away and finding a little grace of his own.

Father Teague placed his hand on Malcolm's forehead while quietly speaking holy words.

Malcolm whispered, "What you teach me will see me through, won't it, Father?"

Father Teague smiled and nodded his head. He gave Malcolm some books with pictures of angels, Jesus and God. Maybe if he prayed earnestly enough, long enough, and loud enough, he could reach up into the arms of the angels – his Julie angel, his Mummy angel. And maybe he could fly higher than the clouds.

For now, though, he was exhausted with the effort of piecing together the jigsaw of his memories, and fitting them together to form the truth. And from his heavy black boot that dragged him down, made him different.

He asked if he could talk with the nice young doctor some time soon. He was told Yes. When he walked across to this appointment, he knew what he would ask.

"Doctor Burt, am I getting The Leucotomy?" he said bluntly.

"Not at all, Malcolm. No, not you. Why do you ask?"

He felt an immense wash of relief. "Just talk."

"No, don't you worry yourself about that. You're coming along fine." The doctor said this as he wrote notes in an open file on his desk. "Is there anything else you would like to talk about? Any worries?"

"My memories. Some are gone. I know they are gone."

"And they will come back again, I assure you. Has that been troubling you?"

"Yes. I have some memories, but others aren't there. Just dark holes with nothing in them."

"I understand, but they'll return. And, Malcolm, I hear you're enjoying working in the gardens."

Since he wasn't going to have The Leucotomy, he knew it would be easier to get on with living without the fear many others lived with.

He smiled broadly. "Yes, I like flowers and trees. I like working outside."

On another fine day, he set out to climb Mount Charlotte again. After days of rain the air was thick with the abundance of summer. The din of birds: fantails and chaffinches, yellow heads or red heads, sparrows and thrush, and birds less common whose names he didn't know but was determined to learn. The whirr of insects vied with the scent of trodden grass. The sky a bright shade of blue and trees decked out in their summer leaves, the straw in the surrounding fields ripening in time for harvest.

He'd worked out the easiest route to the top so it didn't take him as long as the last time. Though there was a breeze higher up the hill, it was not chilly. Beyond the hospital's main buildings and farms, he could clearly see Maeve's ward, where she'd told him the patients weren't mad and budgerigars were no longer allowed. He could see Ward H, the men's isolation ward. And the fenced paddocks where men and women trudged for their daily exercise, barely clothed. Separate and apart from each other.

In another direction he saw a procession of staff run across a paddock in chase of patients hot-footing it toward the dense bush. There was no need to hide his amusement up here. There was no one to see. He laughed long and hard. And he felt good.

He was fascinated with one particular fight that took place in the dayroom. The sun beamed softly through the open windows. The scent of flowers seemed at odds with the unfolding drama. There were fights from time to time but he'd sensed this was going to be different. Rather than taking himself off, he stayed to watch. In these fights he found a thrilling unpredictability and a spontaneity that eluded him in the rest of his tranquil existence. He made sure he wasn't close enough to become physically involved.

Old Sammy had got himself worked up over Phaedrus' constant crotch-grabbing, his maniacal cackles that too often turned into shrieking, and because Phaedrus hogged the morning sunlight with his comfy chair.

Malcolm saw Old Sammy leap to his feet and pad over to Phaedrus, yelling, "I'll give you something to cackle about, you disgusting bastard."

And with that Old Sammy downed his corduroys and dumped a load right on Phaedrus' knees.

Malcolm was astounded. He'd expected Old Sammy to fart in Phaedrus' lap, as he'd done in the past when pushed to the limit of his tolerance. Everyone was shocked silent. Then one man began to giggle while surreptitiously lowering his trousers. Malcolm's eyes bulged. Could that man truly be manufacturing ammunition on the spot?

Sure enough, he lobbed his lot indiscriminately.

Father Teague was left with his glasses hanging off his right ear. He blinked slowly before wiping the back of his hand across his face. Malcolm watched in horror as tears formed in the holy man's eyes, before sliding down his cheeks to run off his chin. Malcolm wanted to go to Father Teague's aid, but was riveted to the spot. He turned back to the thrower, equally shocked, his gummy mouth now working overtime.

Meanwhile, Phaedrus sat dead still as Old Sammy's poo came to rest on his slippers. Pressed to the absolute limit of what his nose could stand, Phaedrus rose to spew in the curtains.

Old Sammy was back in his chair. His shaking hand picked up his cup of tea to slurp. Clearly distressed at the climax of his fury, his mouth worked furiously in his deeply flushed face.

Father Teague stood still, muttering silent prayers. Malcolm wondered sadly if Father Teague was right now in that place of despair Satan had warned about.

Those of a more delicate nature, including Mr Desmond Markby who had coquettish, almost maidenly, poses and postures, had taken shelter in the furthest corners of the dayroom or behind the curtains, though Phaedrus' untimely spew forced some to scramble.

Then Old Sammy, in his blundering fashion, took further advantage of the fight to unleash his own pent-up compulsions, bellowing like a madman.

Malcolm never flinched. He stood where he was, truly intrigued, noting the different personalities. He was learning from this.

In came the domestics, the clean-up brigade and the attendants to deal to the fighters. All became quiet with everyone sullen or bewildered. The Ward Charge bustled Father Teague away, him still crying quietly.

Some patients were sent to cool off in the lockup.

Can't have shit fights in a dayroom with new curtains.

Chapter 19

More Secrets

Malcolm was happy to be working in the gardening gang. He'd always liked flowers and trees, and the ornamental shrubs that filled the hospital grounds and made them look like a park. Like the Queens Gardens he remembered from his way-distant past. He was issued a sturdy wooden wheelbarrow with an iron-rimmed wooden wheel made in the workshop. Although still set and ordered by the clanging of the morning tea and lunch bell, his life was somehow changed. It seemed to him that even the keen chill in the early spring air parted to allow him through.

With a barrowful of weeds, he headed to the rubbish dump past the willows. He thought of Ned The

Accountant and wondered if his sister knew he'd hanged himself in the willow tree. Over the previous autumn and winter, he'd listened to various talk but he'd never heard mention of the man again, or of any enquiry. And it wouldn't be wise to ask anyone about it. He glanced at his boots, the traces of bog dirt long gone.

Even so, a cold shiver raced down his spine.

He turned at the sudden howling behind the wooden fence to the right of the main entrance. The barrier was thirteen-feet high. No chance of climbing that one in a hurry. Abandoning his wheelbarrow, he pressed his good eye to a knothole. He'd used this hole before to observe with horrified fascination recurrent and boisterous bouts of extreme unreason. He was only grateful to live outside this fence, away from the many and varied forms of greater madness. Beyond this courtyard the bad patients were housed. Yet who decided they were 'bad' and what did 'bad' look like compared to 'mad'?

Paddy lived here, freshly delivered from Dunedin Prison, along with other prisoners who showed the vaguest sign of instability; shunted out to the country airs. He'd chopped his wife's head off with an axe, and tossed it in the rubbish tin.

Behind the fence, Paddy was yelling at the top of his vocal range, "Slut! Slut! Slut!" and wildly galloping hither and yon whilst constrained awkwardly within his straitjacket, even though the buckles had come loose. One of the bigger attendants tackled him to the ground. The rest took it from there, dodging as he kicked out with his bare feet.

Some patients egged him on while another group wearing an assortment of pyjama tops and bottoms stood quietly by. Some drew closer to the fence as if to make them invisible. Malcolm felt a wash of emotion. The place was overwhelmingly dreary and dispiriting.

"Slut!" bellowed Paddy from beneath the scrum of arms, legs and boots.

Malcolm removed his cap to run his shaking fingers through his hair. How could he possibly survive if he ended up behind this fence? His throat constricted painfully. Then he became aware of talking and shouting from farther along the fence and recognised the two different voices of Alan Bowcock.

The first Alan whimpered, "Shut up. Get away."

"Don't you tell me to shut up," boomed the second voice of Alan.

The first Alan whimpered again, "You keep your dirty hands off me. And stop looking at me. I don't like it when you look at me."

"What about him then? Is he still your friend?" This second Alan was strong and overbearing.

"I hate him. He hates me."

And then it was quiet for a moment.

"I'm scared." The tremulous whisper was right beneath Malcolm's knothole. "Eye? I'm scared."

"Shut the hell up with all that cryptic crap," the second Alan shouted back to himself. "Talking to an eye. You're a bloody insane imbecile!"

"Eye? Can you feel the hate? Can you?" The madman's mouth, wet and pale, was hard up against the knothole, his voice filled with horror.

Malcolm stepped back, wiping spittle from his eyelid.

The second Alan was now even more menacing. "Haven't you ever wanted to kill someone?" he goaded.

The first Alan said, "Get away from me! Oh, God!"

"Who'd you kill then? Your son?" His taunts were provoking all kinds of fear in his other personality.

Timidly he asserted to his own self, "Not my son. Not my boy. I never done it."

Malcolm peeped again through the knothole.

"You pathetic, locked-up demented sod!"

He jumped violently when Alan's fist slammed into the fence. He remembered those fists, sometimes bloodied, sometimes bound within a straitjacket. He often wondered what this man's life must be like. Clearly much worse than his own.

There were so many noisy distractions behind that fence. He didn't want to end up in the lockup. He'd heard all about it. Massive keys and locks, a prison, a padded cell, straitjackets, haunting darkness and dismal noises. So on he walked, as fast as his gammy leg would allow, up the road to the dump to empty his wheelbarrow.

Malcolm was re-assigned the care of the tennis courts since the previous chap had been discharged. Now he spent some time each day watching the game until he thought he'd got the hang of it. Martin, a junior nurse, appeared to be a mediocre player. He had a decent serve that made use of his height, and he could hit the occasional beefy shot from the baseline, but at the net he was clumsy and stupid. His backhand was mutinous and he seemed to prefer to run around balls to his left. Perhaps he was scared to win against the senior attendant, Carlos.

Carlos was in another league altogether, a player of fast and accurate strokes, and with a surprising prancing vigour for a man of his age. He took the first set six-one, the second six-love, the third six-one, but what astonished Malcolm was his fury whenever the junior Martin managed to snatch a point. Though aimed at himself for being such a dunderhead, it was a tangible fury nonetheless. Cussing and blaspheming he made it obvious that he didn't want to simply win the game, he wanted every last point.

Once the game was over, Carlos was amenable again and thanked his opponent for a 'bloody good game, cobber'. Martin in turn gave Carlos a vigorous handshake along with promises of another game. Soon.

This exchange of courtesies amused Malcolm.

When the tennis court was neat and tidy, he was sent up to the Chief Engineer's house to rake leaves and trim thorny hedges. A young male nurse was his escort to ensure he didn't do a runner or cut himself. He was leaning against a tree smoking Pall Mall filter tips when Malcolm arrived.

"You can call me Joe if you like." He offered a cigarette to Malcolm. "Go on. I've got plenty more."

Joe had tattoos on his brown forearms, and across his knuckles the words 'Love' and 'Hate'.

Malcolm thought Joe was quite possibly a Maori. There weren't a lot of Maori folk in his world. He politely shook his head. Those patients who worked were paid at the end of each week. Most accepted a packet or two of Government Issue tobacco and lollies.

"Thank you, anyway."

"What do you get then, if you don't get tobacco?" Joe asked pleasantly.

"Mutton pies."

"Mutton pies? Well, I'll be damned." Joe blew a smoke ring into the air. "Hey, I heard you were the one who went to live down in the big smoke a couple of years back."

Malcolm nodded. Here he was talking with this nice young chap who could be around his own age. He reckoned he was more than thirty now.

"Where did you live?" He wasn't used to asking questions of staff, especially personal ones. Normally he just answered theirs.

"Down country. Down south a bit."

"What's it like?"

"The country? Well, it's – umm." Joe's face lit with amusement. "Let's see. Less buildings and more cows. Yep, that about sums it up. Lots of sheep."

Joe stayed nearby while Malcolm trimmed the hedge with the shears. He talked easily of his life in the country.

Malcolm marvelled at how he was engaging in normal conversation just like the staff or the patients from Clifton House. He liked Joe. Joe could prove to be a good cobber.

Joe took a turn with the clippers as Malcolm filled the wheelbarrow. "What about where you're from?"

Malcolm tried to find words to describe where he came from, what he'd seen. But he couldn't find them. He spread his arms wide. "Big... Many houses..."

"Do you have family, Malcolm?"

Malcolm thought about the cosy meals around the table in the roughcast house up the high street with the others, the roasts and the puddings, the coal sacks and icy windows in the winter. After a time, he smiled. Yes, he had a family.

The hedges and bushes were neat. The crocus spikes poked golden or purple heads through the hard earth. There were pansies, hyacinths and alyssum, pretty to look at though alyssum smelled like piss. Flowers he would never have introduced to Julie.

Julie had liked roses, stock and violets. The jonquils, alyssum and bright daffodils flowered in the hospital grounds alongside vibrant polyanthus and snapdragons. Now they were flowering, the gardens were beautiful, reminding him of the Queens Gardens.

Violets made him maudlin.

He, who had long ago learned to listen, vowed to speak more, like he did with Joe.

"I beg your pardon?" he practised on the yellow daffodils, and to the bluebells, he said, "I'm not sure I follow you." And, "I'm not sure I quite understand," he said to the park bench. "I don't understand what you are saying," to The Twins, Leonard and Margaret, who were twittering at him. And as he grew more comfortable with his assemblage of words, "I do believe there will be sunshine today. I do believe there will be. Oh, my, isn't that something? That tree over there."

A large cloud covered half of the sky. The fresh bright colours in the garden turned grey. A woman was picking little purple flowers and tearing them up.

His memory was returning in dramatic spurts, usually triggered by a comment or a smell.

Or like now, when he suddenly thought of Bazza for no reason he could fathom. He recalled everything he could about him. Bazza said he was suffering from some form of acute mania, that he was suicidal because of money worries. The attendants fed him with oesophageal tubes, twice daily. It was a wretched time for him when he didn't want to live as a failure or a burden to his family. He was being forced to live.

Soon he'd be discharged to deal with his money worries all over again. He told Malcolm that being disruptive at night was another form of insanity, as well as stripping naked. So he deliberately became disruptive and naked, especially at night. But, inexplicably, he'd burst out crying. He said he hadn't planned on the crying.

Malcolm listened to nearby attendants discussing Bazza. His new persona appeared to be viewed with more concern than his depression and failed suicide attempt. One attendant said Bazza was rambling in his speech, unmanageable and in danger of doing some harm to himself or others. Clearly he was outside the bounds of normal behaviour. He was scheduled for The Treatment.

Malcolm studied Bazza when next he saw him and was saddened by the change in the man. Bazza was now docile. Fed daily by tube, he also accepted spoonfuls of mash. The remains of the man were discharged into his wife's care – fully recovered.

The next time Bazza attempted suicide he was successful.

Sometimes when his memories returned they were plain sad. Malcolm climbed Mount Charlotte again to explain this to Julie, to tell her about Bazza and how he died. And like each other time he talked to his memory of her, the shuddering in his chest set up again.

Chapter 20

Martha and the Whales

"You'll have to be quicker if you want to see the whales, so get a move on, man."

Malcolm tugged at his stubborn tight boots.

"Don't you want to see the whales, Malcolm?"

"Yes, I do want to see the whales."

"Then get your wits about you!"

News of the stranding buzzed through his ward. A nurse from Warrington had seen them as she left for work – a dark pod cast like wet slugs on the beach. But it was Keith and Martha who held them up because Keith lost his teeth and would not budge without them. They were eventually found on top of the radio.

Martha was in the lavatory.

Clambering onto the bus she gave the driver a telling-off for tooting, saying in her Southland drawl, "I wasn't finished. If I wet myself it's all your fault."

"Get to your seat now, girlie." He laughed lightly. "Hurry along, there."

"You men are all the same. Never any consideration." Crying quietly now.

They were off. A bus full of inmates – or patients as they were called now – going to watch the whales die. Around the winding dusty road above the ocean to the car park by the white beach, not to the waters behind the pine trees where they played football and where the sea crept in and out, nor across the grey flats of Blueskin Bay where the whalers came ashore many years ago.

The whales came ashore on their own, onto the white sands.

An attendant yelled, "Keith, you get down now!"

Keith was walking up and down on top of a whale, muttering unintelligibly.

"Who do you think will pull you out if you go through? It won't be me, you stupid blighter."

When Keith got to the tip of the tail the second time, he stepped off onto the sand, not because he had been told to but because he'd reached the end of the whale's body.

"That's cruel," Martha yelped. She was given to tears, and now others had followed Keith's lead to clamber over the dying whales.

"They're still alive," she wailed louder, before suddenly clutching at her crotch. Too late. A pool of yellow piss formed at her bare feet to soak into the sand.

Malcolm limped on to examine one magnificent bull set apart from the others. It feebly waved a fin. He walked the full length of his chosen whale, but on the sand. He bent down to look into its tiny eye, seeing the life slowly fade from it. He moved on so he could pat its flipper before coming back to speak to the eye.

"It won't be long now, whale. You'll be all right. Say hello to Mummy and Julie for me. And Ned The Accountant, and Bazza. Say hello to God too."

When Keith stumbled onto the tail of that whale, Malcolm shoved him backward onto the sand. Keith, flat on his back, spitting red from his bitten tongue, roared. Malcolm heaved him up onto his feet, brushed the sand from his trousers and jersey. Keith made for the whale's fin. Malcolm aimed him toward another whale.

They weren't the only ones watching the whales die. A group of locals had arranged themselves into teams. Countless times they attempted to refloat the calves, only to find them beached again to be near the mothers calling them back. Working against the tide, the teams carried gallons of seawater in tin pails to wet the still-living whales, and dug deep trenches between the sea and the whales to refloat them.

Back in the bus Martha sat on a towel. She let rip with her take on cruelty. Blood pooled under Keith's chin, soaking his jersey. Malcolm had not harmed his whale nor climbed on it. He had talked to it.

Over time, he collected Martha's disjointed stories until he had a fairly cohesive mental picture book. The family once lived on a farm down south, where she cooked her husband meals, when she was not tormented by constantly pissing her pants, when she was a hard-working mother and farmer's wife.

But what she and her husband possessed they always seemed to lose and in any of their new enterprises they failed. Her husband managed to keep himself out of jail, but gave himself up freely to all such sins and weaknesses – drink, wife and child abuse, gambling – as human beings can indulge in without breaking the law. Martha said Ross was not such a bad feller. There were many worse than him. He was likeable, even talented in his own way. Only he'd not got the knack of living properly. That's what Martha told Malcolm. He listened closely.

"We ran sheep," she said. "Ross alternated his farming and working at the freezing works, so I'd be busy milking, calving and lambing. I dug the veggie garden, cooked meals for shearing gangs, crutched and docked lambs too. Then before he came home at night I'd have the kiddies in bed..."

Whenever Martha got to this part she would whisper as if she were right back there.

"He's coming. He'll get angry and beat them."

Drawn into her fear, Malcolm lowered his head to better hear.

She talked of how she might drop a plate and collect a cropper for her efforts but dare not cry out. If she did the kiddies would cry and they'd be for it. So she'd finish the dishes even if they weren't washed properly. Shove them in any cupboard. Haul out the spuds while Ross sat boozing.

"He was a right bugger," she said.

He'd deserted from the army and gone into hiding in Central Otago, getting work on different farms. When the army pay stopped she had no money for food, existing on scraps she'd normally feed to the pigs. Before he came home from anywhere Ross stopped at the local – he always had coins in his pocket. By six o'clock closing time he'd loaded himself with a few jugs. He'd be right cantankerous.

Malcolm was intrigued with how others lived outside The Building. He knew Martha had five kiddies, and the eldest, Ronald, was fifteen.

"Ronald would distract them with all kinds of shenanigans. He'd stand on his head and make funny faces, anything to make them laugh," Martha said. "I was scared I'd spill Ross' dinner because then he'd smash my face in it."

She ran her tongue over her empty gums. When she spoke, her voice was low. "Bloody mongrel. He'd scrape his plate outside for the dogs. Wouldn't share his scraps with us. He'd kick me out in the rain or snow too. Better than being around him. He'd drag a bunch of Frenchies from his pocket..."

Martha said the last time Ross had bashed Timmy, he'd broken the boy's arm. Abruptly she burst into tears.

"Timmy was only six. My kiddies lived in fear."

He looked into her swollen red eyes. He reached his hand to pat her arm. He considered her size; she was no match for a strong farming man.

"He'd do me on the floor." Her face softened and the red colour faded. "Next morning he'd say our love would overcome his dark moods. He was just a red-blooded Southland bloke. And after a hard day's work… Well, you know, the kiddies whining and all."

It seemed to him that Martha needed to believe Ross, what with no money and seven mouths to feed.

"True, he loved us fair enough. He rough-housed with us, was all."

She'd coached the kiddies to go to their room when their dad came home, not to come out whatever they heard.

"He tied my hands, burned me with cigarettes. For sure, I cried as he did me over the table. He got his orgasm."

This was the part Malcolm got a kick out of. He'd turn his head slightly to watch the others. At the word *orgasm* a few who'd pretended to nod off woke up, and some of the more genteel patients left the room. He stifled his mirth as someone snickered.

"I was pregnant again, see, so I planned to leave. I had to keep this one safer than I'd kept the others. Whenever he started on me, I'd imagine me curled up in my womb saving my baby from his beatings. If I were to die, they'd probably all die with me."

He let Martha tell her story often. He wanted her to get well so he listened. He knew about fear. He recalled his various fears about getting The Treatment, being in the men's lockup with the murderers, The

Leucotomy and the beating by the bully attendant who said he was on The List. Though Dr Burt said this was not true, he wondered if The Leucotomy would hurt more than The Treatment, and if anyone would know that answer after they'd had it.

"He held my hands on the coal range. I never lit it again," she said with a gulp. "And Ronald wanted to kill him because he belted Gwennie, her just coming up four."

The skin on her face stretched, making her hard-faced, and her eyes glinted. Perhaps she was mad after all. But he still liked her.

"Ross came in drunk. He pulled out the rest of my hair. So he roars for his beer, only I crush pills in it. He went to bed. When I poked him he didn't move."

Martha described how she'd taped her husband's hands and legs together before piling blankets on top of him. She turned the electric blanket on high and the radio on loud. After banking the fire, she and her kiddies were out of there.

At this point she'd mop her moist eyes.

They found a row of beach cribs before Brighton, though they were locked for winter.

"Ronny wanted to break in but no kiddie of mine would do crime if I could help it. After the fifth crib we were dead beat. But it was my kiddies, see. I had to find somewhere for them. It wasn't a palace; it was a miracle it still stood. It overlooked the Pacific Ocean and the weather had stripped the paint off and etched the windowpanes so they couldn't be seen through. Ronny lit a fire to heat water for baths and we ate canned food from the larder. With vegies from the garden and scones from sacked flour, who could ask for more? Ronny hunted rabbits in the dunes. It was idyllic, our stolen home."

Malcolm imagined Martha's view, the sea with its bubbles of creamy foam gathered layer upon layer on the wet beach. And the kelp glistening and popping. The kiddies scooting the bubbles onto their feet, jumping on them. They collected chunks of kelp to boil up for dinner. And their father was never referred to again – except much later in the court.

"We lived in the stolen crib for months. Murder, they said, but my lawyer said How could anyone plan such a cruel death unless they were insane, Your Honour? I did it all right, Malcolm. The court people were all there but who among those could hurt us more? Who among those could touch our souls? Now Ronny's got a fair chance. And the others are doing fine with my sister. I hadn't noticed they got so skinny after the larder food was gone. Guess that's because none of them complained. They wouldn't though, would they?" she said. "They all come visit me."

"That's real nice of them."

And she added softly, "I miscarried."

So that was Martha's story. Malcolm knew that within her sunken bosom she had a greatness of soul that enabled her to scorn her ongoing misery in the wake of the horrors of the past. He'd met her kiddies often. Each week without fail they came on the train to Seacliff Mental Hospital to visit their insane mother.

Chapter 21

Sports Day

The hospital sports grounds were beyond the brick building, Clifton House, which was occupied first in 1917 – a fact tucked safely away as part of Malcolm's memory training. The grounds and the tennis courts had dried out after the wet winter and spring. Maintenance teams, when they weren't patching up the decrepit buildings or plastering over cracks, helped mow and roll the corrugated surfaces ready for the new season's Sports Day. Malcolm had had a good shot at using the heavy rolling machine. They also groomed the bowling strip and trimmed the edges. Trimming and pruning trees was something he enjoyed.

Joe, the young tattooed attendant he'd first met a few weeks back, climbed up the ladder to hack and saw broken branches while Malcolm gathered them into his wheelbarrow, trekking back and forth to the dump all day long. Joe eventually climbed down the ladder, leaned back on it and lit a cigarette. After a few drags, he stubbed it out and put it behind his ear.

"Right, mate. Let's crack on, shall we?"

For those who could think, or at least feel, Sports Day was a time of great excitement. Mr Treweek, another attendant, usually organised the entire affair down to the cricket teams, the bowling and the running races. Whistles were blown at the start of each race and later the Medical Superintendent gave out the various prizes.

At last the big day arrived. The hospital staff and families from the village below all contributed in some way. There were banners and brightly painted signs, areas were neatly cordoned off, and soft drinks, club sandwiches and fruit-packed cakes were brought over from the kitchen. There was a loudhailer and a podium for the announcer to stand on.

The day was a real scorcher. Most of the patients wore sunhats tied beneath their chins, though some who didn't know better spent their day huddled beneath a blanket. Busloads of patients from both Cherry Farm and Orokonui Hospital arrived to stand in tight little groups or rush about to meet an old mate they'd not seen in ages.

Visitors came from miles around: Dunback, Pleasant Point, and Palmerston – home to the mutton pies. Children raced about while adults sat on their car's running board with tablecloths spread on the ground before them. Cordial, hot corned beef and hotter tomatoes. Lettuce leaves wilting on crockery plates. A thermos of milky sugary tea. Baskets covered with damp tea towels. Malcolm sniffed the air around them, trying to guess if they contained bacon and egg or mince pies. He dawdled among the visiting cars, so he could sniff the various flavours, name each one.

Although he didn't participate in any event, he waited at the finishing line to see if Davey McPherson won his heat. Davey was a fast runner. Everyone cheered, yelled or screamed for the sheer hell of it. Malcolm bellowed as loud as he could, happy to express his support for his mate. Attending were doctors, Matron and the sisters, nurses and attendants, all the maintenance staff, kitchen, laundry, sewing room workers and others he couldn't bring to mind. Like the farmers.

There was the fat lady from the sewing room whom he had long ago decided had some odd mental problem of her own. Her head jerked to the right far more than was necessary in a uniformed staff member.

Father Teague stood some distance away. Malcolm waved to him and he waved back.

Wheelchairs and red vinyl-covered dayroom chairs lined the racetrack.

A few patients were absent because they were in lock-down, alone but secured.

Malcolm cheered as loud as he could, "Davey! Come on, Davey! You can do it!" He tried a wolf whistle.

But Davey fell down.

First he'd staggered a lot, running in the wrong direction, before ploughing heavily into the ground, his arm pinned beneath him, feet still kicking erratically, trying to win his race. While some attendants tore off in Davey's direction, Mr Treweek announced through the loudhailer, "That's it, then. We have the winner of the men's race. Eric Coombs!"

A bellow of congratulations beat in waves upon Malcolm's ears as he pushed closer to the loudhailer. Pulling at the trouser cuffs of the attendant, Mr Treweek, who was atop some box arrangement, he said, "Davey hasn't finished his race yet."

"What's that, Malcolm? Oh, of course, you're right."

After a lot more whistle blowing, Mr Treweek said,

"Hang on a minute." Phee phee-ee. "Wait where you are. Nobody is to move. Davey has yet to finish his race. *Davey has yet to finish his race.*"

Everyone waited; they understood. Davey hadn't finished his race. Two attendants had him upright though clearly dazed. His eyes rolled lazily in their sockets while blood ran freely from his mouth. As Davey and the two attendants stumbled and lurched across the finishing line the cheers that went up from all patients, staff and visitors alike was deafening. "Da-vey! Da-vey! Da-vey!"

Malcolm ambled off to the bowling green. He'd always been interested in bowling but was too clumsy for it, what with his height and boot and all – it was difficult enough weeding on his knees. The one time he'd given bowls a go, he'd fallen head-over-kite before releasing his ball. Now, standing quite still alongside the bowling teams, observing the neatness and precision of them, no one shoving or jostling, all intent on perfect bowls, he looked up to see Mr Treweek approaching. Malcolm lowered his face and scuffed his boot lightly on the manicured green grass.

"Good on you, man." Mr Treweek patted him on the shoulder. "Good team spirit." Then he was off to organise the cricket teams.

Everyone knew about Davey McPherson's fits. He often complained of blurry vision and headaches, talking slurred. He'd find an attendant or nurse and they'd whisk him away to have his fit in private. Sometimes they didn't make it in time and there he was, lying on the floor or in the middle of the road, kicking his feet wildly, arching his head back, eyes rolling, slobbering red froth.

One time he bit clear through his tongue and there was blood all over the show. The staff whisked him away smartly. And the doctor did a jolly fine job sewing Davey's tongue back on. It healed all right, only with a big pink bobble on the end of it. And Davey talked as though he had a mouthful of scone.

Days and weeks merged. Malcolm considered that perhaps this life of his was as good as it got. He'd made more friends since he'd learned to talk more, including Davey and Joe. And there was Martha. He started to list them off on his fingers. Mr Antonio, Jack, Mrs Green, Sandy…

Most staff at Seacliff Mental Hospital were kind. It was like one big family. There were those who got on with everyone and those who plain didn't. From what he'd gathered in his listening, he thought that was pretty normal. He made a mental note of those he admired most, counting on his fingers, first one hand and then the other. There were many more than ten. And as he watched them daily go about their work, the number of them grew. By doing this exercise, he was able to focus more on those who were kind and less on the few who were not.

Nice ones were those like Big Harold (though he was a patient) and Bill The Blacksmith, who made pokers for the staff members' fires, and boot lasts. Big Harold's job was to hold the farm horses steady while Bill prised their old shoes off and then worked over the hot forge, hammering, forming and correcting the piece of steel he'd fashioned to fit each hoof. Big Harold held the horse firmly by its leather halter, stroking the velvety muzzle, crooning and breathing in the straw-scented horse breath. Malcolm sometimes stood next to the horse's rump to watch.

Bill said to Big Harold, "Next I'll show you how to heat the iron until it glows white hot."

The horse clattered off on four newly shod hooves.

Big Harold said he paid careful attention to everything Bill did or said. He knew he was fortunate to be working with him. To Malcolm, Big Harold held out a hunk of stiff leather, saying, "Bill gave me my own leather apron. Ain't he the best, then?"

Malcolm longed to work with horses. He remembered when the draught horses hauled carts of coal from ward to ward until the big lorries took over. Earlier, many farm workers had their own horse and every horse had its own cart. Some of the other carts didn't have a horse, though. Laden with coal and supplies, they were pulled by harnessed men up the hill to the wards high above. Malcolm recalled them doing this when he was a wee lad exploring the grounds. He remembered glimpses of half-naked men and women, in separate grassed areas walking around in aimless circles. He hoped he would never have to do either of those things.

Reclaimed bits of scattered memory like disjointed jigsaw pieces made not a lot of sense. He wondered if his brain might be dying and he along with it. Or he wondered when he would turn into a stranger so that others might not recognise him, or he himself.

He hoped that wouldn't happen soon because right now he was happy and interested in the horses.

Chapter 22

The Farm

Everyone knew the patients ran the hospital. The farms, the grounds and the laundry with the heavy mangles and all that ironing – those were the really big jobs. And the sewing room where they darned socks all day or made uniforms for the staff and clothes for the patients – the whole set-up. The boot-maker took care of the basic essentials for staff and patients alike while the painters and the upholstery workshop workers repaired furniture.

Jack said all of the trades were represented in this self-sufficient farming community with much of the work carried out by the patients, those who were ex-perienced in these fields. Mostly those capable – regardless of whether they were staff or patients – worked long hours because of staff shortages.

Jack said there seemed to be a big change in place. He said there were lots more female nurses than he ever remembered. Male nurses and attendants once dominated the psychiatric nursing profession, as the work was deemed too physical and dangerous for women.

Malcolm made a mental note of how many female nurses there were compared to male nurses and attendants. Often the nurses commenced at 7am and finished after 8pm. They worked four days on with one day off, then four days on with two days off. He compared them to the patients who worked all day and every day; the patients had no rostered off days.

When he saw them wander back to their wards late in the afternoon or evening, depending on where they worked, some patients looked dead beat. He wondered if this kind of job was the same as people did outside the hospital, only the staff and the people outside were paid in money each week whilst he and other patients were paid in mutton pies and tobacco.

These thoughts and others like them had him thinking more about the outside world, and his place in it.

Jack would explain more to him.

For now he observed the nurses' behaviour when the doctor did his ward rounds. There was a definite regimented structure in place for the nursing staff that brought to mind a new memory about some lead toy soldiers. If a charge nurse happened by, the juniors would stand politely with their hands behind their back and say Good morning, Sister or Good afternoon, Sister. Matron did her rounds with the doctor from 9.30am and each ward attendant or charge nurse walked behind the pair to stand at the end of each bed with their hands behind their back.

In the main kitchen it was always cheerful.

Jack was saying, "The patients milk all those cows. They're a basic part of the whole establishment. Those who're able to help, at least, or those who want to."

He explained again how Seacliff Mental Hospital was essentially conceived as a prison, but the then Medical Superintendent, Dr Truby King, had turned it into an efficient working farm by combining various medical treatments and procedures with labour. Unless they were physically incapable, the patients were trained as farm workers, which had the end result of improved fitness, exposure to fresh air and the occupying of their minds with healthy outdoor activities. The ongoing benefits were the nutritious diets enjoyed by both patients and staff, for Dr Truby King insisted the staff ate the same meals as the patients to keep things fair and square.

Malcolm thought about all of this as he drank his milky tea. *Whole*, was what they were. Without the mad ones there would be no hospital, without the hospital there would be no mad ones, without – without – without-

But the horses and carts were important too. So he left the warmth of the kitchen to go back to his current job, mentally noting the approaching cart loaded with muck from the pigsties, the horses plodding over to the dump and back, an endless procession, all day long. Ah, but to have his own horse…

Malcolm was to work in the vegetable gardens. Mostly women worked in the flower gardens – weeding, trimming, planting out and weeding some more. He was fit and strong so he worked with the men in the main gardens. There were many gangs of workers in different groups. For every ten patients working there was a supervisor. Some of the patients hoed and a few of them never knew when to stop until someone took the hoe from their hand and shoved them in the direction of their ward to have lunch or tea.

"Damn fine workers, that lot," someone said of them. "Digging and grubbing and hoeing without stopping. Some of 'em can't talk to save 'emselves, but they're damn fine workers."

Malcolm was part of a group of damn fine workers. He dug row upon row of spuds, brushing the soil off before dropping them into sacks. He didn't hoe.

He wondered if he could get a job on the fencing gang. That fencing gang, under the control of Bill Morris, would be well into their day by now. They mended as well as built new fences. They had put them up from the hospital all around the coast to Puketeraki, a settlement on the craggy bluff above Karitane.

"Jack, how far is that? From here to Puketeraki?"

Malcolm saw him at smoko.

"It's a bloody long way, son."

Because Jack had worked at the hospital for so many years, he'd had lots of different jobs: kitchen, pigs, fencing, gardens. As Malcolm saw it, Jack was a source of great knowledge. He wanted to try everything too.

Maybe he'd go with Bill Hight on horseback, droving a mob of cattle to the nearby slaughterhouse. Only he'd never been on horseback so that might be a bit of a problem. Perhaps the piggery would be just fine and dandy. Or the chickens. He would like to feed and collect their eggs. Or perhaps join the bush-felling gang with Bob McMillan or Arthur Little in charge. He looked toward the sun, gauging the time. Yep, they'd all be hard at work in the native bush, chopping and sawing. Any excess wood from the surroundings was carted to Dunedin to use as firewood for the public hospital.

Though he knew the lawnmowers were reserved for others, he considered what it might be like to get hold of a lawnmower instead of a horse, or be part of the gang clearing scrub. Instead, after digging up tons of spuds, day in and day out, he was to plant seedlings from trays in the glasshouses. Cabbages, Brussels sprouts, cauliflowers... He worked on his knees for hours at a time until he feared his legs would never straighten up again. Yet he was being useful – and that was surely good.

Some said the atmosphere at the hospital was like that of a large working community, a description often used in general conversation within his hearing. Patients capable of working were asked to help with various duties, partly because of the staff shortages (due to the war years). Some were not asked. They were told. He pondered why that might be. Probably because of their poor communication skills, someone thought their answers would be unintelligible and best be taken to mean Yes.

Only those considered dangerous weren't asked to do anything. More often than not they were confined to the high-walled yards attached to their specific wards, supervised constantly by attendants. At night, for the safety of staff and patients, they were locked into single rooms.

When the weather was fine, along with beach picnics, some were allowed to go fishing. Malcolm didn't enjoy fishing after the first time he went. All that water disturbed him and there was something about the glazed eyes of the fishes that stirred up half-memories that troubled him.

He would hitch a ride in the hospital van to Karitane, a coastal settlement a few miles north of Seacliff, along with those who did enjoy fishing. He waited on the jetty or on the high concrete wall until they returned. Sitting in the sunshine, looking around, he enjoyed being away from the hospital, being a regular bloke.

Dr Truby King had long ago established a fishing business at Karitane. Those patients who caught fish were said to be contributing greatly to the fishing industry. Originally there was a fishing crew of only one attendant and three patients who, reportedly, caught tons of fish. Half were smoked and used in the kitchens at The Building and the rest were distributed daily to other public institutions in the South Island, as far away as Seaview Mental Hospital in Hokitika, on the West Coast. Along with dozens of fresh eggs.

The other hospital farms shipped their excess produce around the country in much the same way so that each was helping the other. Years later a much larger fishing vessel was brought in and doubled as a pleasure boat to the delight of those patients interested in the sea.

Everybody said the sea had health benefits.

He had no inclination to try fishing again. He was still holding out to go on the fencing gang with Bill Morris.

Chapter 23

Cats, Cold and Companions

The hospital was in a state of frenzy. Staff raced about with sacks, wheelbarrows and garden spades. Some patients galloped around with their shovels while others screamed, tore out their hair, or scratched tear-streaked faces and arms until they bled. Some stood in the garden rocking to and fro, their eyes wide in shock, soundlessly crying.

Malcolm grabbed his wheelbarrow and hurried to the kitchen to find out what had caused this outburst.

Mr Antonio already had most of the story pieced together. Apparently one of the male staff, and no one was letting loose exactly who that person was, had been instructed to dispose of the wild cats and keep his yapper shut about it.

There were large numbers of cats at The Building: orange, striped and grey, black or white, or mottled combinations, and dozens of kittens of each and every colour imaginable. Over the years some had become ward pets and some individual pets, of both staff and patients.

So, as Malcolm saw it, there were cats that yowled, meowed and kept up a racket the whole night, but those cats took care of mice and rats.

And mated publicly to the amusement of most.

So the staff member was instructed to dispose of the wild cats. Belatedly he was ordered to explain to his superiors exactly how he'd done it. Meat scraps from the kitchen laced with a powerful sedative from the ward.

At this part of his story, Malcolm's eyes widened and Mr Antonio winked largely at him.

"That's on the low-down, boy.'

Malcolm nodded. Sure enough, he'd seen his cobber, Joe, leaving the kitchen with a plate covered over with a tea towel. He stifled the laughter bubbling inside. Was it appropriate to find these shenanigans amusing?

Apparently Joe was close-mouthed about lacing the meat. He scattered the bait far and near and then went off home to his cosy bed in the village. In the early morning he returned to carry out the rest of his carefully-formulated plan. His intention, he later explained, was to collect the sleeping cats and kittens into sacks, load up a wheelbarrow and take them to the rubbish dump where he would shoot them and bury their remains. The gun was his.

However, circumstances orchestrated against him. Some cats had been fed in the ward kitchens so only nibbled at the baited meat. Some wandered, dazed, into the middle of the road, and were dispatched by various vehicles driven around that early morning. Seems the drivers fully expected those cats to dart out of the way as they usually did. In fact, not one driver had thought to apply the brakes, so now there were a fair few upset drivers griping on about their 'mental state'. Other cats drowned in the farm water troughs, or wandered into styes and were eaten by the pigs. A fat ginger tom from Malcolm's ward staggered into the path of the lawn-mowing tractor to be splattered over the laundry hung to dry in the early sun. For this cat, Malcolm was truly sad.

A fair few sleeping cats were carefully buried in the gardens, beside the standard roses or between the rows of cabbages and leeks. Unfortunately, the individual doses were insufficient to actually kill the cats. Once this news was broadcast, the patients who had buried 'dead cats' raced helter-skelter to dig them up again, so they could be collected into sacks, loaded into wheelbarrows, and killed humanely over at the rubbish dump by a bullet.

Though Malcolm spent the whole day searching the hospital grounds, he didn't find one live feline to transport in his wheelbarrow. Did cats truly have nine lives, and if so, how had they used them all up?

Patients who witnessed the carnage had immediately gone madder than they were originally thought to be. For days on end dead cats were discovered in the most inaccessible places: curled up in the copper spouting thereby turning the fresh water rank; under the floorboards of the wooden wards, creating a right pong; even in the linen supplies where they'd made a nest for their latest litter.

For days to come the staff and patients were in a weird state of shock. True, the cat infestation had reached toxic levels, yet seemingly each cat had found that one person, whether they were staff or patient, who considered it their own.

Soon the hospital was over-run with rats and mice.

Malcolm was frozen blue and shuddering, even though he wore two jerseys, and miserable before the unrelenting winds. Wet brown leaves swept into whirlwinds then clung to his trouser legs. He recalled the time when the snowflakes last fell, the blanket of white turning the hospital into a castle, draping Mount Charlotte like cottonwool. The hospital woke that morning to silence. Snow continued to drift over the hills. The late mornings and early nights cut into the day, eroding the daylight hours until, somehow, it was time to sleep again.

Locally it was called 'the great snow'.

Often male staff members would ski down through the white farm paddocks just for the hell of it. Details later emerged of how they also skied down to guide crowds of stranded passengers and train crew up from the Seacliff Railway Station, through a foot of snow to rest, eat hot food and sleep in warmth in the concert hall.

Yet this day, standing alone through gale and tempest, Malcolm was bitterly cold. He longed for the change, when the howling wind and biting rain would cease, and snow begin again to fall. In his imaginings it had already changed; he heard the gentle swish of a spring breeze, studied the dew caught in spider webs, and realised he was content.

That was a feeling to be kept inside.

It was a secret.

"Take these pills, Malcolm. There you go."

"Am I sick?" he asked. The new pills were blue and his pill quota usually stayed the same.

"These are to make sure you don't get sick."

A chill quickened the back of his neck.

"Am I getting The Treatment?"

"No, not you." The nurse shook her head, smiling. "So there's nothing to worry about, is there then?"

The pills slid down into his belly.

"They're for your condition," she added kindly.

He wasn't convinced. He'd heard of the typhoid outbreak at nearby Orokonui Hospital; how, of the four cases, the two youngest had died. He'd heard how their kitchen was at the bottom of a long hill so the meals for the top wards were taken up on a cart. On the return trip, the bodies were brought down. Perhaps he had typhoid.

A young woman, Esther, called to him from her armchair by the window. She was winding colours of wool into strands then cutting them into lengths.

"I take those pills now. They don't do any harm. Maybe they don't do any good either." She giggled.

He'd already figured she was about his age.

She lined up a hank of wool and snipped it with the scissors. A pink-uniformed nurse stood guarding the scissors.

He gave a single nod, relieved to know he wasn't the only one on new medication. There was an empty chair next to Esther, so he sat among the piles of coloured wool, thinking back to Julie and her stack of coloured rags, and that part of his life back at the house up Maclaggan Street. The tightening inside his chest began again, making him oddly glum, yet he knew he must hold on to his memories if he were to live well. It was his goal to remember as much as possible.

The nurse took the scissors from Esther and left.

Outside, the gardens were breaking into new growth now the cold wet winter had passed. More often the rain stayed away allowing the sun to warm the soil. Soon he would be back in a gardening gang with his cobber, Joe, pruning the dead wood from the new, sorting out the hedges and shrubs. He liked this time of year. He liked spring.

He liked Esther too. She didn't jerk or constantly nod her head, or dribble, or shriek into the quiet of an afternoon. She was cheerful and always wanted to talk to him. Nor did it seem to matter that he rarely talked back when, in the puzzle of his life, he lost some of his spoken words.

Today was different. Today he wanted to listen *and* talk to Esther. She'd once told him she wasn't always bright and cheerful. She understood how he sometimes felt, and that the highs and lows were always interchanging, and nothing stayed the same for long.

"You know," she said, "each time I come in I have to be restrained. Straitjacket and all. And sometimes they stick me in the covered bath. It's so cold. I think they freeze me. Then I have the – ah – you know. The Treatment." She shuddered violently at the word. "They say we don't remember it, at all, but we do, don't we?"

Sudden tears wet her cheeks.

He nodded vigorously. He never ever forgot that stuff.

"The covered cold bath, the straitjacket, the cell," he said. "Too right, we remember all that."

"And the hand that pokes our food through, don't forget that, either," Esther prompted. "It's always cold. That hand with no body, only a plate of cold food. How can they say we forget any part of it?"

"We don't forget a thing, Esther. We don't want to remember, is all."

"I hate it. I dread it," she cried vehemently. "Even though I know the cycle, I still go home to my husband and bubbas and take the new bubba with me. Even though..."

He wasn't used to Esther in a state such as this. Normally she was bright and cheerful as she went about mixing or sorting her woollen strands.

"The knowing is worse," she mumbled. Shoulders slumped forward, whispering, so low he had to lean closer to hear. "I don't choose it, you know. The bubbas and all. They just come. The first one came early. So much blood and pain. Alone at home, I was, John not being due back from work until later. That wee baby came in the lavatory. He was nothing but a tiny wee mite, barely bigger than a puppy, and mewing too. I wrapped him in a towel, this tiny puppy of mine. I wrapped him in a towel and put him in a shoebox..."

When she paused, Malcolm asked quietly, "A shoebox, Esther? You put your new bubba in a shoebox?"

"Yes, a shoebox with white tissue paper. I buried him in the corner of my garden."

Malcolm's heart lurched, but still he asked, keeping his voice low, "Was he still mewing, this bubba of yours?"

"Yes, he was still mewing. I stayed with him, though. He deserved that. He was my first wee puppy."

"I think he was a bubba, a boy baby, Esther. I think the wee boy should have had the chance to grow up. He could have had some fun."

"Oh, no. I didn't have a choice, you see? It was the pain, they said."

Then all signs of distress abruptly left her. "This one's name is Henry Walter Reid." She smiled down at her newest baby, which the nurse had just placed in her arms. "That's a nice name, isn't it? A strong name to make him feel safe and loved. That's very important."

"Yes, that's very important."

He thought about his own name. Malcolm. Not enough to make him feel safe and loved. Not enough to hang a life on. He wondered what the shoebox baby would have been named, and he felt sad for him.

Esther told him this was her fourth admission.

"Each time I have a baby my brain goes wrong. The doctor says the pain of the delivery is too much for me, so they take my baby away from me as soon as it's born. Just in case…you know, like I told you last time. I sort of want to punish it for the pain it caused, but not really, because I love my bubbas. I love all of my bubbas, I honestly do."

Malcolm watched her face redden and screw up as she stroked the baby's cheek, crooning. He waited for more tears, but they never came.

After a long while, she said, "We'll be fine. It's just the first few weeks until the memory goes."

He wondered which was worse for Esther, the pain of the delivery or the pain of The Treatment afterward.

He often made sure he was around when the pink-uniformed nurse carried Esther's baby in for her to hold. There were always two nurses until they were sure she wouldn't harm it.

He gazed at the tiny hands and feet. Oh, how he ached to hold this little boy in his arms and blow kisses on his bare tummy like he'd seen Esther do. He ached to pass his hand over the soft downy head. Yet he did nothing. He watched from a distance, even turned his head a little away.

Henry Walter Reid was loved.

Sister Hodge was having another meeting in her office. A tall rangy woman, she pinned her long black hair tightly on top of her head. Malcolm wondered how many dozens of shiny hairclips she used to keep it in place. Sister Hodge had hands like a man's;

broad with fingers that were squared-off and flattened at the tips. Her nails were filed short. Some days her hands shook worse than others. Every six weeks without fail, Sister Hodge would go on holiday.

Esther told him this.

"Where are you off to this time, Sister Hodge?" she asked outright one morning while he was sitting in the dayroom. Over her floral frock, Esther wore a grey and pink cardigan with sleeves, which bulged at the wrists where she tucked handkerchiefs.

"Up north," was the curt reply.

"She sure goes up north a lot," Esther whispered to him, "Maybe even up as far as Hanmer Springs."

"Where's Hanmer Springs?" he also whispered, caught up in her mood.

"Top of the island. It's a drying-out place for alcoholics. My brother-in-law goes there. Anyway, wherever she goes her hands have stopped shaking by the time she gets back. I reckon that's where she goes, though. Or maybe she has a feller up north."

It was often hard to tell who were patients and who were on staff. Malcolm recognised a man (a former attendant) who wore a uniform one-week, and the next he was shuffling about in pyjamas. Perhaps employment in mental hospitals afforded some camouflage for the likes of that man. Perhaps he was madder than those incarcerated for life.

There was another kind of meeting – hand-over, they called it – to ensure each patient in their ward was accounted for. Before she departed, Sister Hodge handed over her ward. All present and accounted for, like Buzz Bars, biscuits, toothpaste and bottles of fizzy raspberry drink. Mrs Green counted boxed Jaffas, nylon stockings, trinkets, expanding rings, envelopes and tobacco. She called it stocktaking. To him, it seemed that handover and stocktaking were pretty much the same thing.

Such a hot day for late spring, everyone said. Flies buzzed slowly around the pig slops in a tin outside the kitchen. Fat ponderous bumblebees beat themselves up against the locked windowpanes. Outside, heat rose off the bitumen, melting it, causing shuddering patterns in the air.

When the late afternoon sun dropped low enough to shimmer across the polished dayroom floor, tea rattled in on the trolley's crooked wheels. Malcolm watched and listened as the new man slurped, Jimmy supped and Mr Desmond Markby, still in this ward even after the shit fight, sipped daintily with his pinkie finger stuck out like he'd broken it. A fly landed on his checked shirt. Just before, one male attendant had called Mr Markby a dirty faggot and had stuck his foot out to trip him. Mr Markby had gracefully risen to his feet, dusted off his clothes and touched his hair to make sure it was in place before returning to sit quietly in his chair. His cup rattled ever so slightly in the saucer.

Malcolm saw tears track the gentleman's face. He moved his chair closer so as to impart some of his own physical strength. There were lots of flies in the dayroom. He watched one climb the length of Mr Markby's arm; Mr Markby had fallen asleep. He listened to the rise and fall of the man's breathing. A particular arrangement of mucus in his nose caused a faint high-pitched sound like a blade being sharpened, and then it faded.

Malcolm drank in big mouthfuls, his tealeaves too. Patrick tipped his tea into the saucer and slurped at that, most of it going into his big lippy mouth but a fair amount slopping down his front. Patrick didn't care about anything; he'd broken his teeth, those that hadn't rotted out and they'd removed that lot anyway. He said false teeth hurt his gums. He refused to wear them. Asleep in his chair now, Patrick made soft chewing sounds with his tongue against his gums. Perhaps he dreamed of being hungry or thirsty.

Malcolm was alert to the compulsive movements of the others, the constant nodding and endless jerking, the wall-slapping and pounding, how one man wrung his hands constantly, nervously twisting them this way then that. In her ward, Cynthia was probably tidying and realigning the chairs, the curtains and the mats, sitting down and then getting up again, and then there was her nervous cough. He watched, listened and learned.

He noticed that Patrick, apart from slurping and slopping his tea, had this daft thing of blinking. Up down, open shut, up down, open shut. You'd think his eyelashes would wear out. Malcolm wondered if he did any of these things, like the wringing of his hands, head bobbing, the blinking and stuff. As far as he was aware he only scratched his head. Usually he removed his cap to do this but sometimes he did it from underneath his cap without taking it off. Now he sat and stared unblinking, long and hard, to see if he could, or if he was just like Patrick.

On days when he was not so sharp, his observations, like his memories, ran together like blood and water –gone down the drain. Vaguely, he wondered why he would describe it like that.

He liked best the peace in the dayroom when the coughing and hawking ceased, the rhythmic clicks of the heating pipes and the creak of floorboards when someone approached on rubber soles thinking they moved silently. Sometimes the hospital never slept. Sometimes it never woke.

Generally the long silences were broken only by the tea trolley. Playing cards: solitaire or patience or patients. No one knew which. There were few rules in this ward. If he wanted to, old Patrick could go outside the kitchen for a fag.

Myrtle came over from the women's ward. She was very interested in men, and now she was bearing down on him, with her lips already puckered up. He furrowed his eyebrows and stood up quickly, straining to his full height of over six foot. With his head held backward he knew Myrtle couldn't reach his mouth. The worst she could achieve would be a slurp on his Adam's apple. He shut his eyes and held his breath, but she tore on past him to zoom in on the new man trapped in his wheelchair, whose face, all too late, registered shock, disgust and revulsion.

Soon enough everything became unpleasantly heavy with the heat of the sun's rays pouring through the locked windows. With the curtains wide open, the patients all wilted like garden flowers deprived of shade.

Sister Hodge came in, causing the floorboards to creak. She sniffed the air like a rabbit, glanced at Patrick with the tell-tale stain of piss spreading in his tweeds and shot him a look of disapproval. She briskly snapped the curtains closed and left them to cook up a stench.

Chapter 24

Slut

Malcolm listened as Jack and Mr Antonio nattered to each other. He was allowed to listen; at least he'd never been told not to. They were on about the latest lobotomy patients, how at best they functioned at the level of a domestic pet, how they'd lost the usage and understanding of words. Then, as he stood by quietly shocked, they talked about other goings on around the hospital.

"Yep, that happened in the men's lockup as well, so I've been told," Mr Antonio said. "And Mouse, he nearly drowned himself in the lavatory. Said he was just off for a crap in private."

"Ah, Mouse," Jack said. "He's tried that lark before."

"They found him bare-arsed, feet waggling away, coming up for air and going down again."

Mr Antonio knew all kinds of stuff. He was a popular guy and in charge of the food and meals. When Jack shook his head slowly from side to side, Malcolm thought he looked real sad.

"Stuffing his pyjamas down first and pulling the chain until it filled up? Not so crazy, eh, but that must be the hardest way to go."

Malcolm had been in that ward with its atmosphere of desolation and helplessness, with the same unanswered question – Why am I here?

"I've known Mouse for a long time," Jack continued.

Malcolm thought of that bitterly cold ward: no life, no colour, high up windows like in a compound, like in a cell, the scratchings on the walls like real words though he couldn't read them and dates that went way back. Peeling paint, pools of rust and water in the yard... His thoughts trailed off into bleakness.

Mr Antonio said, "You can't blame him, can you? That cell-like environment."

"There's no breeze or sunlight." Jack shook his head again. "Only little slide-holes high up in the doors for the attendants to peer through."

"Damned if I could survive in there." Mr Antonio had a real family and home he went to each night.

Malcolm had wondered why Mouse should ever want to live. Yet when he'd been in there he'd still wanted to live. Now he wondered why Mouse should want to die. He remembered another time Mouse had tried to drown himself in the lavatory. The attendant got a towel, hauled the pathetic little man onto his feet.

"Enough of your shenanigans, Mouse," he'd said, not unkindly. "Next time you try that you get the jacket. Got it?"

Mouse shuffled off bawling, his nose streaming, the towel dragging on the wet concrete floor.

"He'll probably get The Treatment," Jack said. "Hopefully it'll fix him." No one at the hospital wanted any patient to be like Mouse. "Or maybe they'll shave his head and do The Lobotomy. Maybe then he'll come right."

For some patients, the days and seasons ran together. If it was sunny, some of them thought it was the height of summer. If it was raining, they thought it was winter. At the mention that tomorrow might be a cool-ish day, the working women queued to get a job in the steamy warmth of the laundry.

At the crack of dawn, with the weak sun rising to dispel the mist, the dirty linen from the wards started to come in, piled high on carts. Mountains of sheets, pillowslips, towels and nightwear, growing ever higher as each horse cart dumped a new load. The first job was sorting them into two piles, whites and non-whites, scraping and scouring. The patients bundled and lugged the piles, stuffing them into enormous coppers of boiling soapy water.

These same women wielded heavy wooden paddles, laboriously stirring, surrounded in warm steam whilst outside the temperature continued to drop. They'd guide and pull sheets through the mangles or wringers for hours before pressing endless pillowslips and tea towels.

The radio was always turned on.

The laundry was near the main kitchen. Sheltered from the chill blast in the doorway, Malcolm kept an eye out for Jack. He had another question to ask, but sometimes he lost it. He wanted to ask Jack before it got lost again because Jack would know the answer.

But Jack never came that way on that day.

With autumn gone, a new season of southerly winds howled and whipped around the naked stick-like trees. Thunder and lightning reverberated, flashing through the long empty night. Malcolm stood throughout one entire night with the lightning flashes right before his eyes. He waited patiently for the gentle rain that followed the storms. After many weeks of raging the storm calmed, but by the next week the chill winds were back.

Then it snowed for days.

Malcolm ventured up the hill toward the ward where the budgerigar used to live, where nobody was mad and everyone wore clothes. Through windswept snowdrifts, hard and crunchy, he laboured, just to go and see. He figured he'd follow his boot prints back down to his ward afterward, but it got dark early and he couldn't see them because it was snowing again.

Lost in the darkness, he groped about until he found a wall, and then a set of stairs. But the snowdrifts covered holes in the stairs. He made his way cautiously up on his hands and knees only to find they led nowhere, the door and room above having been carted away during the current demolition. He began to reverse slowly down. At the base lay a snowdrift higher than he was. When he fell through the rotting timber he was consumed by snow.

He was not afraid.

He thought he heard the voices of staff changing night shifts, too distant to pinpoint. What might have been hours later he heard another group of voices. He steadied himself, clambered upright and stumbled toward them. The light from The Building welcomed him home.

Another day. The ceiling above, the floor beneath and all in between achingly cold. Under the watchful eye of the pale moon, he stood quietly dispassionate to consider the freezing temperature. And he marvelled at the sight of the snow-covered trees barely dwarfed by Mount Charlotte.

Those patients who caught colds weren't allowed in the quiet dayrooms, but remained in their squeaky iron beds on damp mattresses, hacking phlegm or blood into enamel bowls. Clawed hands clutched thin blankets to their chins. He was glad he didn't catch colds or he'd have to lie there among the others, row upon row of them, mouths open, hacking and gasping for breath.

He liked the dayroom when it was peaceful, with no one there to make it otherwise.

One morning he went off to find Jack. He had remembered his question from months before.

"What's a slut?"

Even as he asked, he knew a slut was not a good thing.

"What's a what?" Jack peered into his face.

"A slut."

"Oh, a slut, now, is it? Well, let me see. But – ah, tell old Jack where a nice young feller like you heard a word like that?"

"At the lockup. And I remember Mummy called Bella a slut." He had a flashback of his gentle aproned mother in her fiercely ordered domain, before Bella came.

Jack seemed to give it good thought. Eventually he said, "Well, son, there's many kinds of slut, as I know it, but I need a bit more to go on. Best sit yourself down and tell me the story."

So he told Jack about his recollection of that day in his parents' front bedroom across the passage from the sitting room. About the brown wedding photo of his mother wearing a long creamy dress, his father in a suit, tall and strong with his black hat on, standing next to her. On the mantelpiece above the sealed-off-fire was the framed photo of him as a baby, sitting on a blanket holding a ball.

Fixed in his mind was a particular memory of his father, who held a pipe in his hand, which he did not light until he had finished discussing some issue or other with his wife. He maintained a purposeful grip, forefinger curled around the bowl, stem poised a foot or so from his mouth. He wore a creased collarless shirt. His manner was careful, somewhat distant – this was a conversation he must have had often.

When he spoke this time his gaze sometimes moved from his wife's face to his son's as though to more precisely evoke his wife's condition or to watch for the boy's reaction. He put his hand gently on his son's shoulder, an unusual gesture for him those days, and walked him outside and along the few yards to the end of their garden where the section continued with swathes of buttercups, like a bright yellow picnic cloth.

They stood side by side while his father lit his pipe, at last. Malcolm, with the adaptability of his years, accepted this strange little feast of affection as the new normal.

He told Jack he'd realised something was different with his mother; she was more often mounded with fluffy eiderdowns and she rarely got out of bed. He had never for one moment thought of her as having a 'condition' and at the same time accepted she was different. Like when his father wrapped her in a blan-ket and set her down in the armchair next to the fire to read stories to him. *Once upon a time there was a little prince...*

With his father, he'd once collected pinecones in coal sacks and stacked them in the back of the wood-shed where the black woolly spiders spun their webs. On cold nights he'd toss cones into the fire, making them spark, or watch his father snap branches across his knee. His father was a strong man who rarely raised his voice or belted him as most fathers did with their children. Yet he was uneasy, and he couldn't reason why things abruptly changed around his sixth birthday. A space began to open out between his father and him, and between his father and his mother. Their little family was now hard-edged; he experienced it as a lonely sensation that made him feel somehow guilty.

He was with his father, feeding the fire's never-ending appetite.

"Don't sit too close," he was warned. "You'll burn your knees. Move back, boy. I said, move back!"

Whack!

Less now his father nursed his mother before the fire while she cried quietly against his shoulder. The boy watching him stroke her hair and nuzzle her neck, heard the whisper of soft words meant only for her to hear. She had become a ghostly figure, a gaunt and gentle sprite with sparse tousled brown hair, who drifted about the house as she now drifted through his childhood, sometimes communicative, sometimes sad or crying; always affectionate.

She could be heard at any hour of the day or night fumbling through the house, bumping into furniture or doorjambs, pausing to stand and stare into her kitchen. Some days she would be found pottering about in her garden or perhaps standing dead still in the centre of the narrow lawn. Or painting water colours – smeared scenes of church spires and verdant countryside. But she never washed her brushes or finished a canvas and her nightie was dotted here and there with daubs of softly-hued or strident paints. Sometimes she spent days cutting pictures out of books, gluing them into a scrapbook with messages added beneath in her tight and tiny writing. She wandered slowly about the house, with discarded paper clippings and canvases everywhere underfoot. Paste or paintbrushes hardened where she left them on chairs or windowsills.

He often heard her murmur to herself as she cut a particularly sentimental picture from a book, say a family of four, or two little boys playing on a slide or see-saw, or merry-go-round, happy together. "There, there, there," she might say.

It never occurred to him to question if she was happy. She certainly had her times of anxiety when her breath came in quick snatches and her thin arms rose and fell and all her attention was fixed on a specific need she must immediately take care of. His nails were too long. She must sew name labels into his new school clothes. His ears needed cleaning.

She would fuss ineffectually, hugging him to her, brushing his hair with her fine hairbrush, kissing his face or doing all together, storing up these affections ahead of time, before drifting into a deep sleep.

Sundays his father took him to the store to buy ha'penny ice creams and acid drops for his mother.

Bella arrived with her suitcases on a Sunday. She was his cousin from far away. She sat on the other side of the room popping bubblegum, scowling behind the adults' backs as his father nursed his mother on his knee, the bigger family eating ice creams.

He watched Bella.

Bella shook her head slowly and rolled her eyes when no adult was looking to indicate she thought him weak in his head.

When his father gently sat his mother in her armchair by the fire, Malcolm went to her side, unspoken questions on the tip of his tongue.

"Are you happy, my darling boy?" she would ask instead. "Are you truly happy?"

"Of course I'm happy."

And his mother held him too tight.

Less and less she came out to the fire. He'd visit her dimly-lit bedroom and snuggle up beside her.

"Night-night, son," she'd say. "Be a good boy. Sweet dreams, then."

In the sitting room, his father leaned over to light Bella's cigarette. Bella tilted her frizzy head back and drew on it with her bright red lips, coating lipstick on the butt. Bella always chewed gum, sulked, sang pop songs, flooded the washhouse, slammed doors, hung out washing, smoked, made noise.

In the morning she was in the kitchen making lumpy porridge and burning toast.

He dressed, ate breakfast, cleaned his teeth and went back to his mother's bedroom to draw stick men on the windowpanes. Sometimes he huffed on the glass to erase a mistake; three arms, or one big boot, like his. He learned to write his name, M... in big letters. It was his writing exercise. A, B, C in big letters and a, b, c in little letters.

Then he pulled his small square suitcase onto his mother's bed and checked it ready for school.

"Slut," Mummy hissed to no one else there. The tone in her voice snatched his attention. Yes, she was crying again, but until now she'd never sounded angry. And she wasn't yelling. She was talking low.

"Mummy?" he whispered, so his father didn't hear.

Whack!

"Go to your room, boy. Now!" He'd heard all right! Daddy with the big ears: Daddy who was always cross now, who wouldn't help him do his reading or writing, or walk him down the long stairs to the garden shed to get pinecones when it was dark.

"You're old enough. Go on your own," he would say.

As Malcolm passed by with his suitcase pressed against his chest, his father lammed another whack into his shoulder. He winced. He knew enough not to cry. His father, who was a giant, who was an ogre…

His mother shrieked, "Leave him alone!"

Yes, he was old enough.

Things had changed…

He passed Bella's bedroom, and since she was the one who'd upset his mother and since she was still in the kitchen noisily burning stuff, he kicked the door to her room. It creaked open and he held his breath tightly as he reached to shut the door before his father came along the passage.

He paused. Bella's room smelled like his father on Friday nights, like ale and Swedish pipe tobacco. On her bed lay the package of Cadbury chocolate cream-filled eggs his father had brought home from the corner store, wrappers strewn on the floor. He'd been especially good lately, waiting for his father to share them. Bella didn't share.

After school that day he sat crossly on his bed, rotating his shoulder to ease the ache from the morning's wallop. His room was damp and chilly, so he pulled his knees up under his chin and huffed warm breath in them. His marble bag lay beside him with his favourite bull's eye, his cat's eye and the new shiner he'd won fair and square off Billy, though he said it was his best marble and Malcolm wasn't getting it. They'd had a fight over it until a teacher came and grabbed them by the scruff of their jerseys and marched them off to the headmaster's office. They sat there forever, waiting for punishment. When they got tired of waiting, they forgot why they were there. Billy and he snuck off and became best friends.

Behind the bus shed, Billy said, "Nah, you keep it. It's not me best one. Me best one's me spinner."

His parents were fighting behind the wall. His father shouted. His mother spoke in a low voice as she said, "Get that slut out of my house. Do you think I'm deaf and blind as well?"

His father punched their bedroom wall with his fist so hard Malcolm expected it to come through into his room, right next to where the high-up picture hung on its nail.

"It's my house!" his father yelled. "It would pay you to remember that! I choose who goes where!"

Malcolm eventually won the spinner and a lucky farthing off Billy. Marbles and farthings...

Words were stealing through the walls and under the door, but he didn't hear the fighting any more because he was singing loudly, rolling his favourite marbles around in his hands with a glassy scritching. Singing at the top of his voice, "There was an old lady who swallowed a fly-"

His mother screamed real loud, "No! You can't possibly mean that! Oh, no. Surely you wouldn't."

Malcolm stopped singing to listen hard. Big growly voice... Big growly voice...

His mother sobbed. "It's out of the question, Colin. I simply won't have it. He'll stay right here. It's his home, for pity's sake."

Then it was quiet, only gulps as she sucked air behind the paper wall.

Hot tears fell down his cheeks as he lined his lead soldiers in two rows, one row red and one row blue, hurling the marbles back and forth to kill the enemy...

"Mercy, Colin, I beg of you. He's my only child. Surely he can stay until-"

His father cut his mother off with the deep voice he used often now, growly like a bear, like a tiger in the night. Marbles, spinners and tiger's eyes. Bright and shiny colours, so smooth... Scritching...

"Get her out of here. Anywhere – get her out. We're a family. Please. For the boy's sake, please!"

Wham. Slam.

Inside the wardrobe the voices were closer, right behind the wall. He tugged the door shut and buried his head in his pillow, pulling it tight around his ears – can't hear can't hear can't hear can't hear...

Inside the wardrobe it was dark. Safe.

He hummed a little tune...

There was an old lady who swallowed a spider that wriggled and wiggled and tiggled inside her she swallowed the spider to catch the fly I don't know why she swallowed a fly perhaps she'll die

Chapter 25

Mr Brown the Rawleigh's Man

Once upon a time...Mr Brown the Rawleigh's man came up the front steps and through the front door to talk to his father. They walked into the front sitting room without speaking, and then closed the door behind them. They talked in quiet voices. The boy overheard that Mr Brown had come to take him away.

His mother came out from her bedroom and stood clutching the doorjamb. He went to her side and hid his face in her nightie, his arms wrapped tightly around her skinny legs. On and on she screamed when his father tried to pull them apart. He clung to his mother, his hair sodden with her tears.

Pulled this way and that, he bawled louder.

"I don't want to go. I promise I'll be better. I'm sorry, Daddy, I'll be good. *It was an accident!*"

His father bundled him roughly down the stairs and thrust him into Mr Brown's car, slamming the door. Then he walked back inside the house without a backward glance at his son who clawed at the car window, scrabbling on the glass, mouth stretched open and cries muffled by the noise of the motor.

Mr Brown lived in a tall white house way above the water in Portobello, with hundreds of steps to climb to the porch. His house was stuck high up the bushy hillside as if born there.

When he eventually stopped climbing, Mr Brown was puffing and blowing, his medicine suitcases banging against his legs.

"Never mind, lad. The steps will be good for you, make your leg strong. Take your time now. Easy, easy."

He stumbled along behind the man's bottom, wiping his eyes on the sleeve of his school jersey, letting out occasional wails of misery. Mr Brown carried his little square suitcase tucked under one arm.

"You can see Port Chalmers from up there. You wait until we get to the top. It's a wonderful sight."

Mrs Brown was happy, fat and round. Her kitchen smelled like Monday's baking, like his home used to smell before Bella came and burnt stuff. Mrs Brown stopped what she was doing, wiped her hands on her pinny and came over to inspect their acquisition.

The boy's head pounded. He was not hungry. He didn't want to sit at the red table pushed right up to the glass and look at the wonderful sight.

Look at the water, lovie.

Look at Port Chalmers.

Look at the seagulls.

Look at the city.

Though he was upset he no longer made a sound. But he felt like he might throw up.

Off to bed in the attic room – more stairs – where he cried silently all night with his head beneath the feather pillow with the bits sticking out. He wasn't sure when he stopped crying or even if he did, though it was still dark when he picked the last of the bits out of the pillow and hid them under the mattress. The pillow was no longer prickly, now it was flat. At daybreak he saw that it was a blue room, an old playroom, with a kind of alcove.

And still the tears flowed down his cheeks.

There was an old lady who swallowed a bird how absurd to swallow a bird she swallowed the bird to catch the spider she swallowed the spider to catch the fly I don't know why she swallowed a fly perhaps she'll die

One cold night he climbed down the stairs. He needed to pee. The dunny was out past the back porch through the hanging coats and lined-up gumboots. He crept through the kitchen where the grownups sat gazing out at the night view, with the rain dashing across the windowpanes. They drank tea and ate cake and talked quietly together.

It was never likely to be good when grownups talked quietly together.

"...quite mad...says she's rambling...can't have long..."

He stood there for a memorable few minutes before bursting out into the driving rain, along the narrow path to the dunny – the long-drop – the lavy – through bushes that grabbed at his pyjamas with dank branches. In the deserted garden tears dripped from the trees.

He climbed onto the wooden seat of the dunny to howl his eyes out. His mother wasn't mad. He knew about mad from the boys in his street. They picked on him and said he was mad and made rude faces and stuff. He might well be mad but his mother was sick. Something was wrong in her tummy that made her bleed.

If one of the boys had said she was mad to him, he'd have been obliged to thrash him. His mother was very sick, and he could no longer fight this enormous truth. He began to accept that she had been sick for a long time, and that he'd always known.

Much later, still sitting there in the dunny, he listened to the sad call of the morepork. Did owls cry too? The storm was over but an angry wind continued to rage. While he waited in the dark, he counted how many sleeps he'd had in the high-up attic room, where the branches of the tallest trees scratched at the windowpane all through the night.

Let me in, let me in, let me out, let me out...

It was more than a few weeks yet he'd not been sent to school. It was maybe a whole month. Maybe a year. He didn't know. It was a long time. He had new pyjamas. It was safe in the dunny with the owl crying and the steady sound of rain pelting against the tin roof. Sitting in that dark place he watched until the sun came up.

There was an old lady who swallowed a cat fancy that to swallow a cat she swallowed the cat to catch the bird she swallowed the bird to catch the spider she swallowed the spider to catch the fly I don't know why she swallowed a fly perhaps she'll die

Mrs Brown made toast and porridge (without lumps) every morning. The grownups had more quiet grownup talk, when they thought he wasn't listening. "...good job they have that lovely Bella. She's his niece, I understand. I don't know how the poor man would have coped without her, it being his second loss. And so close too. That poor mad woman. Poor, poor man..."

Mr Brown said something else but the boy couldn't hear because he was crunching his toast so loudly. When he swallowed the last of it, Mrs Brown was saying, "...poor, dear wee soul."

He scuttled off as fast as his gammy leg could scuttle, half-dragging, half-pulling himself along in his pyjamas as he clambered back up the narrow stairs, up to the attic. He hid beneath the cold covers on the bed. After a long time he started crying softly. His mother needed him. Not Bella. Not his father. Him.

Frantically, he looked around the attic. There was no wardrobe, no comforting small place so he crawled beneath his bed once again and lay cramped there in the cold dust. He pulled his flat pillow tight around his ears. He ignored the spiders that crept across his feet and up his pyjama legs.

He hummed a little tune.

Another day.

Another night.

He slept.

Before it was completely daylight, before the bell-birds woke at crack of dawn, he dressed, packed his school suitcase and quietly left by the back door. Down the slippery concrete steps, twenty-five, twenty-six, watch out for webs wet with dew. Down, down, down, forty-eight, forty-nine, careful – the moss and the spiky creepers reaching out to catch at his ankles, eighty-seven, eighty-eight, arriving on the roadside far, far below.

In the greater distance, over the other side of the city beyond the grey water, he had seen pine trees high on the hills in the early morning smoke. From down on the road, he could only see the bases of the closer buildings in Dunedin across the harbour water.

"I'm going home," he yelled at squawking seagulls diving from on high. "She needs me! I'm her big boy!"

He ran, unaware of how high he was stepping, his suitcase bumping against his knee. He walked. He limped. He dragged on and on until he could no longer see the big town, only the Caversham shops. He stumbled into a cemetery, cold and damp, no hope of direction or comfort there. A red telephone box stood tall and secure, scorning his confusion.

Miserable, thirsty and hungry, he retraced his steps and made off in another direction to go higher. He slumped into an exhausted sleep beneath some bushes in the town belt, the cold gathered around him, a brusque wind nosing beneath his tight school jersey and up his tight grey shorts. Early the following morning, down, he stumbled, down, down. Then up, up, up he plodded until he neared the top of yet another hill from which he could see the long skyline in the distance clad with stark pine trees. Passing terraced cottages all of a sameness, chimneys poking holes in the clear morning sky.

The afternoon sun shone weakly. Dry fire spread up his throat, and his tummy gnawed away at him. But he knew his way home now. From way up there he'd once collected pinecones to stuff in a sack. His father had carried the sacks over his shoulder.

Not far now. Cresting the hill – nearly home.

Visitors.

Dragging his heavy boot, he moved slowly, intrigued by the long, shiny black car pulling slowly away from his gate. There were lots of other cars too, and uncles wearing church suits and hats, and aunties swathed in black and wearing church hats with veils pulled down to hide their faces. Like magnificent tragic columns. Dressed up for a wedding, for church. Was it Sunday?

He spied his father among the group.

"Hey, Daddy, it's me. It's your boy. I came home." His voice a hoarse whisper.

Propelling himself faster now, limp, hop, limp, red from exertion and the chill of the cold southerly wind, he waved and called again. This time no sound came out from his mouth.

Everyone left. Gone in the cars that drifted silently away from the gutter, windows as secret as early morning mist, one following another.

He stopped running. His boots were making his leg muscles scream at every step. On his heels were huge water-filled blisters where his too-small boots rubbed against them. His throat stung from the cold air, his legs ached, his knees were splotched purple.

It rained.

From Portobello it was a long way to the top of the hill with the pine trees. Looking back to where he'd walked from, he could barely see the houses dotted along the peninsula. Try as he might he could not see Mr Brown's house up the hundreds of steps, hidden in bushy shrubs where sad moreporks cried and creepers grabbed his ankles. Hauling himself up, boots in one hand, suitcase in the other, he limped on to find his home.

His mother would be surprised to see how big he'd grown. He'd been away forever. He pushed the back door open with one hand, the kitchen oddly chilled without the constant warmth from the coal range.

Walking down to the front bedroom on tiptoes in case she was sleeping, he whispered, half-singing, half-laughing, "It's me-ee. I came ho-ome."

Cold shivered through him, raindrops dripped from his head down his back and shoulders, as he dropped his boots in the doorway, his balled-up holey grey socks closer to the bed.

He reached for the rose geranium talcum powder tin on the dusty bedside table, shifting it from hand to hand before putting it into his pocket. Then he pushed his hand down under the eiderdown to the emptiness below. The hollow shape of her body was still there, but it was cold. Damp.

He sat at the foot of the bed and waited for his parents to return home from wherever they had gone.

Chapter 26

Fox Furs

Bella rushed in from the street, high heels clunking, up the stairs, two at a time. The door banged back on its hinges. She stoked the fire to heat the wetback for her evening bath and filled the kettle, humming a commercial jingle. She set out cups and saucers. Clink, went his mother's best tiered cake plate and rattle went his mother's best flowered china – onto the trolley.

Better be careful, he breathed.

Clink, chink, rattle came the trolley down the passage to the sitting room opposite the cold room where he sat on his mother's bed.

There was an old lady who swallowed a dog what a hog to swallow a dog she swallowed the dog to catch the cat she swallowed the cat to catch the bird she swallowed the bird to catch the spider she swallowed the spider to catch the fly I don't know why she swallowed a fly perhaps she'll die

The house was filled with the whispering of grownups. Tall relations and strangers alike were bowing in toward each other, talking in muted tones, ignoring the darkened room opposite.

...such a lovely woman...so young...that poor man...his second loss, you know...

"Is it really?"

"I believe so, dear."

"Oh?"

"Indeed. Shhh!"

"Do you know where Mummy is?" he whispered to the old black taffeta lady who peered down at him from beneath a dark cluster of feathers like a black-bird. "Do you?"

"Come, come, young man." Her voice firm, she helped him down off the bed. "You be brave now. Come along and greet the others, there's a good boy. They're all your family. They'll look out for you. So never you mind."

Standing barefoot and drenched below the moving sea of black, wave-crested with feathers, flowers, veils and satin hats, his eyes danced from one to another. Brown fox furs stared back, sharp little eyes, warning him – of what? Words travelled along invisible strands of wire among the feathers and hats; words full of meaning and importance – to tall people.

The curtains were closely drawn though it was daytime. Stiffly standing at various points in the darkened room were vases – on the mantelpiece, the oak dresser – filled with white velvety lilies. He inhaled the different smells of sweet sherry, malt whisky, cigar smoke and mothballs.

His father in his too-tight wedding suit was shifting oddly from foot to foot. Whisky glass stayed between hand and lips, he noticed the boy in the passage holding onto Great Aunt Gert. His face tensed and a muscle set up a rhythmic twitch beside his mouth.

He reached his arms up. "Who are these other people? Why are they here? I can't find M-Mummy."

Words tumbled urgently from his mouth as he bravely held back his tears.

"Not now, boy," his father said, strained and low, smiling narrowly at the grownups. Taking the boy by his cold hand he pulled him along the passage to his bedroom, shut the door, hauled him onto the bed.

The boy prepared to be cuddled and told where his mother was and who the grownups were.

"What are you doing here?" His father's voice was solid with familiar anger.

"I...Mummy...my boots–," he wailed. "They're wet."

"You're supposed to live with the Browns, you ungrateful little bastard!"

His father shook him fiercely by the shoulders, making his head jiggle and bounce, before hurling him flat on his back on the bed.

He shrank into the bare mattress as his father's face loomed fiercely above him. Wham! The fist pounded the wall, making a hole, tilting the picture on the high-up nail.

Though he was afraid, he managed to say, "I'm truly sorry, Daddy. It was an accident."

He howled as he dodged a second blow to his head. Then his father clapped his other hand over his mouth, fingers blocking his nostrils so he couldn't breathe. Struggling, his blistered feet kicked wildly at the mattress, the wall, the dresser. His tongue probed the palm of his father's hand that tasted of familiar Swedish pipe tobacco.

His eyes pleaded. *Daddy. It was an accident...accident...accident...*

Images swam in his head, around and around, a fish swimming in water, or a seal tumbling in the waves, rolling black thunderclouds on a cold day scattering the leaves...

His tongue slackened against his father's hand.

His bare feet stopped kicking.

His eyes watching, watching...

High above the room all was peaceful...

Watching...

There was an old lady who swallowed a cow I don't know how she swallowed a cow she swallowed the cow to catch the dog she swallowed the dog to catch the cat she swallowed the cat to catch the bird she swallowed the bird to catch the spider she swallowed the spider to catch the fly I don't know why she swallowed a fly perhaps she'll die

The man left the room, walked smoothly back to the guests in the sitting room, a tight smile slapped on his face.

From high above, through the ceiling, the boy watched him fill his whisky glass too high, laugh too loud. The women folk tsk-ed, appreciating his grief, empathising. He watched him pull open the curtains, letting the bleak sun shine her reluctant rays inside the house of secrets and death.

He watched Bella serve cups of tea and fresh cucumber and tomato sandwiches.

He understood everything – from his new understanding high above the rooms.

Such a dear girl you are.

Barely out of your teens.

Helping your family in their darkest hour.

Where would one be without family, I ask you?

Bella curtsied, lowered her eyes and smiled, her bubblegum tucked into her cheek.

She had a secret.

His father had a secret.

He had a secret.

Chapter 27

Coal

This time Malcolm didn't bawl. So far Jack had said nothing, and that was all right. There was learning in nothing too. After scratching his head for an age, Jack eventually said, "Well, son, that's a big story so I'll just tell you that a slut is a bad woman. She's not good for anything, so make no mistake there. You mind me and keep clear away from sluts. Okay?"

"Okay," he said calmly, and he got down from his chair by the window in the warm steamy kitchen. Just so long as Bella was a slut, was all.

Everyone had a story to tell.

The gardens near Clifton House and The Cottage were well cared for. Often as Malcolm sat on a park

bench among the many-coloured rhododendrons, pe-
onies in full bloom and standard roses, lush, full and
rounded, someone would join him to talk or maybe
just nod or jerk. The more senile patients, those who
couldn't do any of that any more, were housed a distance away from the main building.

As time passed Malcolm had become interested in
the hospital as a whole, as a unit, and in its history.
He'd heard that The Cottage was opened in 1898 especially for those women who were convalescing, or
were now well enough to prepare for a return home.
(Clifton House was for the men.) The Cottage gardens
were designed to be peaceful so those women patients could live more normal lives for the remainder
of their stay. Those in residence were there primarily
because of minor breakdowns or financial worries,
some because of home troubles, childbearing, or
overwork. Even diabetes.

He recalled a young girl whose parents had her
committed because she would slip away to the lake
whenever there was a full moon. The lake, the night...
The lake beneath some torrential rain. Oh, anyway,
somewhere else. Somewhere far away.

Some horses, some men and women he knew,
poor resigned creatures hunched over in the rain. He
switched off the mental picture, and told himself, "I'm

nothing like them," yet felt himself bound to them by invisible chains.

He *was* different from the mass that lived in the crowded isolated wards, each housing fifty or more.

He was waiting for...

He recalled how once he'd laughed at the word. Waiting. It was anything but amusing now. What else did he ever do but wait? He waited for...

He wandered through lifeless rooms and lifeless gardens. Another two hours. Another three. Then dinner. Then the sound of some key locking some door. Then the sound of footsteps crossing the gardens or roads to lock other doors or gates. Then more waiting...sometimes feverish and strange...

The sound of a horse neighing from afar. The clanking of metal or a motor starting up. Voices. Music. Then the nights, the stormy nights with their great gusts of wind in the oak trees and the distant rolling thunder. And then what, then what?

He sat quietly on the seat and he waited.

A patient called Dick Clough joined him, speaking fast and loud in his strong deep voice. Sometimes Malcolm didn't understand a word Dick said. Today he was saying, "I realise I have no other home. Can you believe that, Mal? I just live at the men's house."

He watched a sparrow flit past. He'd known Dick for a long time now. He knew Dick's story.

"I used to have a home back in England when I was a nipper. But I was a bit of a bother to me mam. Gave her the lip once too often. Ah, me dad warned me good and proper but I was just a kid. I was too young to care."

Malcolm understood about England and the English people. He'd heard Jack and Mr Antonio say there were loads of Poms working in the hospitals as nurse aides or attendants, all meeting the terms of their assisted passage from England. The English staff were contracted to do two years employment in order to repay their passage over. There were far more women than men arriving and most of the young women did their two-year stint then shot through. They didn't like the mental hospital, the patients or the conditions. They said it was dirty and the work expected of them too hard, unsafe.

Jack said most of them were city chicks from the old country and they expected too much from their new life. He doubted they'd ever set foot in a mental hospital back home. As well as their not liking the place, they spoke a different English, hard to understand. Now there were Dutchies arriving and Scots,

Irish and Pakis, even Abos. Well, it was a circus all right, Jack said.

The two houses – Malcolm was somehow intrigued with them – Clifton House and The Cottage, they each had a kitchen where the men or women made their own meals and sorted their own medication. They didn't sleep in noisy dormitories – he'd been inside – they shared private bedrooms. He wondered if he would ever make it to Clifton House and have his own room and make his own meals.

Dick was still talking. "...and so I got into a few fights down at the wharves, broke a few noses. Dad said I'd best get meself on a merchant ship before someone done me in. He was glad to see the backside of me. Blimey, I'd give someone a bash and get a thick ear meself. And me mam, she'd had enough of me. It was just lads being lads. I know that now. What do you reckon?"

It didn't matter what he reckoned. Dick went on talking anyway.

"So I set sail when I was thirteen, getting up to some right shenanigans. But it weren't no different from home. I still got in lots of fights. So they packed me off to the mental asylum. I don't have a lot wrong with me, though. I'm not deaf, dumb, blind or lame. I'm none of that. Musta been me ugly moosh."

He took a long hard look at Dick's face. It seemed all right to him.

"And I'm not a homo like them homo chaps. What with their lady clothes and all, no wonder they were committed. They get The Treatment regular. It's the only way to control their deviant bodies. They're kept well apart from each other. Matron gets their special drugs from her dispensary. None of us regular blokes take the coloured pills they do. I checked."

Malcolm wondered what colour the homo pills were and if he were taking any of them. He was about to ask Dick about the colour but he was talking again.

"...so this here has been me home for nearly fifty years now so I'll stay put. In the beginning, I must admit I got pretty down. It was once a real castle, you know, like the old castles of home with the turrets and the battlements. I saw them in the photographs on the walls. Now it's just a building. But the grub's good, eh?"

He nodded. Yes, the grub was certainly good.

When he considered Dick, he was reassured that Dick wasn't such an odd fellow. Using Dick as a gauge, he decided one didn't have to be mad to be here. And if this were true, there was hope for him yet.

Dick patted his big belly. "I used to work in the boiler house with old Bill way back. I'd be down the railway station, filling the horses' carts with coal. They were Clydesdales then. Bloody beautiful animals. Socks and Mac they were called. Then we'd come back and dump it all in a ruddy great heap outside the boiler room. That was before they got that six-ton Albion lorry with its solid tyres. That was a damn fine lorry, with an especially high tray for carting coal. Did I tell ya it was chain driven?"

As Malcolm opened his mouth to reply, Dick continued, "And the next lorry we got had those pneumatic tyres on it."

He thought of all that coal, shiny clean and black, and he asked, "Was it Ohai or Kaitangata coal?"

"Sometimes 'twas hard to tell the difference. Sub-bituminous, I think."

"I love coal," he said quietly.

"I love coal too," said Dick. "Go figure that? Maybe we're both crazy. Maybe we're both normal, eh?"

They laughed heartily, and then sat for a while as each pursued his memories about coal.

After a time Dick said, "It was an important job I had. Bill got me a black woollen singlet same as his. Some o' the wee boys helped. They filled their own wee trolleys and carted the coal up into the boilers.

The boiler room churns out all the heating for the hospital now. Remember the old days, Mal? No heating in The Building. Some poor sods froze to death. You remember, don't you, the frozen ones?"

Malcolm vividly remembered those patients frozen in their beds or outside against a wall or under a tree. Now there was plenty of heating for the laundry, kitchen and the engineers also. Everyone benefited from the steam the boilers produced. The wards were heated that way and all their water too. The boilers were stoked each night with wood chopped by the attendants, and they were stoked with coal. Sometimes the water was almost boiling when it surged along the pipes then churned through the taps into the baths.

He told Dick of Cynthia who used to cry all the time and tidy furniture, how she might have been sent home once she became normal after her operation. But Cynthia was scalded to death in a bath of boiling water. A patient had forced her into it and held her down. Tears burned his eyes as he outlined the new policy of encouraging the patients to dress in clothes more like those worn by normal people, how Cynthia had been given her new outfit.

She'd worn a floral scarf to cover her shaven head and some lipstick to make her even more normal after her lobotomy. She no longer annoyed everyone with her incessant tidying. She no longer spoke or cried either; she stared around at her bright new world from her big startled eyes.

The other woman wanted Cynthia's new scarf.

Malcolm stayed on the bench with Dick. Generally Dick was a cheerful character, but now he knew about Cynthia his mood was sombre.

"Aside from you, me best mate is old Jim," said Dick. "The blokes at Clifton House are me family."

But now Malcolm wanted to talk to Jack about what he remembered of the coal and grit at the station.

"Dick, I'll see you later, right."

"I remember my father and me on the train."

"Slow down, son. Take it easy."

Malcolm talked about how the train approached Seacliff Railway Station, the white plumes of steam over the back of the on-following trucks with the passenger carriage tagged on. Steam hissing impatiently beneath the iron wheels, the screech of brakes on iron tracks.

His father had said, "Out you get for a spot of exercise. Don't trip on that step. We'll soon sort that silly old boot out. And when you've finished you sit on that bench beneath the sign. Bella and I will exercise our legs too. Off you go now. Off you go."

He recalled his excitement when his father and Bella described the new life they would have in Christchurch, becoming a new family.

Even as the strangers left with most of their furniture and all of his mother's things – the delicate china tea set and fancy tiered cake plate; even as the Salvation Army collected her clothes, packing them in her own suitcase as if she were going on holiday, along with her mirror and music box, he had still been elated.

While they poked through the house or continued to rummage, one grabbed the calendar from the kitchen wall, and his eyes fixed momentarily on the date, 1927, with a circle around the day his mother had died. Bella did that.

Someone commented on his bedroom and the lack of sunlight on that side of the house, the damp mildew patches on his wallpaper, how the paper was peeling off. They noted the gaping hole his father had punched through the wall. One adult glanced at the boy then down at his boot.

Yet he was still elated. The death of his room – his first ever bedroom – despite that he was in high spirits. He watched the final burning of things. Bella called it rubbish. As the bonfire raged in the backyard well into the night – burning photographs, his mother's unfinished watercolours of church spires and verdant countryside, her hard-bristled paintbrushes, her scrapbook, nighties, horsehair clothes brushes – he was racing around, poking the fire with a broom handle, laughing hysterically.

After the clamouring confusion, leaving the dead house behind to the slam of the front door, there was new hope ahead for him. New friends at a new school to replace those he lost, like Big Billy and his tiger's eye, spinner marbles, vain promises to write.

He packed his most treasured possessions in his suitcase; his marbles, lead soldiers and storybooks. And his lucky farthing. His too-small clothes had gone off with the 'calendar' people.

"We'll get you all you need in Christchurch."

"Even real boys' shoes, Daddy?"

"Even real boys' shoes."

"Brown!"

Never again would he wear ugly black boots, boots that robbed him of saying goodbye to his mother before she went to live in heaven.

On the Dunedin Railway Station platform some people were stepping forward to greet the exiting passengers. Some stepped down before the train had even stopped, down onto the platform with a little running skip. Malcolm moved among the throng of busyness, standing enthralled at the sight of the train engine in the stained glass window above the entrance that seemed always to be coming toward him no matter where he stood.

He jumped when his father jerked his arm.

"Into the tearoom. Choose something or go without."

He was the only child waiting on the platform, gripping his father's hand lest he be drawn under the wheels of the train, down into the steam and noise. And later, when the train chuffed through the Mihiwaka Tunnel north of Port Chalmers, the adults leapt to close windows against steam-laden air and billowing soot. Once through the darkness, the train crept higher through beach settlements clinging to the hills above and below the railway track.

He put his head a long way out the window.

"Look, Daddy!"

His words whisked away. Far below, the heavy sea pounded against the rocks and farther along past Doctor's Point. He leaned his body out of the window to view the engine as the train snaked along the tracks. Now they were crossing the mud flats of Blueskin Bay, the tangy air swishing across his face, making his eyes stream.

Bella scowled as he put his mouth against the rattling window, licking off the salty condensation. Endless hours of rickety-rackety travel on the serpent's tail.

Again, he asked about new shoes.

"Whatever colour you want." His father spoke offhandedly. "In Christchurch."

"Not black. Not boots. Just regular shoes."

Bella mimicked *Not black, not boots, just regular shoes,* a smirk on her face.

He no longer cared when she pulled faces. He was getting new shoes in Christchurch, and they would be brown, regular boys' shoes.

So for now he exercised by waving his arms about and walking the length of the platform. Then he sat on the bench beneath the sign and spelled out Seacliff Railway Station, waiting, like his father told him to. On this family day of adventure and new beginnings his father wore his tight wedding and funeral suit. Bella wore her red and black dress, black gloves, and red high heels that matched her handbag and her red lips and her cigarette butts.

He huffed and crossed his arms, suddenly annoyed.

"Not again," he muttered to no one in particular.

His father and Bella were arguing. They always argued. Not like before, while his mother was fading away in her bed, while Bella sat on the kitchen table and chewed bubblegum. She used to make bubbles that burst across her cheeks encasing her mouth in a glistening pink spider web.

Back then his father told Bella she was 'quite a girl.' And when she had her birthday and his father gave her chocolates and nylons, he told her she was 'quite a *big* girl now.' He told Malcolm to show her more respect because Bella was a grownup. He told Malcolm blowing bubblegum bubbles was a dirty habit and he'd get the belt if he caught him at it.

Then his father would go check on his mother, supporting her head as she drank the medicine from a spoon. It's to calm her nerves and imagination, he'd said, before sending Malcolm to the dairy – not the one on the closer corner, the one farther down the hill – to buy sugar. But he had counted seven bags of sugar in the cupboard in the kitchen.

"Daddy, we've got lots of sugar now."

"Don't question me, boy." *Whack!* "I've warned you about not respecting your elders."

Yet each time he got back with a new bag of sugar his father patted his head and said he was a good boy at heart. But he still wanted to know why they needed more sugar, and why his father was in a good mood when he returned from the dairy, and why Bella smirked and played soldiers with him for a while, her hair reeking of his father's pipe tobacco.

After his mother had gone to heaven, Bella started to sulk. His father would smile a lot and be nice to her, but she'd pout and stomp off to her room. Sometimes she cried; maybe she missed his mother too. Then his father would check she was all right behind the shut door. Much later Bella would come out to make dinner, and they'd be happy again.

Until the arguments started over, even before he went to bed. They said mean grownup things to each other until his father took off to the pub. Then Bella was nasty to Malcolm. She poked him in his chest with her pointed red fingers, pushing him backward down the passage into his bedroom. She'd flick his cheek with the tea towel, or flick it across his bare legs. She'd smooch his face up tight in her perfumed hands and squeeze his cheeks and mouth until it hurt and he couldn't cry. She'd make him stay in his bedroom until his father returned.

"Do your homework, you stupid idiot. And keep out of our way. We don't want you, understand? Nobody does. You're a nuisance, imbecile."

"I hate you!" he bellowed back. "You're not Mummy. I wish you were dead!" And he stuffed his idiot hands into his imbecile eyes to kill the stupid tears there.

His father eventually came back and asked where the boy was.

Bella called out gaily, "He's been in his bedroom doing his homework for ages. He's no trouble at all. He's a lovely boy, aren't you, Malcolm?"

Now Bella stood on the platform at the Seacliff Railway Station, her hands firmly placed on her hips and her feet set apart. Her chin jutted high and her fiery hair fluffed out around her face in the breeze. He'd seen her paddies before. He stifled a laugh, thinking Oh, my word, what a face. His mother said a face to curdle milk.

Sometimes he was scared of Bella.

Right now he thought she was plain silly. They were on their way to Christchurch, their new life. He grinned inside, careful not to let his mouth betray him. Sitting on the bench, he watched his father and his cousin fix tight smiles to plastic faces so anyone passing would think they were happy.

Like tigers, more like, Malcolm thought. Faces like birthday tiger masks.

He started to giggle.

Bella had been horrid to him ever since he'd come home from Portobello. She'd tell his father Malcolm is no trouble at all. Yet when they were alone she called him a dumb cripple or loony and hurled his boots around the room so they left Nugget streaks down the wallpaper.

What he wanted to know was when Bella was grumpy with his father, what did she call *him?* For sure, his father was grumpy right back, like now, hands stuffed deep into his trouser pockets making fists. He kept walking in tight circles, first away from her, then back to angrily face her. Occasionally he'd throw a sharp word or two at her.

Anyone would know his father was grumpy.

Toot! The northbound train for Christchurch. Toot!

Bella flounced onto the train. His father yelled at her, words drowned by the urgent sound. Toot! Toot!

There goes Bella, he thought, amused. Better wait for me and Daddy or there'll be big trouble. The steam train's wheels started to slowly turn, shackled together with steel, like his boot. Chug-a-chug-a-chug. Gathering speed, groaning, huffing and chuffing as it drew away from the platform, faster, past the water tank leering down from its tall spindly legs.

Malcolm, still wearing the traces of his smile, turned his face toward his father. His eyes and mouth widened in dismay as he watched the man race along the platform and grab the handrail with one hand, to swing his body onto the bottom step of the train.

"Hey! Wait for me! Daddy! You forgot me-e-e!"

But his father didn't look back. One twist of the door handle and he was sucked inside the carriage.

A voice wailing, "Daddy, what about me? It's me, Daddy. It's your Malcolm. You forgot me-eee." Confused, the boy waited, expecting them to wave out of the window, or call out goodbye.

My suitcase...I haven't got my marbles...my soldiers...

The train rumbled and roared, picking up speed as it passed the Presbyterian Church, over the cattlestop, around the corner. Gone from sight, with a long mournful too-ooot.

Well after the last whistle, he pictured his suitcase in the string luggage rack, his books and things, and Christchurch where he would have got new clothes and new brown shoes like a normal regular boy. Not like now when his ugly black boots caused only bad things, like making him miss saying goodbye to his mother, like Bella calling him a cripple, an idiot boy, like making his father forget him. He looked along the dusty tracks, listening to the wind in the telegraph wires, the wind blowing from place to place past him and there he was, in between, listening to the moaning wind.

He felt again a familiar burden of sadness or loneliness as if something had begun or happened that he knew nothing about. A sadness that had no relationship to him; it belonged to the world.

It was dark when the lights were turned off and the Station Master came to him. The grownup stood there for some time as Malcolm stared down, still bewildered, at the broad polished shoes. Then the grownup sat beside him, looking hard at the talcum powder tin in the little boy's clutched hand.

"Is it your mum's, lad?"

When Malcolm didn't answer, the man leaned back, stretched his legs out and rolled a cigarette.

"What's your name, then?" The Station Master's voice was gruff but kindly.

He stared toward the dark ocean water that reflected the rising moon and the far hills where the train had come from, above the pounding water on the rocks, until he couldn't see anything more out or beyond.

"Guess you'll be coming home with me." The man patiently puffing on his cigarette. "Big boy like you must be, what, five or six, huh? Maybe seven?"

He stood, tucked his newspaper beneath his arm, and offered his hand to the boy, who didn't move. He put the newspaper down and reached both his hands out and lifted him beneath his armpits to stand on the seat. Turning around, over his shoulder, he said, "Climb on my back, lad. It's going to be a bumpy ride."

It was raining now so Malcolm pushed the talcum powder tin deep into his pocket before he climbed onto the stranger's back. That's how he rode to the house alongside the railway tracks. On the Station Master's back.

Mrs Roger was a wee woman who wrapped her hands in and out of her pinny before rolling it up in a ball in front of her. She darted shy smiles at Malcolm as she scrambled some eggs for their dinner.

"It's raining," she said to the man.

"It started raining before. Just a shower."

To Malcolm he said, "Sit here a while, lad. You warm up by the fire."

Then he made a phone call in the dimly lit passage, boisterously cranking the telephone handle, talking to the operator in a clear voice. Though he'd kicked the door shut, Malcolm still heard. The man was saying something about it being another case, remarkably like that of young Donna. Did her parents ever make contact? Malcolm heard him exhale sadly.

When he returned to the kitchen, he said, "She'll be right, lad. Eat your tucker, then."

Malcolm stared forlornly at the plate of cold scrambled eggs.

"Not hungry?" the man said. "You look healthy enough. So they fed you, did they?"

Mrs Roger asked brightly, "A glass of fresh milk?"

When Mr Roger had eaten his eggs and a stack of toast, he sat in an armchair by the fire.

"Come over here, lad. Nothing to worry about. You'll be fine and dandy."

Malcolm got down from the table and went over to stand in front of him. When Mr Roger pulled him onto his knee before getting out his tobacco tin and rolling a cigarette with Zig-Zag rolling papers, Malcolm gulped and looked away. Cold sweat made his neck prickle. He shuddered.

"So you got a daddy, then?"

Mr Roger breathed out a small puff of smoke before making circles in the air.

Malcolm yawned. He should be sleeping in the high-up place in the train's compartment with the blinds against the window tap-tap-tapping in time with the clacking of the huge wheels.

Mr Roger said, "Your daddy smokes hand-rolleds?"

And his pipe, Malcolm thought. Don't forget his pipe.

Mrs Roger ran a deep bath.

"To help you sleep," she said. "And some cocoa."

Mr Roger lifted the boy off his knee and led him into the steamy bathroom. Malcolm stood rigid as a pencil when Mr Roger knelt to unfasten his tight boots. He stared at them as they lay on the shiny linoleum. And his eyes still dragged back to them when Mr Roger peeled off his tight woollen school jersey, checking the faded label inside.

With the shirt and singlet off, Mr Roger drew a slow breath. He traced his fingers down the bruises and scars that covered most of the boy's body. He turned him this way and that, whistling through his teeth. Wide red welts raced across the small bottom, only the edges showing signs of healing. Cigarette burns. Pinch marks. Cuts, bruises and scabs.

Lifting the boy into the bath, Mr Roger said sadly, "So you have got a daddy."

No, the boy whispered silently.

There was an old lady who swallowed a horse she's dead of course

Chapter 28

Regular Brown Shoes

Malcolm stood still while the staff looked him over. One tall man said the boy might be eight years old. A nurse disagreed. While he was a big boy, he was probably only six. Seven? They agreed on seven years old, and the tall man wrote something on the paper.

The noises, the smells and the vast concrete floors terrified Malcolm. Strange other children, not at all like Billy or the boys at his school, made weird noises, grunted, or scuttled over to pick at his tight clothes. One boy spent most of the time in a corner of the dayroom. He was cowered down, head butted into bony knees, arms wrapped tightly around his thin body. A tiny ball, constantly mewing.

Malcolm was on the alert.

On the constant lookout for the ginger-haired, freckle-faced boy skating around the floor in his socks. On one sweep past the boy grabbed the talcum powder tin from Malcolm's hand. Then he stopped where he was, and stood grinning on the far side of the room. Malcolm limped over and reached for the tin but the boy dropped it on the floor and stomped on it.

With a loud bellow Malcolm flew at him.

The boy, with shrill cries, head-butted him and gouged at his eyes. He kicked and punched and bit Malcolm's ear until it bled. His jersey, red-soaked, was ripped from his shoulders. It took three male attendants to separate the pair after their long noisy fight. Both had bloodied noses and flushed cheeks, bites and scratches, and torn clothes.

Malcolm had clumps of ginger hair in his hands. The other boy held tatters of grey jersey. One pair of eyes flashed fury. The others narrowed with manic spite.

A man gripped Malcolm's hand. He watched helplessly as a nurse scooped the flattened tin, bits of jersey and ginger hair into a rubbish basket. He struggled free and rushed the nurse, bringing her down with a tackle to her knees. The attendant again over-powered him, hauling him off by the scruff of his neck. He dumped Malcolm roughly in the corner and told him to stay still or there'd be big trouble.

"And I mean big!" he roared.

The nurse walked away with the rubbish basket, and gone were the sole tangible remnants, or proofs, of the life he'd shared with his mother.

"Mummy!" he screamed to no one understanding.

"That does it, my boy. You've been told."

The attendant held Malcolm by the shoulders. Another held his chin tilted high. The nurse poured bitter medicine between his clenched teeth.

This old man he played one he played knick-knack on my thumb with a knick-knack paddywhack give the dog a bone this old man came rolling home

He dreamed he woke in a frozen room with high walls damp with running water. It was dark; only the moon slanting a feeble ray of light through the high-up window. He tried to be quiet, but he was scared and freezing. His teeth chattered.

"Mum-m-my? D-dad-dy? I'm lost. Please find me. It's me. It's your M-Malcolm. Find me."

Within this pleading he lay drenched in darkness until in utter confusion he screamed loudly.

"MummyMummyMummy!"

A fat English night nurse came on soundless feet and filled him with more bitter medicine. She cradled him in her arms for a long while, and hummed a song.

"You'll be fine, little man. You'll be fine."

This old man he played two he played knick-knack on my shoe with a knick-knack paddywhack give the dog a bone this old man came rolling home

In the dayroom, there was one boy who had a face like the flat backside of the moon. He never moved. Another child with pale unseeing eyes glided around, hands outstretched, bumping into things yet always smiling. Her chin had a running gash on it, and cuts and bruises covered her arms and legs. They called her Julie. Often the nurses would do their rounds while holding Julie's hand, or take her outside into the gardens to touch and smell the flowers.

This old man he played three he played knick-knack on my knee with a knick-knack paddywhack give the dog a bone this old man came rolling home

To begin with, Malcolm did not wet his pants. He was not like the others. Even the nurses said that.

"He's not like the others, is he?"

He listened attentively as a senior nurse explained him to a junior nurse. She thought he had a mild hemiplegia – a symptom of cerebral palsy. That would account for his gammy leg, weak arm and clumsiness.

The dreams were relentless: the loud toot-tooting...his school suitcase...lead soldiers...his mother fading away...

He woke in the night and cried for her and the same old night nurse came silently as the night itself with her torch, to feel under the sheet – wet boy. It was she who pulled the bedding apart and wiped the brown rubber before remaking his bed. Crooning to him, she changed his pyjamas.

"You'll soon settle in, dearie. You'll be fine, little man."

She hugged him on her knee until his sobbing ceased.

Long, fearful nights she would sit with him, cradling him in her arms, warm and close against her plump breasts while he whimpered himself to sleep, curled into a tight little ball on her lap.

Still he searched for his mother's talcum powder tin in all the rubbish baskets, or sometimes in the pockets of the nurses' uniforms. Either they pushed his hands away or hugged him tightly.

This old man he played four he played knick-knack on my door with a knick-knack paddywhack give the dog a bone

> dreams upon dreams
> layers upon layers
> all mixed up now
> now now Malcolm rest now
> now this moment is a new now
> every new moment is a new now
> how long will it be like this now

He found his thumb, his comforting, sucking thumb, rocking back and forth on the floor like the other children who sucked and rocked, rocked and sucked. Some of them crooned or moaned or screamed or sang or hummed or dribbled incessantly. Or peed or messed. Few of them spoke any words – real words. Children with round staring eyes full of nothing watched in moon-faced silences. The Down's syndrome children were lovable, often walking over to stand in front of him, reaching up a hand to touch his face and smile a little.

He had no love left in him to give them.

The senior nurse drew up a chair and watched him for a while. She told the junior nurse, "I fear he is regressing. He'll become like the other children in time. He should go to school, keep his brain active."

I'm not like them, he thought. I want to go home.

There were seventy-three adult patients in this ward along with the fourteen children. When Malcolm overheard this, he wondered vaguely where they all were and where they had come from.

One morning he was taken by the hand and led into a small classroom where some other children were already seated. It was explained that he must be a good boy and learn well. A kindly teacher returned his pencil to his hand whenever it fell to the floor. After some time she switched the pencil to his other hand, his better hand. The books were familiar, as was the pencil and rubber. At the end of each lesson, everything was gathered up and accounted for prior to the children being taken back to the dayroom.

Regularly, with all the children together and some of the adults, a nurse brought jugs of fresh milk into the dayroom, while another nurse carried a square wooden tray heaped high with orange quarters. Yet another had a tray with dried bread crusts and plastic mugs.

Malcolm sat rocking back and forth with a honey crust dripping slowly down the front of his pyjamas until some boy, screaming like a fire siren, scooted over and grabbed it from him. More crusts and honey on toast, screaming on toast, toast on toast...

Always he watched and listened.

One child was only a baby, a boy of about ten weeks, he'd heard. Everyone seemed to love him, both the patients and staff alike. The baby had been abandoned at the public hospital. His mother saw how his head was shaped like a moa egg, and she said she had tried to love him but couldn't. She didn't ask what would happen to her little boy once she left him at that hospital. She had, however, named him Derek. It was written on his birth certificate, which she'd pinned to his blanket. The family name had been cut out, as was the serial number and date of his birth. So just a piece of paper with Derek written on it.

Another called Bryce lay still in his iron-framed bed. Malcolm heard the white-uniformed nurse say he was quietly fading away. He stood for a long time watching him, waiting and wondering if he would actually see him fade. Bryce had arms like skinny twigs. He was far smaller than Malcolm, yet the nurses said he was more than twenty-three years old. But how could that be? Twenty-three was a grownup. Yet Bryce was small – and fading fast.

On a hook near Bryce's bed hung a little shirt and pants set. Malcolm studied the tiny brown shoes hanging by their knotted laces. His own boots were so cripplingly tight now he couldn't wear them. Watching the small boy fade, Malcolm leaned over and smelled his neck. Then he searched beneath the sheet to find the boy's hand, to stroke and maybe squeeze it a little, to tell Bryce all was fine and dandy.

Sister Daly dragged Malcolm and his wordless protest away, and dumped him in the dayroom.

"Bad boy! You have to be good to go to school."

That night he lay stiff and tight in his stiff tight iron bed.

That night he fell silent.

This old man he played five he played knick-knack on my hive with a knick-knack paddywhack give the dog a bone this old man went rolling home

The butterfly. Malcolm watched it grow on the outside of the barred window ledge. A wriggly fat caterpillar, a cocoon, but once it got out of its old skin it was brand new and beautiful.

Cockroaches – he watched the little shells break open and they hatched running, fast and shiny.

One boy sat in Malcolm's corner of the dayroom picking constantly at his skin. A nurse bound his bloodied hands and arms with bandages and tied them behind his back. His name was Douglas Bad Boy.

Malcolm wondered why Douglas Bad Boy picked his skin off. Maybe beneath his skin was a better boy, a brand new boy, a good boy. Same as Douglas, Malcolm felt an overpowering need to be out of his old skin to find himself beneath. A brand new boy, he would go home to his mother and father and his new baby brother, Geoffrey, too. They would be a regular family once more.

He picked at his skin.

The sun shone and the butterfly flew away.

Cockroaches – they grew the fastest. On the walls. Behind the curtains. They scurried into the corners of the floor, beneath the door. They scuttled along window ledges. And grew bigger. At night they came out to feed. At night he heard them.

Cockroaches!

But who will hear you scream? In the dead of the night, who will hear you scream? Lying paralysed in fear as the cockroaches scurried across his bed. In the dark he heard them clicking. In the dark he smelled them, and felt them clawing his feet beneath his pyjamas. Who will hear you scream, Malcolm Bad Boy?

If he were to become new again he knew exactly what he had to do. At first it was difficult. He used his teeth and blood slicked down his wrist. But the new boy remained inside, and it hurt so he stopped.

On silent bare feet he limped toward the kitchen. They were baking crusts. All brown and straight on a wire rack, like little soldiers. Malcolm stood at the open door waiting to be noticed. He stood very still. He was very polite.

You don't have to wait all the time. Use your brain, boy. Go get the pinecones yourself. Go fill the coal bucket. Have you got a brain? That's what it's there for. Whack!

He walked to the far bench where there were crates of oranges alongside a chopping board. He couldn't find a bandage. All he found was a wooden spoon.

This old man he played six he played knick-knack with my sticks with a knick-knack paddywhack give the dog a bone this old man went rolling home

Malcolm lived in the children's wards, always shifting, always changing. He lived how they all lived, growing together until he was the same as them. His limp worsened in bare feet until they gave him new boots, larger and heavier and uglier than the last pair.

Black.

Vaguely, far beyond his moon where his memories collected, he had expected regular brown shoes.

For now, he sat cross-legged on the floor and rocked. He held his new boots cradled in his lap. He dreamed that he held his mother while she faded away and he rocked her gently in his arms. Sometimes he was peaceful inside his clouds. Sometimes he rocked his baby brother, Geoffrey. Sometimes he wondered about the brand-new boy, the good boy trapped inside him. Sometimes he didn't – anything.

Bryce was gone from his iron bed and the little clothes and brown shoes gone as thoroughly as he.

Another secret.

A boy raced insanely by, whirring fire-engine siren noises until a nurse gave him a good slap and a spoonful of medicine.

It was quiet

No more noise

He rocked

His mother and Geoffrey and Bryce gone

This old man he played seven he played knick-knack up in heaven with a knick-knack paddywhack give the dog a bone this old man came rolling home

Chapter 29

Socialising

Some of the older girls and boys were escorted for two hours daily down the rocky road to the Seacliff village primary school. Malcolm knew he went to school though he couldn't remember where. He had worn grey shorts and a woollen jersey. And he had a school suitcase with his name on the front. M, and then something else... B? Malcolm Bad Boy? Was that his name?

When he was much older he went each Saturday night with the other patients to watch moving pictures at the village hall, down from the primary school. He learned to sing – though he didn't sing out loud – and soon knew all the words and tunes. The hall in The

Building was disused. The staff often talked of how it was going to be renovated and refurbished later on. Not this year, though. Not any time soon.

Monthly dances were held in the village hall. Mrs O'Connell, who had dark hair and dark-rimmed glasses thumped away at the piano. A chap called Ralph played the drums, and Jack Green squeezed tunes out of his piano accordion. Once they were warmed up, the other men would go outside to drink beer from a keg mounted on a post. The ladies weren't expected to venture outside. They went downstairs for a secret smoke.

Malcolm stayed where he was told. He was intrigued with the tea chest strung with tight wires that made a bass sound when strummed. He considered how he would like to play an instrument such as that, or an accordion like Jack's.

Though he hadn't spoken a word for years, he was thinking about speaking again. This idea was brought about by a new attendant.

"It's time to go. Hey, you. What's your name?"

"M-Malcolm," he began.

"Malcolm who?"

"M-Malcolm."

"What's your surname, your other name, man?"

The attendant jollied him along quite nicely.

"Malcolm B-b-bad B-b-"

"It's all right. In you get, then."

He climbed into the waiting bus.

Both attendants spoke loudly to each other.

"Ya hear the news tonight, Fred?"

"Nah, missed it."

"Labour Government finally fell. Some news, eh?"

"No shit! After fourteen years?"

"Hard to believe, eh? Malcolm, sit in behind the driver. Easy goes it. Watch your step, man."

He liked going down to the village hall to the pictures. The local men and women dressed up pretty sharp, hair wetted down, or curled and lacquered to stay in place. The patients sat on hard forms at the back of the hall next to the doors, in the spot that was said to be the coldest and draughtiest.

Going to the pictures helped Malcolm remember a life somewhere else from amongst his young past.

There was a new patient, Monica. She refused her food. The staff saw that as a form of unco-operation. But Monica just wanted to get out and go home and grieve. Her only son had drowned when a lorry spooked his horse. It had bolted across Waikouaiti Bridge, farther north of Seacliff, and thrown the boy into the stony river below.

Monica sang dirges. She sang of her heartbreak and her confusion, lamenting the tragic death of her son. Malcolm could see this. But her constant mournful singing was deemed auditory deviance by some staff. That she never made any attempt to comb her dishevelled hair and sang songs of which she created both the words and melody worked against her.

Another patient named Mark – a different case although it appeared to Malcolm to be similar – staff often discussed within his hearing, how Mark's singing was a positive expression of emotion and recreation and to be encouraged. Apart from her indications of heartbreak, Malcolm thought Monica was no worse case than he or Mark.

As he grew up, he listened to every word spoken around him, to him and about him. Often it seemed that physical difference was perceived as linked to 'madness', as if patients had to be seen as different to those employed to care for them and the wider public. He'd never seen a staff member or visitor wear a boot like his. Somehow these physical differences justified their confinement. Staff would comment that this patient 'had a wild stare' or that one 'wore a sullen expression'. If their shoulders slumped, or their face was cast down, or they shuffled when they walked or had a genuine limp, like his, did that help to remind the staff and public that they were mad and therefore needed special treatment? Was madness visually recognisable? If so, what did his clumsy limp, his shuffle, his weak hand and more often downcast face say about him?

Chapter 30

Death at The Building

Dick Clough sat on the bench outside Clifton House. They met there on a regular basis, by chance not by arrangement.

He brightened when he saw Dick.

Every single time they met, Dick greeted him enthusiastically.

"Gidday, Mal!" His grin widened. One day it would split his face and open it up right to his ears. "How are you, then?"

"Fine, thank you, Dick. Are you all right?"

"Right as rain. But I've got a bit of a secret."

Malcolm had guessed as much from Dick's fidgeting, the covert glances he sneaked over his shoulders. They were surrounded in secrets.

"You know Pete Durham is gone?"

"Where's he gone to this time? Town?"

"Death by Request." Dick snuck more covert glances over his shoulders into the empty space of the gardens, his voice raspy and rank with spittle.

"That's the word on it in the house, though no one's really talking about it."

Malcolm was shocked. He'd not heard of such a thing for quite some time. Poor Pete. He'd liked Pete.

Dick settled in to tell him what he knew.

"Well, Pete had been going to Dunedin, see, Friday afternoons for ages. He was a voluntary patient – not committed like the old Chinaman; he's in for good. He can't speak a word of English to save himself so he'd be dead within a day if he got out. And they now say that unless we get discharged within six months of coming here, we're here for life. Guess that's why they started turfing the fellers out a bit back."

His stories were like old Jack's, as rambling as the ivy clinging to the red bricks of this building.

"Anyway, old Pete, they discharged him. Just like that. Said he was finally allowed – no," he corrected himself, "*free* to go for good. So off he went taking his belongings in a paper bag. Only he came back because there was nowhere for him to go to. So he was back to living with the rest of us at the house again. His problem was with the bottle, eh. Try as he might he couldn't beat it. Last Friday, when he said he might try leaving for good again, he didn't come back from Dunedin."

Anyone on leave who didn't return had their leave cancelled and were listed as escapee.

"But he wasn't supposed to not come back that time, like. He was just on ordinary leave. So the attendants were sent out to scour the city. They found him in the gutter by the Leviathan pub, drunk as a coot. Some blokes from the paper printers' early shift sat with him a couple of hours because he'd been done over proper. Waste of time though because Pete didn't have no money. He'd spent every last penny of his Comforts Allowance in the boozer."

The two men reflected quietly on Pete Durham.

Dick spoke again. "Well, they brung him back, sobered him up and started again, but Pete – he said he was too old for this kinda lark and his guts was giving him gripe. It was killing him to be alive and he wanted to go home. Sad thing is he *was* home. So he talked to the attendants, they talked to the doctors. Yesterday, it were done. *Death by request*. Gone now, anyway. Home somewhere. Poor Pete. Poor bugger."

Dick fell silent. He might have wanted to continue talking. Malcolm neither encouraged nor discouraged him. He just sat there quiet and receptive until Dick burst into boisterous tears. Malcolm waited while the noisy torrent was spent. He wasn't new to crying. He'd seen it most of his life in one form or another.

Dick drew a grubby hanky from his pocket and rubbed it all over his face.

"He were me best mate, Mal. Him and you are all I got. I didn't get to say goodbye."

He was thinking Pete was probably better off dead what with the gripe and all. Better than being sent home when he had no home to go to.

The Welshman died, Idris Llewellyn Lloyd from Malcolm's current ward. As he saw it, there was nothing dramatic about his dying. No death by request. Idris died in his sleep, that's what the word on the ward was. A doctor was needed to say if he was properly dead, though; an attendant or nurse wasn't allowed to make that call. So the staff stood around the bed, jawing on about the grey-faced man with the sunken eyes, until the doctor came. Idris was pronounced dead. The doctor said he'd been dead for hours. Or at least he hadn't breathed for hours.

Malcolm was well aware that people died. All of his life people had died. Some years more died at The Building than others, especially during the coldest winters. He did wonder whether or not all the deaths were necessary. He decided from now on to take a particular interest in who died and how.

He'd heard tell the Welshman's family thought him a wee bit peculiar, best put the odd feller into the mental hospital. He could, just maybe, be suffering from some gradually deteriorating degree of dementia.

"We're a close family, but this – it's incurable, you know. It could even turn out to be dangerous," said the Welshman's sister one day, when she'd come to visit. "Imagine waking up dead one morning, shaken to death by a madman."

That same close family went so far as to have Idris committed; a ward of the state needing two independent doctors to sign him out. Just in case. So the Welshman, Idris Llewellyn Lloyd was committed to sleep among creaking iron beds beneath high-up barred windows for the rest of his natural life, amidst hacking and coughing and the incessant screaming, pacing and wall slapping.

He'd once told Malcolm, "It seems I'm mad for sometimes choosing to sleep in the bush to get away from my family's squabbles. Just sleeping outside. Watching for shooting stars and comets in the southern skies. Is that wrong? Is that really mad?"

Malcolm said, "I'd like to sleep outside sometime."

Stars – had he ever really looked at them without bars cutting right across the night skies?

"I've been jinxed all right," Idris said. "On account of being a bachelor. They think that's weird, that I oughta be avoided, might be dangerous. My sister got them all scared over nothing. Ah, well..."

"I think you're fine, Idris."

At least he had been when he first arrived; not bad enough to be committed. Like, he didn't have fits or run around naked and screaming, or shake his head and drool or bang his head on the concrete until it bled. Idris only sat by the window staring at the sky through the bars. Smiling.

After a time he did go a bit loony – like some of the others did. So maybe he had been mad all the time. Maybe he was even dangerous. Maybe his family were right and he was suffering from some gradually deteriorating degree of dementia.

Or maybe he would still be alive if his family had let him sleep beneath the stars.

People die here, Malcolm thought, and this made him remember his mother when she was dying, how shrunken and grey she was, like a living ghost. He wasn't scared of impending death, or frightened to touch the dying.

More recently Father Teague talked about immortality, but Malcolm had no sense of that. Was he going to die here in Seacliff Mental Hospital, and how might that be?

So Idris died in a squeaky iron bed, one over from him, and Ned died in the willow tree in the bog. Bryce died (he imagined they said that, though he knew the wee boy had faded away) as was expected of him. And why that sudden long-distant memory of Bryce when he couldn't remember the rest of long ago?

Some died on the rocks at the bottom of the cliffs. Some were whisked away in the night to a far away mental hospital to forestall any local family embarrassment.

Or because they were proving to be tiresome, like the Italian, Mario. He didn't stay long enough for anyone to decide if he was insane or unable to manage his personal affairs, though some did say he was thoroughly unhinged.

Initially they said Mario was an excellent vocalist, with a superb voice of great volume. Daily he walked the grounds and sang out melodies in his mother-tongue to the pleasure of visitors, who were not treated to his continuous rehearsing of his repertoire, day and night. On and on and on. Often as not, Mario sang hymns. Even such noises as Malcolm thought should be acceptable were recorded as symptomatic of madness.

Some said the thirty-year-old shipping clerk had suffered from a hereditary adolescent insanity for many years. Finally he'd pushed his family over the edge and into dealing with it, and him. If he were at the beach, on a stage or in church, his singing might be deemed appropriate, if not beneficial, or at the very least outstanding talent. Here, because Mario sang in an unspecified place, at an unspecified time, he was 'acting in a deviant manner'.

Both Mario and the woman named Monica had violated the constraints by singing out of accordance with the correct style, time and place. Mario was whisked off to Sunnyside Mental Hospital in Christ-church.

Malcolm had no clue as to why they were all dealt with differently. Few of the patients knew why the staff did what the staff did. He shrugged it off; it was just how it was.

But death? He found that intriguing. Joseph Merchants discovered a sneaky cave tucked into the ocean cliff, dense with black popping seaweed and inhabited by little blue penguins. When the searchers came, he covered himself with seaweed. As the tide changed the little blue penguins waddled out from the cave. The water closed the entrance and filled the cave.

Pete Durham died by request.

Esther's mewing boy baby was buried in a shoebox.

Malcolm had secrets about death.

He had many secrets.

Chapter 31

Geoffrey Humphrey Bennett

Once upon a time there was a small white box on a sitting room table.

The father was not looking at the mother and she wasn't looking at him. The father blamed the mother who blamed herself. Both of them were crying. Malcolm was six years old. He was bawling the loudest of all.

Their baby's name was Geoffrey Humphrey Bennett. He was sleeping soundly in the small white box.

Malcolm's father repeatedly yelled at him.

"You're a bloody big boy. Help with more things. Be less clumsy, if you can. For goodness sake, don't slam that door! Idiot! See what you've done?"

Whack!

Yes, Daddy.

"Surely you can fill the coalscuttle without spilling it all over the path. Just once? Oh, leave it on the steps. I'll bring it up myself. Leave it!"

Yes, Daddy.

"And make sure you help your mother. Got that? You're the eldest now. You help her with the baby."

Yes, Daddy.

"Sit over there. Go away, boy. Just – go away."

Yes, Daddy.

He sat where he was ordered to sit, or went where he was ordered to go. Sulking and fearful, his eyes fixed on the leather strop, poised to leap to his feet the moment his father's hand reached for it. Why had his father changed? He used to let him sit on his big knees. He used to teach him nursery rhymes and tell him stories about rabbits that wore real clothes and had real families, and other stories about cargo ships, clippers and steamships that sailed from one side of the world to the other. Back in the olden days. Now his father barely spoke to him.

...come here boy do this boy do that boy get over there boy be quiet boy go away boy go away boy...

On a Friday night his father came home from the pub, stumbled up the pathway, knocked over the rubbish tin, lost his door key, hammered and hollered, woke Malcolm who lay quietly in his bed listening to his parents fight.

"...retard! That's what they call him at the local! A bloody retard!"

His mother's voice was shrill. "Don't you dare call him that, Colin! Don't you dare!"

"Bloody bumbling idiot! He's no son of mine!" His big fist hammered on the adjoining wall. It vibrated through the boards.

Malcolm dove under his bed. He didn't like his father drunk. He smashed things. Like him.

"He's *your* son and he loves you very much!"

"Sometimes I wish-"

"No! No, you don't. We're a family and we don't wish anything different, do you understand? Now go to bed. Sleep in the sitting room. It's late and you've woken half the street..."

Malcolm loved his parents and he loved their new baby. His baby's name was Geoffrey Humphrey Bennett. Geoffrey chuckled when Malcolm tickled him under his chin. He gurgled like bath water going down the plug-hole. After his mother put him on her breast, she draped him over her shoulder and patted his back to make him burp. Mostly he burped up his feed.

His mother changed Geoffrey's nappies. That was the pattern: cry, nappies, feed, burp, nappies.

Malcolm stood on a chair at the end of the table and watched her fasten the safety pins in the border of her cardie. Then she peeled the wet nappy back and washed the chubby boy-body with warm soapy suds. He watched as she rubbed her face in Geoffrey's tummy and made his podgy feet and hands dance. Geoffrey chortled and screamed and grabbed at her hair. Her smile was always soft and sometimes she had tears in her eyes. When he asked her why she cried, she said it was because she loved her boys so much. They were happy tears.

He kicked his boots off and crawled nimbly along the tabletop to play with his brother.

"What more could I ask for? You're such a great help, Malcolm. What on earth would I do without you?" She scrunched up his hair. "Now look after Geoffrey and see he doesn't roll over while I get the talcum powder."

He was trusted. She often said so.

She returned to dust Geoffrey's pink bottom with powder. More often than not, she let Malcolm do it.

Geoffrey, with his big smile or fat angry tears, was then tucked tightly into his cane pram, his white shawl almost covering his face. Only his eyes and the top of his head poked out. He wore a little knitted helmet with a button at one side.

"Daddy, will you read to me?"

Malcolm carried an armful of his favourite Lucie Attwell storybooks to his father and began to clamber onto his big knees. When his father abruptly stood up, he fell backward, spilling the books across the floor. Though his face screwed up, he didn't cry. He was the eldest now.

"Get off," his father barked. "Your boot digs into my legs. And you're far too big for that lark, anyway."

His father stepped over to stand close to the hearth. He pulled a tin box from his pocket and lit a smoke. Then he leaned with his back on the mantelpiece, his head tilted upwards as he breathed in the smoke. He expelled it in bursts through his mouth and his nose, ignoring the boy on the ground. He inhaled sharply, before saying a bit gentler, without looking down, "Those books are too old for you. Put them away until you grow up, there's a good lad."

Malcolm hunched over, making himself smaller, quietly turning the thick pages of the book about a white goose, his fingers tracing the inscription on the first page. Happy 6th birthday, Malcolm, 1926.

He said this over and over in his head.

His mother ironing in the passage.

"He'll grow into them, dear," she murmured. "It's all right for him to look at the pictures."

He could also read some of the words.

But best not make his father angry again. He sighed loudly, like the grownups did, and piled his books together to take to his room. When he returned, he flumped down on the carpet square in front of the fireplace, catching a stern look from his father. When he smoked his pipe he was far nicer. Hand-rolled meant he was cross. He was rolling another now.

Malcolm fidgeted a bit. He spied a loose piece of paper sticking out from the unlit fireplace, the start of a Jiggs cartoon strip. He reached for it.

Whack!

By now the boy was feeling wretched. He got up and wandered outside into the dreary street. He thought he might collect round pebbles from the verge to roll down the gutter. This time some might roll as far as the stormwater grate. Instead, he hunkered down to count tiny red spiders on the concrete, pretending they were miniature soldiers marching back and forth, left and right.

"Look, there's loony! He's counting spiders again!"

"Loony! Loony! Counting spiders!" chanted the bigger boys. "Bet you a tiger's eye he can't count."

But he *could* count. He could! He was the best counter in his class. Teacher said that last week. Oh, how he hated his boot. He hated how he was labelled 'loony' because he was born with a weak leg and a weak hand.

He knew the names of many spiders including the red ones that raced across the hot concrete, and the bigger hairy spiders that hid in the coal shed. And red admirals and white cabbage butterflies, and some moths. And the flowers growing in their garden and along the fences in their street: onion plants, nasturtiums, gladioli, buttercups, pansies, bluebells and crocuses. He concealed this information, but to him it proved he was not loony.

He stomped back inside his gate and searched out his mother, who never teased or scolded him. She loved him. She was on her knees busily scrubbing the washhouse floor. She smiled, and she stopped what she was doing.

"Goodness me, dearie. Where does the time go? Fill the kettle will you, luv. I'll soon be done here."

He climbed on the kitchen stool and held the kettle under the sink tap. He knew how high to fill it. Not too high. He put it ready on the bench and climbed back down off the stool. He fetched the milk jug and the biscuit tin. Soon they would have a nice hot drink together. She would have a refreshing cuppa and he would have cocoa made just right, with two teaspoons of white sugar.

His father had gone to the RSA to talk with some blokes about a dog.

Geoffrey's face was ruddy with rage at being ignored whilst his mother scrubbed the floor. Malcolm carefully lifted him from his pram, flicking the pom-poms that jiggled across the front of the hood. The baby stopped crying.

Since his mother was now hanging nappies on the outside line, Malcolm put Geoffrey on the blanket, which was folded over the table, like he'd watched her do. Carefully, he removed the two big safety pins from the nappy, pinning them onto his jersey front.

"You're a big boy." His father's words echoed inside his head. "You can help more around here. Don't wait to be told. Use your brain, boy. That's what it's for. You're so bloody clumsy!"

Clumsy...clumsy...clumsy...

"Stinky baby, stinky baby," he sang into Geoffrey's happy gurgling face.

And Geoffrey kicked his legs so hard he got poo all over his feet.

Malcolm decided to bathe him. His mother was still hanging nappies so he raced down the passage to run the bath. Geoffrey was too small to roll over, his mother said that. He filled the bath to the same level she always did, and then headed back to the kitchen to collect him.

"Stinky baby," he crooned happily.

He hugged him close, ignoring the poo on his jersey.

But lowering the baby into the water, as he had so often seen his mother do, was far harder than he'd anticipated. Geoffrey was strong and he thrust his arms in any direction and kicked his feet all over the show. Then, as soon as his feet touched the water, he gurgled in ecstasy and arched his body high, wildly, legs and arms thrashing out non-stop.

Malcolm grappled with the frolicking baby, naked and noisy, leaning right over the bath to tighten his hold.

His weakened hand let go.

His boot came in contact with the splashes of water on the linoleum.

He slipped.

Geoffrey disappeared beneath the water.

Stunned, Malcolm stared, amazed, for a split second. But as soon as he struggled to his feet, he slipped again, cracking his head against the hard rim of the bath. Blinded by the blood, he struggled upright, dizzy now.

And Geoffrey...

Geoffrey looked up at him through a film of water, his round eyes full of wonder and trust, still laughing as a trail of bubbles rose from his mouth...

It was an accident.

Malcolm stood rigid with shock. He'd dropped Geoffrey head first into the bath water. Geoffrey had spun onto his back like a wet baby seal. He'd tried to grab hold of the little arms, but Geoffrey kept turning and rolling around and around. He was so slippery. And the edge of the bath was high and sharp. In vain, Malcolm clutched at the empty spaces within his reach, struggling to grasp the wet baby boy.

It was a dreadful accident.

"*Mummy!*" he shrieked. "*Geoffrey!*"

And his mother came running and raced up the stairs two at a time.

Chapter 32

Women

From many years of living at the mental hospital, the loony bin or booby hatch, Malcolm had learned to listen to other people's conversations. He neither commented nor added to the discussions, but paid careful attention to what was said.

On this particular day one attendant commented, "The conditions, especially in the men's building up the top, have definitely improved."

Sister Daly said lightly, "I say it's got worse."

Malcolm had no opinion on the conditions; it was as it was.

This fine day he chose to wander up past Women's Ward 5 Reception. He hadn't walked there for a while, but he'd heard colourful talk about two girls newly admitted from the borstal. He wanted to see for himself what all the fuss was about.

Dumbfounded, he stared at the girls, haughty, fearless and fearful, disruptive and uncaring.

"There's no hope for the likes of them in here," Sister Daly had said to the attendant. "They're living right among the horrors of insanity, either factual or judged. I believe that pair would have a better chance if they were still on the outside."

He gathered that the borstal girls, Lindy and Genna, always together and laughing raucously and punching each other, would strip naked in a jiffy whenever it took their fancy. Just for the thrill of it. They were always in trouble. Their hair, bleached or dyed, bristled with metal curlers every morning. By lunchtime, their faces were painted and their hair teased and frizzed, first one style and then another.

Davey, who'd finished the men's race even after his fit, called them harlots.

Eric Coombs, the bloke announced as the winner of the race, said, "They be hookers, Mal, that's what they be. Straight off the wharf, the pair o' them."

So he went to have a look for himself. He'd never seen borstal girls, or hookers, so he didn't know what to expect. While he stood and carefully observed them they kept their clothes on.

He'd always been intrigued with the variety of people labelled 'mad', like these borstal girls. Over the next week, he studied their colourful ways, always on the move, changing and laughing, so very happy with their antics. It was said they more often than not behaved 'hideously' even 'abominably'. Scolding had no impact on them, or being threatened with The Treatment. Apparently they'd behaved the same for weeks now and would probably continue to do so.

Malcolm did wonder why they had not been separated, though. It seemed logical for them to be housed apart because clearly the two girls, cavorting about the yard in their tropical plumage, egged each other on.

There was a woman in the ward with them called Alva. Malcolm had seen her on numerous occasions. She grunted and groaned, but never spoke. Her thin face was painted thickly with makeup like the women on a chocolate box.

And he'd long been intrigued with another woman from that same ward. She was not a hooker, not according to Eric anyway. She was particularly pale and fat, bloated like a fresh white maggot. Her arms bulged below her dress sleeves and where her elbows should have been were huge folds of white flesh. More flesh lapped over the top of her black unlaced shoes, like white socks rolled down. Her name was Catherine.

He stared openly at her through the high wire fence, as he did each time he visited, and that was frequently now.

She stared back.

He left to continue his walk.

It was time to say goodbye to Esther, the shoebox baby's mother, who'd been readmitted with her fourth baby a while back. She was going home again to her husband who loved her so well, and her other bubbas.

"Bye then," she called, waving cheerfully from their car window. "I've enjoyed our talks." She clutched James Allen Reid against her breast. Another good strong name to live by. "Maybe I'll see you again. We are Catholic!"

He knew about Catholics, Anglicans and Presbyterians. It appeared to him that most on staff at The Building were Roman Catholic and those who weren't Catholic were of the Freemason Order.

He waved goodbye to Esther. In his heart he prayed he would never see her inside again.

The following day he strolled in the warm sunshine back up to the women's ward where Lindy and Genna,

Alva and the fat woman named Catherine lived. He stood outside the bottom fence. He intended to watch them for a fair while to see if the borstal girls would take their clothes off.

This time Catherine approached to stand near him. They said nothing to each other, he on the outside and she inside. He studied the fatty jowls hanging down, the layers that made up her chin spreading out in rolls and folds. Her shoes had been adapted to fit her swollen feet. Rough holes were cut in the front and outer sides for her fat toes to stick through, and the laces had been removed. She moved closer, leaning on her walking sticks. The pair of them, the fresh air, communicating.

And so an almost daily pattern formed over the next months (depending on the weather) with him on the outside and her inside, just looking at each other.

One day she said, "Hello, mm-mmh." And she giggled.

He nearly jumped clear out of his skin.

"I – I always thought you were dumb," he finally managed. "All this time."

"I thought you were deaf. All this time."

They both laughed at that.

"Some of us are. Some of us aren't."

"I wasn't always fat, you know," she murmured, almost confidentially. "Once I was slim. Mm-mmh."

He stared at the pad of flesh stretched and full about her cheeks, her pale lips, pink and meaty. Her eyes squinted through the flesh that formed her eyelids. And she had no discernible eyebrows.

She said, dreamily, "I don't like visiting hours. They only come to gawp at us, especially on Sundays. Do they visit you? Do they tell you lies?"

He was surprised at the volumes of words she directed at him.

"N-no."

"You have no visitors?"

"No."

No visitors ever came to annoy him with anonymous courtesies, or plague him with the discomfort of ghastly, prolonged silences, frantically filled up with platitudes.

"So you've got no family either, mm-mmh?"

She was taking him somewhere he didn't want to go.

"No." Then he added, fast and loud, "I'll see you again sometime. Goodbye."

He headed off to consider what she'd said. He'd never had visitors. He could clearly read how different they considered themselves to be, how they almost had to force themselves to communicate with those inside. Like him and the fat woman, Catherine.

"However do you pass your time?" they'd ask, amidst enigmatic inquiries about health or wellbeing.

"What do you do all day?"

"We think about you often. We wonder how you occupy yourself."

"It isn't as grim as we thought. We thought it would be grim inside as well as outside. It's not grim at all. It's a beautiful place."

"The gardens are well tended. And all those trees. You're fortunate to be here. I hope you're grateful."

The following day he walked back up the rise to visit the fat woman through the wire fence.

She repeated her same question about visitors. But there were no visitors for him, ever. No one cared enough to tell him lies and no one came to gawp at him. Not like her, this woman behind the wire fence. She cared enough to gawp at him. She smiled at him and brought her mouth closer to the wires.

Low and husky, she said, "You've been here a long time, haven't you? I've watched you for some time."

"I've watched you too."

He took a step back from the fence so he could see the whole of her more easily.

"Are you loony?" she asked. "Are you a lunatic? Or are you just mad?"

He laughed easily. "Quite possibly I am. Both. All of them."

"What's your surname then? Malcolm who? Have you got any more?" She waited politely, and then coaxed him. "Maybe? Perhaps?"

He didn't answer. Then, with an unmistakable change of personality, she tilted her head with a genteel, flowing sort of graciousness, as if re-enacting some part of her once-life, her once-past.

A rose flushed in each cheek. And she continued to talk as if he were no longer there. He was used to that. Then she turned and floated off, her enormous white arms and hands gesturing elaborately.

He left the fence.

He recalled he story, how her parents had intended putting her through university, that once upon a time she was considered bright. With that thought he headed toward the library. Although he couldn't read well, the writing in the newspapers was familiar and comforting. He spent hours tracing his finger over the words. Often he studied the pictures and tried to guess what the words beneath them meant. Some words were more familiar than others. He liked pictures and the Jiggs cartoon strips.

He joined the others as they shuffled back to his ward.

It was smoko time and visitors sat stiffly in the clean dayroom. He studied them as he waited for his cuppa. Above them a wall clock ticked noisily. This particular day, for no reason he could discern, he was disturbed by the visitors' laboured exercises in tact or curiosity. Both visitors and patients seemed to wonder How long have I been here? How much longer must I stay? They'd run out of things to say, to ask, to comment on. They were strangers, apprehensive and unsure. The visitors began to resemble the patients, all blank stares and startled looks, seizing on, or grasping at fleeting thoughts – anything to pin a conversation on.

And some of the others, desperate to escape unscathed from this hellhole of insanity, seemed anxious to appear 'completely normal' in front of the other 'completely normal' visitors lest it be thought there was a family deficiency.

Malcolm sat quietly on his chair, measuring them up with a telling accuracy. The patients would all, he knew, be treated to a pitiful kindness, a stealthy condescension that was almost vengeful. After all, they were the certified crazies.

The visitors saying, "You poor thing, it must be terrible for you."

"It's such a dreadful lonely place, and smelly, yes, indeed smelly."

"Do they treat you well? Are they kind, the nurses and attendants?"

"Is there anything you need?"

You could try to see that we're people too. But he didn't say that. It seemed too much to ask.

"We'll visit you again. After we've been abroad. England, you know, to avoid the inclement winter, most of the year. My sister... But, yes, we'll be thinking of you."

Such false niceties battered mind and soul. The patients clutched gratefully at this outside contact, this one remaining person who could offer up a taste of the outside, seizing onto, "We think of you often. We must leave now. Bye bye, then."

"Here, take this," a woman would say, finding a wrapped barley sugar in one pocket, or a folded handkerchief in another. "It's for you."

The more organised would, to ease their leaving, produce a shiny apple or a paper bag of aniseed balls from their handbag.

"From Uncle Laurie" – or Aunty Norma – "who says hello and wishes you well." They'd rise up and put on an expression of warm and loving farewell. Visitors with less forward planning were constrained to sit there for hours, fascinated and yet repelled.

Was lunacy contagious? He saw the question written on some of their faces. (He would hide a smirk.) Another question: how many endless minutes until they could politely leave? The elaborate search for motionless jackets and coats, a rummage in a handbag for another handkerchief, notepaper, lolly... Anything to make departure viable.

Then, "Must make a dash for it. Before the rain sets in. The cows, you know... Picking Patricia up from school... Oh, well then. Goodbye."

Followed by the usual scraping back of chairs and senseless false sighs. Who cared? He wanted to know this. Who really cared? And again he smiled at the awkwardness of the departures.

An older woman stood up, scrabbling for a long lost train ticket. She shook her head as if to suggest this was not the first time her handbag had swallowed up an important document.

Leave-takings were never unduly prolonged. As soon as one visitor made the first move, the rest thankfully followed.

Chapter 33

Catherine's Story

"I was slender once, you know." Catherine, pale and ghostly, was speaking with Malcolm through the wire fence. "When I was nineteen."

Abruptly she leaned on her sticks and propelled her bulk in the direction of her ward.

Over time she told him about herself and the boy she fell in love with when they were both twenty. She told him how her father had taken her down to the cellar and thrashed her with his braces.

"For falling in love?"

She had told the story lightly, and he tried to hide how much it disturbed him.

"For falling in love with the *wrong* boy. Oh, I suppose I was a bit of a handful. I'd brought the whole family into disrepute, you see. They said I had no moral compass, and that no decent man would want to marry me." She laughed without humour. "The fact that my father had a mistress for years was *quite* a different matter, of course."

As Catherine matured, though she was not a regular beauty she'd had the slimmest waist in Dunedin society. She was a well-bred young woman with good manners. As to her moral being, she was once considered, or at least expected, to be the irreproachable impeccable daughter of a long line of capable legal dignitaries.

So the fence meetings continued over time, always ending abruptly. He would watch expressionless as she powered her ungainly body away on her sticks. Surprisingly fast for such an enormous body.

He gleaned as much as he could of her previous existence, putting it all together in a mind-book to try and understand why she was as she was. Before her untimely pregnancy her mother had engaged in charitable work, distinguishing between the deserving and the undeserving poor. She'd entertained frequently, strictly within her own milieu. A fallen daughter and a bastard grandchild had no place in their family social structure.

As usual, he didn't want to reciprocate with any of his few family secrets though Catherine was more than happy to share hers, which came to him in disjointed bits and bobs.

Her father had planned to run for Mayor of Dunedin. Her mental unravelling began when he decreed her unfortunate pregnancy must be immediately terminated.

For the second time in her recent life he bellowed at his cosseted child. "I can't possibly run for Mayor with my daughter up the duff!"

She imitated his enraged tone of voice.

"Do you any idea of the ramifications of your disgraceful behaviour? Did you consider the family firm for even one instant?"

If it had not been for gender, and then her pregnancy, she told Malcolm, sourly, she could have become head of that same prestigious firm.

"Well," she said, "I learned pretty smartly what ramifications meant, but my father was not on my mind when I indulged in my *disgraceful* behaviour."

Yet it was her mother who insisted Catherine jump up and down their internal staircase for three hours, until she was so exhausted she fell from the top to the bottom. And her mother who forced her to sit in near-boiling bath water until it cooled down. And drink half a bottle of neat gin while stewing there.

Her skin blistered and she couldn't sit or lie comfortably, but remained obstinately pregnant.

Again, it was her mother who arranged for a woman to perform the abortion. She insisted it was a safe procedure, that thousands of abortions took place in New Zealand each year.

Malcolm learned how the abortion was performed; how Catherine lay there studying the dandruff in the woman's hair parting, the blackheads on her nose, how to avoid her fetid breath.

He grimaced when she described her pain, her powerlessness. She was old enough to be pregnant, yet her body was being poked into by some dirty harridan, and at her parents' behest. He understood her pain, her powerlessness.

Apparently, all went according to plan until Catherine saw 'it'. There was blood on her bedspread, her thighs, arms and hands. And then she saw 'it'.

Whenever she came to this part in her story her face screwed up and he waited for her to cry. She never did. If she had cried, he would probably have cried with her.

Her voice became dreamy...

She said his name was Roger and together they'd found a swimming hole up the back of North East Valley where the sun filtered through the willows. Malcolm watched her hold her latticed fingers over her up-turned eyes, eyes that were the lightest shade of grey, speckled with brown and gold. She described the shifting reflections and the shadows on the water.

Oh, they were so young.

She nodded continuously to Malcolm. He nodded back.

When she spoke again, she sounded older and warned herself about the sun's rays. She switched voices over and over.

He couldn't keep up.

He said goodbye, turned and walked away.

Another day when they were positioned on either side of the fence, Catherine resumed her story as if there'd been no break.

"My mother said I was an English rose." Imitating her mother's voice, perhaps?

But there was altogether too much switching back and forth for him. He wanted to see if Jack was in the kitchen or if Dorothea might make him a cuppa. Perhaps Mr Antonio had made cheese scones – in a creased slab, not cut separate.

Still, he waited politely for Catherine.

She and Roger made love beside the water hole.

Malcolm wondered if her thighs were slender back then. There was one woman he'd seen recently with slender thighs...

"Roger was a shy farm boy," she said, and then she was silent as if lost in her memories.

He watched intently as her grey eyes clouded over. When her silence continued, he said goodbye, and began to walk away.

"Wait! There's more to tell you."

So he turned back and waited, though he didn't want to hear this part. It confused him, made him feel awkward. He concentrated on the afternoon sun that was creeping behind a bank of clouds. His thoughts wandered off to what they would be served for pudding that night. Sago or tapioca, maybe stewed apples and custard?

Catherine smiled conspiratorially.

He resigned himself to spending the rest of his day up close to the fence; she was intent on reliving her entire past.

"It was the first time either of us had seen a nuddy."

He'd seen lots of nude bodies, all of them pretty normal, like his. He tuned out from listening, recalling instead white layers and mounds of flesh, the dank animal smells early in the morning...

"...and the sun was so hot..."

...steam rising from the concrete bathroom floor in the summer, damp against his face, his hair...

"...and we were sleepy from our hike and warm beer..."

He stared directly into the face of the once-slim, once-virginal, once-Catherine. He watched her eyes as she probed her memory, searching until satisfied, going on to another level, her eyes darkening.

"...we talked about being married, having babies..."

He reckoned she was probably thankful to get out from her family constraints. So now she had a chance at her own house somewhere on a hill with chickens, nappies and peony roses. Even a branch-horned Ayrshire cow. He thought about those particular cows. A patient from the dairy farm told him that Ayrshire cows gave the best yield of milk.

As usual Catherine abruptly stopped talking and turned and walked back to her ward.

The sun crept away to hide its warmth behind clouds.

It was a late autumn day, with sleet skittering through leafless trees, when Catherine came to the fence.

"I remember exactly what Roger told me." She spoke as if there'd been no pause in their conversation. "As soon as he got back from his uncle's sheep station he'd ask my father for my hand in marriage."

On her side of the wire fence she seemed aware of the effect of her story on Malcolm. In him she had perhaps found the ideal audience. Inspired by this discovery she launched into more and more detail.

He decided she was once a spoilt girl given everything she demanded for a smile. So it was perhaps a curious thing to Catherine that he did not laugh or pursue her with mockery. He believed her. Yet even as he watched, her expression changed again, dark and angry, disbelieving.

He found it hard to keep up with her.

In a tone laden with contempt, Catherine spat out her words.

"That woman said I'd gone mad, that lots of girls can't cope with the blood. That was her excuse for destroying my life. She tucked thirty-five quid in her bra, grabbed her bag of knitting needles and other tools with her filthy hands, and left my baby's bloodied remains in a towel on the floor.

"I howled as if there were no tomorrow," she said. "Once started, there was no stopping me."

Her parents bundled her off to the sanatorium.

"Best thing for you," she mimicked her mother's cultured accent. "It won't be for long, dear."

A glycerine tear welled in the corner of her left eye.

"They said it was a sanatorium, a private rest home. Imagine that. And I actually believed them."

Once disposed of, she never saw her parents again.

He understood lies and emotional pain. He ached for Catherine who, after all, was only a woman.

"The last I knew, I was dead. It was in the *Otago Daily Times.* And I had no way of contacting Roger. I wasn't mad, either. Well, maybe just a bit at first. You know, when I saw – *it.* They thought it was the blood that did it. It wasn't the blood."

She leaned closer, mouth working, forming the whispered words.

"It was the hand, Malcolm. I saw the wee hand with its wee fingers, fingernails and all. It was the wee hand..."

He watched her face fold and crumple. She started to mew and whimper, like Esther's shoebox baby, then to cry with her mouth gaping and nostrils pinching in and out. He placed his hand against the wire fence, against her cheek, reluctant to leave her. She reached blindly for a touch of his hand, her face jammed hard against the wires.

A nurse came to drive her away, saying, "Has he been annoying you, dear? It's all right now. You have a little cry and you'll feel better."

Catherine shuffled off blindly.

He stayed at the fence, despair within his heart for Catherine, his friend.

One Saturday night at the pictures they were seated next to each other. After the film was over, with everyone milling around and chatting, Malcolm said, "You have glasses now."

Catherine smiled prettily. "Yes. Yes, I do."

"Your glasses have no lenses in them."

"They took them out in case I hurt my eyes."

She told him that ever since she'd seen her death reported in the *Otago Daily Times,* she'd wanted to be rid of the old Catherine – or rather, the young Catherine; the girl they were so proud of, the girl Roger was coming back to marry. She believed she had shamed her family into writing her death notice.

Malcolm heard from the staff how she'd set about eating, stealing food from the ward kitchen and from other patients, stuffing it down her throat as fast as she could to pile on the weight, to punish them and herself. The doctors prescribed different medication and the nurses put her on a diet and controlled her food intake. She began eating blankets, lavatory rolls, newspapers, even dirt – anything she could get her hands on.

To Malcolm, Catherine, standing on the brink of an abyss, had fallen, an outcast from her parents' place in society.

She said, "Today is my twenty-eighth birthday."

"Happy birthday, then. I'm probably some years older than you, but I'm not sure."

"You never did tell me why you're here. How come you're here?"

"Well, I've never understood entirely but I'm working on finding out," he said.

"Will you tell me when you know?"

"Yes, I'll tell you."

Chapter 34

Visitors

Malcolm didn't like visitors. At least, not since Catherine had said she didn't like them. He didn't like the
interruptions to their normal life, the gawping curiosity of the visitors. But he listened intently to their
words and what they meant by them.

Two young women were visiting today, fidgeting
and screwing handkerchiefs. He thought they were
probably best friends because they stayed so close
together.

Janice and Marie sat in the dayroom, their chairs
pulled close, stockinged knees almost touching. Although visiting Janice's father, they kept apart from
him as if afraid of what he had grown into. A man, old

before his time, he constantly rubbed his forehead, and he clicked his tongue incessantly against the roof of his mouth.

After some time the lack of conversation began to disturb them, and both young women rushed into talk. Predictably, in Malcolm's opinion, it centred on the institution.

Janice lowered her voice and dipped her head. "I hear the patients on parole are welcomed into many homes in the area."

"If I lived anywhere near this Godforsaken place," Marie replied stiffly, "I certainly wouldn't allow anyone associated with it inside my gate. The whole set-up is so remote it's dangerous. I heard a patient even delivers papers to the villagers."

It was Fergus Marie was talking about. For years Fergus had been doing odd jobs for the villagers. He delivered their papers, dug their veggie gardens over, and planted spuds and rhubarb. Fergus was an amiable and gentle character, and though he didn't say much he sure smiled a lot.

Malcolm tensed when Marie said, "Don't say I didn't warn you, but there'll come a time when they regret such lax control."

Then Janice justified her family's need to commit their father to Seacliff from their family home in nearby Palmerston, though she was still unable to begin a conversation with him.

Malcolm wandered outside. Among those who arrived on this afternoon's train were three well-dressed young men who were not visiting anyone; they appeared to be interested in the history of the hospital as a whole. One was maintaining a dialogue regarding The Building, "...built in the late 19th century, it was famous for its extravagant architecture. Ah, but what a pity the construction faults resulted in partial collapse. It has been said it was an architectural exercise in Gothic Revival."

Perhaps they were from Dunedin University; the way they were studying the buildings, observing the patients as well as the staff, and, as he followed close by, one commented loftily on the gardens and the pig stye.

Malcolm could learn facts from these men so he listened as the balding one explained how he'd studied the history of this hospital since his grandfather had been carted off. He'd found that the weak-minded and dim-witted had been shipped out from England. The sheer number cast adrift without any relationship to those about them had astounded him.

The taller of the trio said it saddened him to think of the injustice done to so many helpless souls. Then the portly one put his spoke in.

"Because the patients are so well cared for, many live far longer than if they'd stayed with their own families. Supported, of course, by us, the taxpayers. And they look as if they intend living even longer, rather than dying from old age."

In his shell of hardness, Malcolm decided this portly man was bitter and full of scorn toward those less fortunate than him. The taller man seemed to have a more sympathetic view.

This man said, "They might have been friendless when they were first shunted onto the colonial system, but I wager a new kind of family formed around them, making them feel normal, secure."

In his opinion there would always be heartless people wanting to rid themselves of a family burden. Say a relative, whose plainness of speech and countenance or eccentric behaviour didn't fit in with their social circle. They excused their actions by exalting the qualities of the establishment they were taking advantage of.

Malcolm thought about Catherine. Her family had rid themselves of their only child to suit their social needs.

The chubby man retorted in his caustic fashion that just the cost of housing so many from abroad within a fledgling mental health system must surely have been horrendous, and still was.

"The hospital's so far from the city it's a damned inconvenience to anyone making regular duty-bound journeys."

Yes, Malcolm had overheard staff members, those without family in the village down below, complain about the distance and isolation.

The balding man perhaps didn't agree with the other man's comments, for he said softly, "It's all part of the confused and corrupt state of our world in general."

Malcolm decided he liked him. And he had enjoyed listening to their debate because from them he'd learned more of the history of The Building.

He returned to the dayroom to wait for the tea trolley. From Janice and Marie he'd learned a different side to how those visiting communicated with those being visited. He hoped he might one day introduce himself to Janice, to have a conversation with her, and to practise normal communication.

He would tell Catherine everything they'd said, because she'd brought it up in the first place. Since he'd paid particular attention to the visitors' conversations he'd developed a contrary dislike for most of them. Not that he had ever had a visitor or was ever likely to have one. But he was now aware how much of their conversation was negative.

Visitors were an unnecessary intrusion.

From now he noticed how they'd park their cars along the fence lines or in front of each ward, even on the new bitumen that had No Parking signs either side. The throng walking up from Seacliff Railway Station either admired or discounted the newly-formed gardens: the polyanthus, pansies and rhododendrons, and the bird-life, and some made false comments as if the hospital was connected to them.

He resented them all.

There were big changes afoot. He mentally noted each as it unfolded. One week the surrounding fence to the men's Ward Two was removed. Only the big gate stayed as before, and the gate surrounds with the hinges still attached, still locked, strong and erect. He watched how the men approached their new freedom, some with caution, and some with no idea of any change.

He studied a group of men who had walked over to where the fence had been and gawped out exactly as they had done the previous week and all the weeks before when the fence was still there. Another line of men grew longer while they waited for an attendant to unlock the gate so they could go outside onto the new bitumen to walk in semi-freedom, oblivious of the total freedom that was their new reality.

Big changes made no difference to the likes of Johnny.

Malcolm felt great sorrow for Johnny and the other men who didn't appreciate the freedom they were faced with now their fence was gone. Johnny didn't know his own name let alone the name of his sister. The two had been admitted together, causing a bit of talk among staff. Malcolm heard how they'd been labelled imbeciles from birth. He gathered information on the two family members and stored it in his mind, adding details as he became privy to them.

A constable delivered them in the prison van. Seems their parents were raising their brood in filthy conditions, amidst a dozen or more cats. Even during the coldest weather the children were barely clothed. Like frightened animals they cowered, sucking their fingers, unable to communicate.

Johnny had congenital diplegia. Malcolm overheard his case being discussed, the speculation on what might have caused Johnny's profound retardation. He was unable to do anything for himself. He didn't speak but could certainly bellow. Mostly he sat in the day-room with a vacant expression on his face. He was barely able to get about on his deformed legs. Generally Johnny was hunched over.

Malcolm thought how fortunate he was compared to him. They both had cerebral palsy, but luckily his own brain worked perfectly fine, while poor Johnny's didn't seem to function much at all. Johnny had nothing to do, could do nothing. While Malcolm and the other patients were outside enjoying organised activities, this was impossible for Johnny, given his physical disabilities.

One day, Malcolm heard Johnny was confined to bed.

Johnny died.

It saddened Malcolm that no one had ever visited Johnny, even though he had never had a visitor. The story of Johnny's family was tragic, all seemingly touched by insanity.

Malcolm and Johnny were both in their thirties.

But at least, unlike Malcolm, Johnny had a full name even though he couldn't say any part of it.

Sundays were roast mutton days with roasted potatoes and parsnip, peas and apple crumble pudding. The food was delivered from the main kitchen along with jugs of gravy and fresh cream. Dick from Clifton

House talked of the dishes of slops they were fed years back before Mr Green and Mr Antonio were in the kitchen.

"Pig swill," he said. "It were no better than pig swill. Now it's as good a feast as you could get anywhere."

Wherever that might be.

Malcolm walked up to the wire fence to see if Catherine would come out this time. He wanted to tell her about the visitors. He'd often wondered how she was getting on. If he waited long enough, would he see her coming along in her pale floppy petticoat, on her sticks? Asking everyone she passed Do I look pretty enough? But she never came.

That evening, however, while his dinner plate was being piled high, the staff talked about Catherine.

"You hear what the fat one did?"

"Up the women's ward? Parsnips two and more meat for this one. What'd she do?"

"Cut herself up. Razor blade."

"More gravy? That's all for you, Malcolm. Now move along. How did she get hold of a razor blade?"

"Some are real crafty when they want to be."

"Next. Malcolm, don't dawdle."

He stalled long enough to overhear an attendant explaining to a junior nurse, 'Sometimes they inflict physical pain to cover the emotional pain they're experiencing. That's why scissors, razor blades, knives and the like are always under lock and key and counted time and time again. Also crochet hooks and knitting needles. You'd be amazed at the lengths they'll go to damage themselves, or end it all."

Malcolm hoped Catherine was all right. He sat near the servery so he could better hear.

"Some of them go right over the edge and don't come back, poor sods," said another, as he dolloped mashed potato onto plates.

"Young Catherine comes from a wealthy family, not that it ever did her any good. They've never visited the poor girl. Her parents ordered that de-sexing operation too. They took her fallopian tubes, ovaries and clitoris. And the other two girls from up there, you know the ones I mean?"

"The whores from the city docks?"

"Yep. They're for the chop this week, or so my missus tells me. It limits the number of bastards the dim-witted produce so there're fewer children admitted. They call it eugenics or something like that. The science of eugenics."

"Bloody inhumane. I don't hold with it at all."

Peas atop the mash. Parsnips. More gravy?

Other staff joined the conversation.

"Catherine's father ran for mayor a few years back. Miserable bastard, abandoning his only child. Her arms look like they've been through an egg mandolin."

Gravy, a thick brown pool.

What was an egg mandolin? He'd ask Jack.

"Doubt she'll come back, though."

Catherine apparently now flickered in life without any foothold in reality. Wherever she had gone, he determined he was not going to stop waiting at her fence until she came back again. He suspected she was one of the ones who were far worse off than him. One of those Father Teague prayed for.

As well as the other woman who got pregnant with only the male night nurse to blame. She was oblivious to everything and had to be spoon-fed her meals or she would not think to eat. Her baby was born (the father sacked) and was adopted out with the good matron signing her own name as the baby's mother, listing the father as 'unknown'. The staff talked about that for a while, and then forgot about it.

Malcolm remembered. He made mental notes and sorted each type of information into small categories. He vowed he would never forget his new facts. He wondered how the baby with the matron's name was, if it was a happy baby, safe within a happy family.

Mostly he worried about Catherine as he waited in vain by her fence.

Chapter 35

The Real World – 1953

"It's time for you to have another taste of the real world. *Reality* is what they call it. So get yourself tidied up."

Malcolm wet his hair, ran his fingers through it, and then patted it down. He replaced his cap.

He was intrigued as to why Sister Evans spoke of the 'real' world. What was wrong with the 'unreal' world? It was real too – in its unreality. Why should he face reality? Reality stung. It hurt. It killed. He'd been to reality and he'd decided it was safer here in the unreal world. Yet it seemed that somewhere in his understated intention to remain constant, thereby attracting no attention and earning no favour, or The

Treatment, depending on which way he was viewed and by whom, he had failed himself.

Years had passed peacefully since his last shock treatment. And he was happy with his life as it now was, especially since he appeared to have dropped out of sight. So was his latest punishment to be given another taste of reality, maybe even to be cast out again?

"What are your dreams, Malcolm?"

The current Medical Superintendent, Dr Blake-Palmer, often asked that of him gently whilst calmly stroking his enormous black moustache. His eyes always softened when he greeted Malcolm.

"What would you like to happen to you?"

In all his life Malcolm had no dreams or hopes. He peered in the dim light of the office, his eyes still squinting from the outside glare. Throughout these extended conversations he behaved the same with a silence before each response, not because he was collecting his thoughts but because he found such speech laborious. There was too much of it altogether.

Or Dr Blake-Palmer might say, "Let's see now, what would you like to be? What might satisfy you?"

He felt his indecision melting toward fear. He did not know what his future might bring, or what he might like to be, or what might satisfy him, but perhaps this doctor thought he did. And he could not take the chance of pitting his certain ignorance against this man's possible knowledge. He felt trapped in his ignorance, and would be until he was confident this doctor knew what was best for him.

Eventually he replied, "I like some things I do here. I like helping in the kitchen. I like the lawnmowers. The chickens."

The good doctor smiled and made notes. But Malcolm was not finished. He took a deep breath.

"I have only fears of the real world. I'm afraid of going back to the outside."

"And why is that?"

"It's too big."

"I see. Too big, you say?"

Malcolm still feared the boy who haunted him from the far corners of his memory, the boy from the big children's ward, Tamariki, tufts of unruly hair gone, no eyelashes or eyebrows, beckoning Malcolm to come closer. If he went closer, would he see himself?

He tried to explain more clearly.

"I fear failing out there. Again."

The doctor waited.

"I fear having to come back here again."

If he were to fail and return to the hospital once more, surely the shock treatments would begin a new cycle. Could he take that chance? Was he truly ready?

But it was arranged.

One of the nurses would escort him to Dunedin for the day, his first special outing. The endless summer picnics and the whales didn't count; they were for anyone. The nurse, wearing a starched white cap, sat in the front of the hospital van while Malcolm and Davey sat in the back. No one spoke for the duration of the trip. In Princes Street they stopped at the Dunedin Public Hospital. Davey, with the driver as his escort, went into the X-ray Department to get his arm sorted. Malcolm stayed with the nurse who was busily writing something.

His gut was in knots, his hands nervously twisting his cap. Were they going to set him loose right here in the hospital car park? Eventually he spoke.

"Why am I here? Am I just sick?" he asked hopefully. He was used to being ordered, controlled, marshalled and herded. Yet somehow, somewhere, the dynamics had altered.

"Gracious me, no," said the nurse. "You're as well as you've ever been. This is just your outing. Davey's having his arm X-rayed. He had that fall way back on sports' day. Remember he fell during the race? Maybe he broke it after all."

This nurse spoke easily to him, as if he mattered.

"Come on, mister. Out we get. We'll have lunch now, if you like. Are you hungry?"

He nodded, looking forward to some grub.

Yet his real question was about his Discharge. Discharge with a capital D. He was fearful of how his impending expulsion would actually take place. Others had talked around him and about him going back to Maclaggan Street. So would he even notice it happening, or would it creep up on him like sunshine or clouds? Just be there? Or would it all happen as smooth as clockwork and he'd suddenly find himself out there? Alone – the rest of his life lurking around a corner?

As they entered the tearooms opposite Knox Church. he marvelled at the sheer number of bricks it had taken to build it, including all the steps. One day there might be time to count them.

For now his stomach rumbled loudly.

"What would you like for lunch?" Nurse West asked, indicating the only vacant table, the used crockery stacked ready for the waitress to collect.

He was aware of how much space he took up in the cramped tearooms. He felt he dominated it, taking command due to his sheer size. Aware that most of the patrons stared, some commenting without any effort to be discreet, he tried to make himself smaller.

He said quietly, "A fancy cake, please."

Another man had two hot cheese rolls on his plate.

"And those."

Nurse West hesitated. Their table was next to the door, the serving counter at the far end of the room.

"I won't do a runner," he whispered.

"I know you won't. Thank you, Malcolm."

She'd thanked him. Deep within, his spirit soared. She trusted him. Just like his mate, Joe, with the hedge clippers, and Jack, with his crayfish pot twist. Sitting there smiling to himself, he fumbled his cap in his lap. With all those regular people walking up and down in the street a sense of exhilaration flowed through him like waves, rising and breaking to rise again. Had he started to become a regular person all ready?

Maybe reality wasn't all that scary. With that hope his elation grew. Maybe he could blend in and become a safe obscurity on the outside. Without the walls of formal control maybe he could have a purpose. He could go back to Maclaggan Street to live with Bob and the others. And this time he would go right back to his beginning. He would find the pine trees on the hill.

Over tea, cakes and hot cheese rolls, Nurse West chatted brightly, asked him questions, and told him it was her birthday.

"So when's your birthday, then?"

He considered the size of the question before swallowing to clear his throat.

"To be truthful, I don't actually have a birthday."

"So how old were you when you first got admitted?"

"I was just little."

"Let's see if we can find your birthday for you."

On the busy footpath, merging with the sea of people, Nurse West guided him toward large glass doors and shoved him into the pleasant odours of Arthur Barnett's store. The merchandise was neatly arranged on shelves and behind glass counters. In the men's department there was a vast array of clothes: rows of jackets and trousers, ties, pyjamas and shirts. He was amazed, thrilled even. He raised his hand to trace his mouth and found himself smiling broadly.

Nurse West bought him a set of handkerchiefs embroidered with M, and he chose a toilet bag. Then he was fitted with serviceable work pants and shirts, all of which she signed for on a clipboard chitty. He walked out onto Princes Street wearing his new clothes, carrying his old clothes wrapped in brown paper; his glide into *outside* smoothly in progress.

Inside a bookstore he was drawn to the children's section. There were books the same as those Maeve had shown him with her name and the numbers inside.

"What do you think the numbers inside Maeve's books mean?"

"Her birthday," Nurse West said, "or Christmas."

"I had numbers in my book when I was young."

"Oh, so you do have a birthday? Then listen carefully to what I'm going to say."

Over his lifetime, he'd learned well to listen.

"What were the numbers? Would you know them again?"

"If I think real hard. If I see them."

So they walked farther along the main street until they reached The Octagon. At The Athenaeum Library, Nurse West read the inscription on the plaque.

"Built in 1870. Imagine that. It's very old."

He said quickly, "The Begonia House is older. 1863. Wilson's is older still. It was built in 1862."

"You've been there? To the Begonia House in the Botanical Gardens? And Wilson's?"

"I surely have." He beamed. He'd been places. He had memories. Inside The Athenaeum, in the children's section, he recognised the pictures on the covers of the Lucie Attwell books. And the Hans Christian Andersen books he recognised too.

Suddenly it was everywhere; a strange feeling of wonderment: in him, about him, the rapture of recognition. He continued to probe every memory to do with the book he remembered from his past. A Lucie Attwell book about Mother Goose. A small boy's finger tracing the inscription on the front page.

Nurse West was more interested in the date the Old Mother Goose Nursery Rhyme book was published. 1926.

To help jog his memory, she suggested she visit Maeve and ask if she might borrow her childhood books. She'd take a carbon imprint of the words inscribed in Maeve's books, and then substitute Malcolm's name for Maeve's, and change a few dates. She'd show her work to him when it was done.

Inside the hospital van, waiting for Davey and the driver, he listened carefully as she developed her plan. He even offered some ideas of his own.

Davey arrived yelling and beaming from ear to ear, his plastered arm in a sling, "Two fractures, Mal! Two!"

On the long drive back over The Kilmog toward Seacliff, Davey examined his plaster and picked bits off. The driver chatted with Nurse West. Malcolm revisited his long talk with her. He didn't pay attention to the conversation.

Until the driver said, "You remember Esther? The one with the bubbas?"

"Ah, yes," Nurse West replied, "She's got four now. She was discharged home last month."

"I hear she's done it this time."

Malcolm was shocked rigid.

Davey was gabbling on about his two fractures.

"And her four bubbas. She made mugs of sugary cocoa and rat poison. On the rug all wrapped in a big blanket. She took all her bubbas with her."

"Poor Esther," Nurse West said sadly.

"Released too soon, you reckon?"

"Who knows? That poor husband. Throughout all of her troubles he loved her. However will he cope?"

Malcolm's hand knew the place with absolute horror and authority and touched the collection of pills in the lining of his jacket pocket. His other hand felt his face. Wet. For poor Esther.

Davey frayed the edges of his plaster, whistling out of tune.

Nurse West worked Malcolm hard. True to her word she visited Maeve and came away with a selection of old children's books. Just holding them excited him. With each, he first turned to the inside page where the inscriptions were written in ink. She indicated tracings she'd made, how she'd substituted his name and several different dates. One in particular he seized on. *Happy 6th Birthday, Malcolm, 1926.*

He traced his fingers over and over the writing until he felt he might burst with knowledge.

"November! My birthday. Month before Christmas."

She reckoned he was thirty-two now. So they'd solved the first part of the jigsaw puzzle of his life.

She spent a lot of time with him. She said the main thing she'd noticed about him was that he didn't turn his gaze from hers, but looked her straight in the eye. She'd long been struck by a strange incongruity between the man Malcolm and the child Malcolm. Surely The State was housing a gentle man. She'd more lately felt a deep compassion for him, and she described how, to her, he appeared reserved and selfless. Behind that reserve, she hazarded, were strength and endurance. Not mental illness.

Even on her off days she trekked up the steep hill from the village to work his memory some more. She was teaching him to read from *Noddy and Big Ears*, *The Famous Five* and *Peter Rabbit*.

"And a pair of glasses wouldn't go amiss either."

So there he was, fitted with glasses, one eye covered with a patch to encourage the other to grow stronger. He read slowly out loud. And when she brought him a pot of ink and a pen he learned to write the words he could read.

Many months on, she said, "By golly, I do believe you've done it, Malcolm."

He beamed. "I think so too."

"I've always doubted your official diagnosis."

"I didn't know I had one."

"I'm no doctor, but I've passed my nursing exams. You simply don't fit the criteria for schizophrenia or paranoia. And I've never seen anything to suggest you're delusional or any of the other conditions you've been labelled with for the past two decades. I think you've been wrongly judged as unable to manage your own affairs. Perhaps it would be more correct to say you were never taught the skills required. But if you were taught, you'd probably do very well."

He processed her words, and then said, "Can you tell me why I am still here and what I am supposed to have done to stay for so long?"

"Well – and this is a long shot – I think there was a wee boy with a gammy leg and a lazy eye. His mother died-" Malcolm had told her everything he could remember. "–and for whatever reason he got left behind at the railway station. His pain at losing his mother and then being abandoned was so profound he stopped talking. Then, living alongside the institutionalised children, he sank lower and lower until he was indistinguishable from them. And, sadly, fitting in like he did, he got lost again in the process."

He began to appreciate how he'd been lost forever in some shape or form.

"This is your chance. We'll start at the beginning and take it from there?"

He nodded.

"And you'd like to learn how to talk in longer sentences?"

He nodded again. Still some of the questions put to him by others resurfaced, so he asked her – for the confidence between them was complete – how it had come to pass that he had lost contact with his past?

She couldn't explain the facts of his life to him, but she furnished him with a possible explanation.

"It was by no means unheard of, neither in life nor in books, that even a child of the best most loving family vanished and was lost..."

She stopped short, perhaps feeling the theme was too tragic.

He accepted her explanation, and from that moment saw himself as that melancholy but not uncommon phenomenon of the day: a lost and vanished child.

At the Occupational Therapy room where he went daily to weave baskets, make sheepskin bears and learn how to waltz, he worried and fretted anew. Was he truly ready? Did he really want to go out there again? He was conscious of the world and of the life within it, but here on the inside he was settled and free to walk wherever he chose. The more he thought the more confused he became. He'd come a long way since the anonymity of the lockup and the long back ward where they housed the forgotten. Yet was he content to remain safe amongst them, each, according to some of the staff, the same as any other, no distinguishing markings, resigned to living in the hospital under a rule of obey or face the consequences? He'd long had a strategy for his survival: he was safer when he chose to obey, to conform, to fit in, though often he'd been punished anyway. Was release to be his ultimate punishment?

He spoke of his rising fears to Nurse West.

"Is there truly no middle place? Do I have to go out there? Completely?"

"It will take time to undo the years of institutionalised living. And there is a lot to learn before you're ready to live outside. Your future is uncertain, yes, but to be honest your past was even more uncertain. Don't you agree?"

He nodded, chewed his bottom lip.

"And your future looks exciting. You see, in the end it doesn't matter what they did to you or said to you. That's the past. It can't be undone. But what you believe about yourself is what is true."

"Yes," he said, in his usual slow way. But then he added, "All right." And tacked on the additional words, "Thank you."

"So tell me, Malcolm, who are you now?"

"I'm me." And this time his voice was strong and true. "I'm Malcolm."

"Good. And one day soon you'll say *I want*, or, *I will have*. And you will. All of it."

He practised his speaking, all day and well into the night. He spoke to everyone he passed in the ward or on the road.

"How do you do?"

"How are you, Jack?"

"Hello, Sister Evans."

He practised his sentences relentlessly as the individuals strode past him, some replying, some not.

"Good evening. How are you?"

"Have a pleasant night, then."

"I wish you a very good night."

Perhaps some wondered where this new Malcolm had surfaced from.

"It's cold today."

"It's certainly very cold."

"It's so cold."

"I've only just realised how cold it is today."

There were nine words in that new sentence. He was pleased. Ten, if he said 'I have' instead of shortening it.

"I have only just realised how cold it is today."

"Don't catch a chill."

"Don't catch a chill, whatever you do. Make sure you keep warm." Twelve!

"Wrap up warmly."

Daily and long into the night he practised the art of talking like the visitors talked. He even exchanged small talk with the young woman, Janice, who still came to visit with her father in the dayroom. Oddly enough, though she seemed unable to begin to talk with her father, she did talk briefly with Malcolm on the days when her friend did not accompany her.

Regularly, he attended the dances in the hospital hall, where he could interact with others, to practice. Sometimes just to watch Mrs O'Connell play the piano.

"May I have the pleasure of this waltz, please?"

"No? Perhaps the next one, then."

"May I have the pleasure...?"

"Indeed, the pleasure of this dance."

Speaking to Nurse West one day, he explained his past as he recalled it.

"I was terrified when they first jabbed my arse with the big needle. And when they slapped the paddles against my head and turned on the juice, I thought I was killed."

He held out his hands to see if they were still shaking as they normally did when these memories surfaced. They weren't, and he exhaled, greatly relieved.

"The funny thing is I remember being afraid before they did it. Shocked me, I mean, but other than that I don't remember a damn thing about it."

"I think that's the whole intention. Do you feel like talking some more about it?"

He leaned his brow into his hand, and said, "No, I don't think so. But thank you for asking."

A man walking alone hooted like an owl, alternated with yells of Hell! Buggery! Bullshit! His voice was pitched like a crow's call. 'Buuuu-gery,' the man bawled as he walked toward the gate, keeling off at the last minute to veer to the right. He thrust his head out in front of him as if to get his brain lower to the ground, to bury it in the toes of his hospital issue slippers.

Malcolm said to Nurse West, "I know him. That's Sid." Then he grew quiet watching the limited activity across the grounds, his eyes on the cars on the road beyond.

"They sure go slow around here. Their speed is as slow as walking. Sid's got a swearing condition."

Steady and calm, he reasoned that, like it or not, some people here were dead to certain realities that concerned the rest of the world, and that was maybe a blessing for them.

If he were to return to Maclaggan Street, if he were to have another chance at being outside, at being normal, he needed to be prepared. This was decided at a staff meeting along with the doctor, who in turn explained it to Malcolm.

"You'll leave in two weeks," he added finally.

So they'd told him on a morning so crisp that trails of smoke like writing patterned the bright blue sky above The Building. But two weeks wasn't long enough to say goodbye.

Already he'd waited three days by the high wire fence for Catherine to come out on her sticks, the sun being present and not good for her fair skin. When she finally emerged from her ward he stared at her arms, the deep and rutted scars, and regular and criss-crossed cuts and slices like the intricate detail on a road map he'd once seen.

He'd already asked Jack what an egg mandolin was.

"Gee whiz, son! You don't half ask some curly ones, but that one takes the biscuit. Go ask the missus."

Mrs Green had explained about the wire contraption she used for slicing up cold boiled eggs for summer salads. She'd said it was called an egg mandolin because of the little wires that made it look like a musical mandolin. He'd never heard of that one either.

"Goodbye, Catherine," was all he said this day, against the fence, only pleased she'd come back from the edge, wherever that might have been.

"Oh, Malcolm, I'm so glad you're getting out. I'll be happy for you – if I can. But I'll miss you."

Syrupy tears formed in each eye, flooding the pupil, and her face flushed up brightly before it began to crumple.

He didn't wait to watch her cry because he was crying too. When he was far enough away he turned to wave.

On the bench in front of Clifton House, he waited for Dick. "Goodbye, old cobber. I'll be gone soon. I'll miss our yarns."

"Yeah. Righto, mate. So, goodbye then. And the best of luck out there, eh. Here, take this. I saved it for you since you can read now. It was from Pete's gear, what he left us."

Malcolm took the book from Dick's hand, the pages stained, creased and dog-eared. On the cover was the picture of a cowboy sitting on top of a spotted horse. He knew he'd treasure it.

Mrs Green was busily locking her canteen door when he said goodbye to her. And Jack – well, he was in the kitchen with Mr Antonio.

"Well, blow me down! Look who it is," Jack said. "We wanted to say goodbye to you. All of us. So, hurrah!" He cheered along with Mr Antonio, Dick, Sandy, Martha and Patrick, and on behalf of Dorothea and the other quiet ones.

Nurse West said, "Goodbye, Malcolm. And good luck."

Mr Antonio produced an enormous sponge cake with freshly whipped cream, topped with whole strawberries and sprinkled with grated chocolate.

Then they all stood around as if they expected him to say something. But for all his practising, he couldn't say a blessed word. Tears threatened a second time that day. He blinked them back and swallowed hard.

"Yeah, we know. We understand. We'll miss you too," said Jack. "Just keep ya nose clean, son, and you'll do all right."

Dorothea stumbled to the front of the group. She clutched a large parcel to her wet pinny – Dorothea who once sang opera at the Dunedin Town Hall. The parcel was wrapped with bright floral wallpaper, tied with even brighter string.

"It's from all of us," she insisted. "We all paid."

She shoved it at him and then proceeded to help him untie the string.

The string fell to the ground revealing a box chockfull of so many wonderful things: Pinky Bars, Buzz Bars, aniseed balls, cinnamon sticks and Pixie caramels. There was writing paper, envelopes, stamps and two pens. Shampoo and Cashmere Bouquet soap, Ipana toothpaste and a tub of Brylcreme!

He stood dumbly, his cap fumbled between his hands, hands that could now hold a pen and write his name. With his eyes watering, he waited silently. The gifts were laid neatly out in front of the sponge cake. He touched each one of them with his big hands.

"Bring the teapot, Dorothea." That was Mr Antonio. "Now get some of this sponge into you. There you go, then, lad. You'll be fine. Just fine and dandy. You mark my words."

Chapter 36

Return to the Beginning – 1954

Inside the house up Maclaggan Street in Dunedin, tucked beneath the cherry blossoms, the larch and the pussy willow, Malcolm wandered from his bedroom along the passage toward the sitting room. First he touched the light switch, and then he ran his hand over the familiar linen cupboard and bathroom door. He stopped and stared at the closed door. That was one room he never wanted to go into again. The hairs on his arms rose, and he forced himself to stifle an old sense of horror.

No, he'd be all right. He would go into the bathroom again. Just like he'd go, at some time or other, into all of the rooms in this house.

He had a lot to re-learn, a lot to re-discover, yet it appeared that nothing much had changed. Oh, there was a stain on the carpet and a crack in one of the glass panes in the front door, but nothing else.

Now he stood in the sitting room doorway, basking in the warmth from the well-banked fire, avoiding the inquisitive stares of the few residents he didn't know.

His world stopped!

She was tucked in a wheelchair.

Surely not! He could hardly breathe.

His throat constricted painfully. His heart was pounding within his chest. Something raced through his body as immediate and bracing as the waves crashing down upon the sands at Warrington Beach.

He couldn't move or make a sound. They'd taken her before. They could take her again. And what if this was in his mind, not real, because he wanted it so badly? Then he'd go back to The Building and be lined up for more shock treatments or the operation, and so the cycle would repeat, forever and ever.

He wanted to retrace his steps until he was in his bedroom, or in Bob's kitchen. Still, he couldn't move, in case what he was seeing was true. In case he never saw it again.

Julie turned her head, listening. A smile trembled on her lips, and she bent forward as if to make an enquiry of the air. Her rug slipped from her grasp as her hand reached out toward the door where Malcolm stood, petrified. The light from the window played across her brow, turning it to a pale gold.

"Is it you?" Her voice cracked so she could barely whisper. "Is it really you? Have you truly come back to me?"

Oblivious to the stares of the others, their incomprehension, he crossed the room to kneel at her side.

Gently clasping her hand, he said, "I'm back. Truly. I won't be going away again. Ever."

His doubts were gone. He never would go back.

The others watched. Someone closed the door against the cooling spring night air. No one turned on the light.

"I've finished your rug," Julie murmured, as he wiped her tears away with his thumb and stroked her cheek. "I made it for you, for when you came home."

Home. The words she offered so simply played over and over in his mind. This *was* his home.

"Oh, Julie, I thought you died."

"Just pneumonia, after the accident. But I didn't die."

Pneumonia. But that was in the past and he was done with the past.

"I've got a birthday. I'm thirty-three now. And I've got a whole name too."

She widened her blue eyes.

"You finally got more?"

"Yep!" He stated it proudly. "Malcolm Anthony Bennett. A name big enough to hang a life on."

Then Bob interrupted, anxious to say his piece.

"I heard they be thinking of closing down the main block at The Building. More earth movement. They gonna to be shifting more patients to Cherry Farm Hospital."

"That's right. It'll be good for them there. All new things."

But here at Maclaggan Street, things had changed too. The atmosphere was somehow lightened.

"We've switched to Kaitangata coal." Bob pointed through the wall to where the shed would be, beyond the dunny. "So the roof won't rust up and leak."

Malcolm said he knew about sub-bituminous coal now.

Bob disappeared back into his kitchen to serve tea. Once the empty plates were cleared away, he hauled Malcolm away from Julie to show him the latest garden, though it was nearly dark outside.

"We've been living off it for years. Almost since ya went back in. We've got everything ya could ask for growing right here."

"I've learned a lot about gardens. I'd like to help in your garden, Bob, if that's all right with you. And help you in your kitchen. I learned how to make a casserole."

Bob eyed him dourly. The kitchen was his sole domain. Still, he considered Malcolm's request, and he grunted, "I'm gonna be making pudding sometime so I 'spose ya could get a casserole going for tomorrow. No mess, mind. But I'll have to think long and hard about me garden."

Next morning, Malcolm dressed and went into the kitchen to eat breakfast with his family. Once he'd done the dishes, Julie stood up from her wheelchair and he walked slowly with her outside. They sat in the sunshine on a bench Bob had recently made. And he told her what he'd learned about coal.

"There's some that is dusty, earthy brown, and there's the other that's more brittle, shiny, blacker."

Bob brought them sandwiches on a tray, and they stayed there quietly for the rest of the day under the warming sun, hoping they were heading for a long, hot lazy summer.

"What more do you need?" Julie wanted to know everything. "I mean, more than you have now."

"Nothing, I guess."

"Everyone needs something more, but sometimes you don't know what until you find it."

He fingered the hoard of tablets hidden in his jacket lining, the balls of pale blue candlewick.

He had a secret.

He had two.

Actually, he had more.

He squeezed Julie's hand. "And maybe you're right."

He knew he would tip the tablets into the bathroom sink, and wash them and his past fears all away.

But for now he had questions too.

"Why are you in a wheelchair, Julie?"

"My hip broke that day in the bathroom. I'm a bit crippled by it, but that's all right."

He smiled at that. "You can't see and you can't walk proper but that's all right."

"And I got stitches in my head." She bobbed down for him to see. "There, where my hair's gone. I was so frightened. I missed you when I came back. I asked and asked, but nobody told me anything."

"Ah," he said, and took her hand in his. He knew what it was to miss someone. He knew how people didn't tell you things. And he knew fear; he'd met it head on. He told her so.

She directed her blank gaze at him.

"What frightens you most?"

Only things too bad to think about. Only...

"Nothing really," he said evenly.

The bog under Ned's willow tree, The Treatment, his father, water... In an instant, he fully grasped that he could cope with life on any level.

Here he was with Julie. He scrutinised the old scar across her chin and gazed deeply into her blind eyes, eyes the colour of cornflowers. In that muted accepting blue he saw himself and all his tattered imperfections.

Her fingers on his face in exploration were softer than moth's wings.

Slowly she smiled, changing reality forever.

Ends

AFTERWORD

I always thought the history about the inside of Sea-cliff Mental Hospital should not be lost, especially as so many from my own era who lived at Seacliff are now gone.

Seacliff Lunatic Asylum was an experiment in the early mental health movement, an experiment that too often went wrong. The location of the hospital itself is a significant indication of its basic philosophy – to hide away those citizens society was uncomfortable with.

Beyond that, inadequate engineering reports allowed the largest building in New Zealand to be built on unstable land – again, perhaps, because of who the building was for.

In 1863 there were thirty-six patients in the Dunedin Littlebourne Lunatic Asylum, and it was vastly overcrowded. Public funding for the mentally ill was provided only after every other medical need had been met. Nobody appeared to be interested in providing sufficient funding for humane care in the mental health sector. The asylum's main purpose was to keep the unloved and unlovable off the streets. So with the help of wardens and inmates they built the much-needed additional wooden barracks as wards to accommodate up to two hundred inmates.

Dunedin was declared a city in 1865; the population boosted with an influx of miners and speculators after the discovery of gold in Gabriel's Gully, the first of Otago's gold rush claims. This same influx left in its wake the disillusioned, the broken-hearted, the impoverished, those who had lost any will to continue searching for the elusive gold – and, of course, the genuinely mad. It fell to the state to provide care for these broken people. Hence the sudden and unexpected increase in inmates, coupled with 'lunatics' deliberately shipped out from England, or others whose families seized the opportunity to be rid of.

The Littlebourne Lunatic Asylum shared a campus with the Otago Boys High School. Perhaps in those days the housing of two awkward groups – the adolescent boys and the mentally ill – in close proximity was deemed appropriate. For years newspapers had trumpeted about the increasing overcrowding of the local asylum while the authorities, with one excuse or another, delayed doing anything about it.

Then in 1880 workmen (and it is believed also staff and pupils from Otago Boys High School) began demolishing the Littlebourne Lunatic Asylum, because the school required the land for their own expansion. Slowly but surely the school buildings began to crowd out the inmates.

Staff and inmates in 1874 had already begun to clear a new site along the coast at Seacliff, twenty miles north of Dunedin. First they erected temporary wooden structures, and later transported some of the original Littlebourne buildings to Seacliff.

At first glance it was a glorious place that had been made available to the inmates – the views were simply magnificent. Surely this location would encourage renewed sanity for them all? The sea was close with its healthy air and there was space for a community farm where work would produce food and provide outside activities and exercise. The grounds themselves could be slowly transformed into a park; such a beautiful park that in the future people would journey out from Dunedin to gape in wonder.

But nobody waited for the glorious buildings or the park-like grounds to be completed. In 1884, the women were the first to be moved from Littlebourne and crowded into those cold bleak barracks built by the inmates themselves.

And, unknowingly, the foundations for the new Seacliff Lunatic Asylum, the ample farm lands and the yet-to-be landscaped park, were being established on unstable land.

Robert Lawson, a 19th century New Zealand architect well known for his Gothic Revival style, designed the Seacliff Lunatic Asylum. Building was commenced in 1874 and the main block completed in 1884. Eventually, it was to house five hundred patients and fifty staff. The construction had cost in the region of 78,000 pounds – an enormous sum.

Some suggested Robert Lawson's work had turned to fantasy with its excessive number of turrets on corbels projecting from nearly every corner, and the gabled roofline dominated by a magnificent tower, further turrets and a spire. The extreme Gothic architecture of Seacliff Lunatic Asylum was the culmination of many dreams and plans. The idea was to remove the mentally insane, the retarded or those who were difficult, from the outgrown Littlebourne Asylum out of the city and into the healing countryside above the refreshing waters of the Pacific Ocean.

Healing? Hopefully.

Away from the eyes of the citizens? Certainly.

When the north wing of this architecturally-designed hospital building was finally completed, those women society labelled as lunatics were, once again, the first to move in. With its stone walls, numerous turrets and high tower, the building was a testament to Victorian architecture, a picture-perfect edifice glorifying colonial aspirations of greatness.

Yes, even though it was hidden in the countryside. Accolades from far and wide poured in.

Barely was the first building completed when the poor drainage of the land it was built on made it essentially unsafe. In 1885, only one year after it was finished, the trouble began. Plaster began to fall from the ceilings and cracks appeared in the walls. Ground movement was suspected.

Yet again, the women were evacuated from their latest residence into hurriedly constructed wooden wards until restorative work would allow re-occupation of the building.

Concern was focused on those numerous high turrets on the main building. They'd been built ostensibly as viewing platforms high above the countryside for when an inmate tried to escape. Primarily they were built for decoration. More importantly, they were not accommodation and thus could be sacrificed; deemed an earthquake risk, many were removed. With their removal, the beauty of the new building, so like a castle – perhaps a fortress – was totally compromised, and all within one year of completion.

In 1887, only three years after the opening of the main block, a major landslide occurred – something noted as 'a high risk' by the original surveyors, yet

totally ignored by those in charge. Fortunately, it af-
fected only a temporary building.

Toward the end of the nineteenth century several
more wooden wards – two-storey barracks – were
constructed to house the increasing numbers of the
insane who had to be accommodated by the state.
Later, after the Second World War, the authorities
removed the highest tower and remaining turrets
from the main building and that took care of any po-
tential danger from earthquakes and slips.

The grounds were glorious, the sea air beneficial,
but that building? It could no longer be termed beautiful; the plaster continued to fall and the cracks to
proliferate.

Still, life goes on, and society continued necessarily
to house those afflicted by insanity, and other misfits
deemed unfit for ordinary society. In 1911 the name
was changed from Seacliff Lunatic Asylum to Seacliff
Mental Hospital, and humane care became the ideal.
Only gradually did that concept seep into and begin to
change attitudes and behaviour of attendants and
other employees.

Psychiatric registration was introduced in 1945,
and 'Psychiatric Nurse' replaced 'Mental Nurse' as a
job title.

In 1959, The Building was finally demolished because of further earth movement, while other parts were closed down. Many patients were moved back into the community as improved medications relieved misery and suffering, and society decided it could tolerate those who were different in their midst. However, those unfit for rehabilitation went to other institutions – most to the new Cherry Farm Hospital, sited between Karitane and Waikouaiti, with its modern villa-styled accommodation.

Eventually, like many of my family and friends, I also left Seacliff village, initially to work at Cherry Farm Hospital.

Seacliff in all its glory is now a memory.

And Malcolm? Yes, he did marry his sweetheart, a woman who had also lived most of her life as a patient at the hospital, and, yes, they did produce a family who lived and grew up in regular New Zealand society. Not rich and famous, but regular. Something Malcolm always desired to be. And that's why I had to write his story.

Note: Some details have been changed to protect living relatives and descendants, though, wherever possible and in most instances the correct dates, names and places have been used.

Meet the author:

Author Susan Tarr has been writing for 25 years, and she often draws from the diaries she wrote during her international travels.

Her daughters were born in Kenya, East Africa.

Although she writes mostly from personal experience, she also uses anecdotal information from conversations and other peoples' stories, resulting in her characters taking on a life of their own, becoming larger than life.

She currently lives in New Zealand.

RESOURCES

Christchurch City Libraries.

Sunday Star Times.

Otago Daily Times.

(1972) BLAKE-PALMER, G, MOORE, C.S., TREWEEK, E.C. & TOD, F. The End of an Era. Seacliff Hospital Final Farewell.

Dunedin, Otago Hospital Board.

University of Otago Library.

New Zealand Society of Genealogists (Dunedin Branch) Newsletter.

Google Search: 'Seacliff Mental Hospital' *et al.*

Made in the USA
Columbia, SC
21 January 2018